In a Former Life

Angie M. Hill

Copyright © Angie M. Hill 2015

All rights reserved

The right of Angie M. Hill to be identified as the author of this work has been asserted by her in accordance with the Copyright, Designs and Patents Act.

All rights reserved. No part of this publication may be reproduced, stored in a retrieval system, or transmitted in any form or by any means, electronic, mechanical, photocopying, recording or otherwise, without the prior permission of the copyright owner.

ISBN-978-1511976343

For Jane, Jeanette, Helen, Sally, Joanne, Debbie, Andy, Dawn and Mum.

Chapter 1

The three of us waited nervously in Lucy's kitchen for Becky to come out of the sitting room. Her name had been drawn out of the hat first, so to speak, or rather the box that became empty after Lucy removed the last few tea bags out of it and forced them into an already-full terracotta pot labelled 'tea'.

Lucy couldn't contain her excitement as she flitted around. She reminded me of a butterfly, first perching herself on a high stool at the breakfast bar and then, after only a couple of minutes, leaping off and grabbing an extra-large size bag of sweet-chilli flavoured crisps and handing them round. It wasn't surprising that she had retained her size eight figure. Her zest for life and enthusiasm shone through. Her elfin features were framed perfectly with her short, highlighted hair. If we hadn't all been friends since junior school, she could have easily told us that she was ten years younger than her thirty-nine years.

"Becky's out!" screeched Lucy. "How did it go, what did she say?"

Lucy leaped forward to greet a rather perplexed looking woman emerging from the corner of the room. Becky ran her hands through her neat, dark-brown bob. With her five-foot-eight frame, the lapels of her beige jacket, which were clearly never going to meet, hanging either side of her ample bosom and her sensible, A-line skirt hanging loosely round her size-sixteen hips, she couldn't have been more of a contrast to Lucy, in her stonewashed, hipster jeans and pink V-neck T-shirt.

"I need a drink," Becky announced, as she reached for the Zinfandel and began to fill an oversized wine glass. "She's good. She almost had me convinced," the ever sceptical businesswoman announced. Accountancy and logical thinking were her thing and she had taken rather a lot of persuading to join the other three of us to have a reading with the psychic that Lucy had booked six months in advance.

"Well, what did she say?" Lizzie, the quietest of the four of us, stepped forward, her blue eyes sparkling.

"Oh, she ..." Becky was about to begin when Lucy reminded me that it was my turn next.

"Yes, go on Claire, don't worry. We'll tell you what Becky has said when you come back out, that's if she's even started to speak by then!"

I took one last look at my three best friends, Becky with half of her wine already downed, Lucy urging me on and Lizzie biting her finger nail in anticipation.

I opened the door into Lucy's sitting room. As I nervously closed the door behind me, I looked around the room. The thick, beige and red, patterned curtains were drawn, shutting out the windy October evening. Two large candles on the mantelpiece cast shadows around the magnolia walls. On the end of the rather cosy, well used, deep-red sofa sat a smiling woman. She had long, dark hair, with several unruly, grey streaks defiantly springing out from the rest. She was older than I had expected, although it could have been the way that the candlelight caught her lined face and cast shadows in all the wrong places, which prematurely aged her appearance. I glanced at her rather ordinary jeans and black T-shirt, the sort a forty-something mother might wear, before looking into her kind, grey eyes and took a seat at the other end of the sofa as she told me that her name was Alice. Rather an ordinary sort of a name for a clairvoyant, I thought, as I expected her to have the name of some sort of gemstone like Emerald or Ruby.

"Hello, Claire," she smiled. "There's no need to be nervous, we'll just sit quietly for a short while and have a listen to what the spirits are telling us shall we?"

Her calming voice and kind eyes began to take the edge off my nerves, although I didn't remember telling her that my name was Claire. Lucy must have given her a list of which order we were coming in, although I wasn't sure when, since Lucy hadn't left the kitchen since we had all drawn the names out of the box, or maybe Becky?

"Right. Okay." My thoughts were interrupted by Alice's voice. "What do we have here? I see a lady who recently passed over, probably in the last year or so. Her name started with an S ... Sandra or Sheila?"

Wow, I thought. She had my undivided attention now. My grandma, Sheila, had died fourteen months ago. She had been ninety-two and hadn't left this world without a fight, having recovered from being hit by a car ten years ago, followed by a long list of other illnesses which may have finished off many less-determined, elderly grandmas long before they reached their nineties.

"Your grandma was adopted at birth and never found out who her biological parents were."

"Err, yes, that's correct, how do you ..." My sentence was cut short as Alice's voice gained a more enthusiastic tone.

"She says that she's found out what happened and wants me to let you know."

I smiled. I had always wondered about my gran's origins and had hoped that the secret would be uncovered during her lifetime, but it never had. Several attempts by my aunties, uncles and mum had always drawn a blank and now, here I sat, in front of a psychic who reckoned that my gran had found out for herself from beyond the grave and was going to tell me. I began to forget that I was in Lucy's living room and felt, rather, that I had entered some surreal other world.

"I see a lot of conflict around the time she was born. Her mother did not want to give her up for adoption but was forced to. Yes. I see her parents," Alice continued.

She frowned at this point in her dialogue and then continued in a softer voice, "Oh, that's strange. Usually, mothers were forced to have their child adopted in those times if they got pregnant out of wedlock, especially if they were very young, but your grandmother's parents were married and really loved each other."

I shuffled in my seat and began to feel very warm as my heartbeat seemed to speed up. I rummaged around in my handbag for a tissue and wiped the moisture from the palms of my hands. Alice gestured towards the jug of water and empty glass which were set out on the coffee table in front of us, but had gone unnoticed by me until now.

"You look a lot like your great-grandmother. Same eyes." She gave me a kind smile as her eyes studied my face for a moment.

My pulse began to race in anticipation as I hoped that this woman would be able to tell me why my gran had been adopted. I looked at her, searching her face for more answers.

"Oh, here we go," she frowned in concentration, breaking the slightly awkward eye contact. I hoped that this meant that she had the information I was waiting for.

"It seems that your grandma's parents were in the habit of practising witchcraft. In fact your gran had descended from a long line of witches."

She must have read the horror in my face and continued, "They weren't like the witches in stories who cast wicked spells and have warts on their noses," she smiled and laughed slightly.

That's a relief, I thought, as I slowly exhaled.

"They really believed in helping others and knew that if they wished for something good to happen for the benefit of others and that none would be harmed by the wish, then it would come true. I suppose it's a bit like when people pray; a higher being is asked for help and if the person has enough faith then their prayers might be answered. When a witch casts a spell, she is wishing for something to happen. It all works due to faith."

I shuffled uncomfortably in my seat. *She had a point. So why were witches traditionally seen as baddies?* I wondered.

Wow, this was a lot to take in. I had thought that I had only signed up for palm-reading or someone asking me to choose from a set of tarot cards.

"Anyway, maybe you would like to read up on that one because your grandma has more to say now. It seems that your great-grandparents were being pursued by those who wanted them killed. They fled the village with your grandma who was then only six months old."

Her face became very serious. "She wasn't willingly given up for adoption. In fact, I wouldn't call it adoption at all. She was taken by a childless couple who wanted a magical daughter. Your great-grandparents spent the rest of their lives on the run and were never reunited with their daughter. They are together now though and want you to know that they are all happy again."

She smiled at me. "I hope you found that helpful, Claire. That's all I have for you today, but if you want to see me again in the future, I'd be more than happy to do another reading for you."

I stood up. My legs felt slightly shaky and the words 'thank you' seemed to be coming from someone else's mouth rather than my own. My friends turned as I made my way back into the kitchen. "Where's Becky?" I asked, hoping to delay their questions.

"She had to go. Apparently, she's got an important meeting down in Leicester tomorrow and has some stuff to get ready."

"What did she say about what happened in there?" I gestured towards the sitting room, hoping that if they told me Becky's story, they might just forget to ask me about my own.

"Apparently she's going to get married in about three years. Can you imagine it?"

They all laughed at the thought of our career-mad friend actually having time to date someone, let alone fall for someone enough to get married.

My hands shook as I reached for the bottle of red wine, but then I hesitated. If I drank, I'd have to get a taxi home, which would mean that I'd have time to tell them what Alice had said while I was waiting. I looked at my watch. It was only nine o'clock. I looked at my friends, wondering whether they would think me a total party-pooper if I left now.

"Are you okay?" Lizzie's kind eyes showed her concern.

Now was my chance, "Err, actually, no. Do you lot mind if I go? I feel a bit strange after that. I'll tell you all about it some other time."

"Oh. Okay. Drive carefully then," Lucy turned and spoke before heading towards the sitting room for her turn.

I drove home in a daze. Luckily it was only about three miles and there wasn't much traffic on the roads. My mum and dad would be wondering why I had come back so early when I had asked them to babysit for the evening. I had been divorced a couple of years from my son's dad and had had the painful process of coming to terms with being a single parent after spending all my life since my early twenties being married. I had recently started dating someone else. I smiled as I thought of his cheeky smile, then wondered what he would make of this psychic reading. I hadn't even told him the reason we were having a girls' night at Lucy's midweek. I had just said that her husband was out and she decided that a long overdue get together was needed. I would tell him soon though. I had decided that in any future relationships I would be totally straight about everything from the start. Okay, so I had already been vague about the main purpose of tonight. As soon as I had come to terms with my own feelings I would tell him. What was I worried about anyway? I'd visited a clairvoyant. What she'd said was unexpected but whether he chose to believe in any of it or laugh sceptically was his decision.

I turned into the drive of my semi-detached house in one of the suburbs of Sheffield and fumbled for the keys in my bag. My mum and dad would no doubt have just sat down in front of the TV after getting William to bed. It was easier to let myself in rather than hope that they would hear my knocking over the important part of some six-part drama on ITV.

I found the keys and reached for the door. My heart sank as I heard a car engine and turned round to have my worries confirmed. There, coming to a halt and stopping across from my house was that woman again in the blue car. I turned and looked at her. I had told the police four months ago that a woman kept parking across from my house and was watching me. They had traced her number plate and had apparently gone round and had a word with her, but had informed me that there was no more they could do because she wasn't technically harassing me. I stared at her, afraid to confront her. She looked me in the eye and then turned her head and drove off.

I turned the key in the lock, my hands shaking. First I hear that my ancestors were witches and then, to round the evening off, I get a visit from my friendly stalker. Great. What next?

Chapter 2

I turned back the covers after the snooze alarm sounded on my mobile phone for the second time. Ten days had passed since the girls' get-together at Lucy's. I had admitted to Steve that there had been more to the midweek get-together than I had first let on. He had been sound about it, saying that if that's what we found entertaining then he didn't have a problem with it, although he'd much rather see United.

Steve and I had been together for six months. I had been out with the girls on the night that we met. Last orders had just been called when a group of men caught my eye. I thought that I recognised a couple of them from somewhere and was just trying to work out the answer, when a tall man with the most gorgeous blue eyes turned in my direction as he handed out the drinks which he had been buying at the bar. I looked away, suddenly feeling rather awkward. I tried to concentrate really hard on what Lucy and Becky were saying but when I looked up again, he was there standing next to me. He didn't say anything at first. It was I who felt the need to fill the silence.

"I think I might know some of your friends from somewhere," I informed him.

"Do you live round here?" he asked.

"I used to. I went to school round here," I replied, thinking how attractive he was.

"I might have played sports at your school. Do you know Terry Brown and Pete Evans?" he asked me.

I replied that they were in my year at school. The three secondary schools in the area had often competed in sports events. Every summer we had a joint sports day which included everything from athletics, tennis, and football to even roller skating, the idea being that everyone should join in.

"I remember those two doing athletics," I said, pointing to the two men who had originally caught my attention. "I used to be in the school athletics team, although there were quite a few who were better than me," I told him.

"I used to play football more than anything else," he informed me.

"What's your name anyway?" I asked, suddenly realising that I hadn't even asked.

"Steve. How about you?"

"I'm Claire," I told him.

We went on our first date the following weekend. We went to a quiet pub a few miles from where I lived. Conversation flowed easily and it was difficult to believe that we had only really met properly for the first time a week earlier. I felt comfortable enough to have a laugh but just slightly on edge because I fancied him so much. Last orders were called and we flagged down a taxi which dropped me off first. I decided not to ask him in, thinking that this probably wasn't a good idea on a first date.

The second and third dates had gone really well and it was then that I decided to accept his invitation to go back to his house afterwards. We had coffee and biscuits and talked about the good old days at school in the 1980s. I had taken my empty mug through to the kitchen and was just turning to head back to the living room when I felt his arms around me. I felt a buzz of excitement and turned to face him, anticipating the kiss that I felt sure was about to happen. I wasn't disappointed. He brushed his lips gently against mine at first. I gasped and pulled his head back closer, wanting more. After a couple of really passionate kisses, I looked up at him, wondering whether we should take this further. I was inexperienced as far as dating went, having spent most of my adult life married. As a divorcee, I felt like a teenager again in an older woman's body and was unsure what to do next.

I started to undo the buttons on his shirt and ran my hands across his bare chest. He pulled me closer and began to kiss me again, this time starting to undo my top. I didn't protest. I felt nervous about the idea of us seeing each other naked for the first time, but the feelings I was having urged me to go on. That's when it happened. Steve pushed me away and grabbed hold of the kitchen worktop. His face showed that he was in pain.

"What's wrong?" I asked, concerned and disappointed all at the same time.

"I've just had a sudden sharp pain in my stomach. I'll have to sit down."

He walked through to the living room and sat on the sofa before bending over double.

"Shall I call the doctor?" I asked ten minutes later when the pain still hadn't subsided, but all thoughts of passion had.

The doctor eventually showed up and said that it was probably just indigestion but to go to the hospital if it carried on in the morning.

I eventually went home at two in the morning after Steve assured me that the pain was subsiding. I felt slightly embarrassed sitting in the back of a taxi on my own at that time in the morning and wished that I'd accepted Steve's offer of staying in the spare room. I imagined the driver thinking that I was some sort of tart who'd gone back with a bloke she'd met and was now going home to avoid awkwardness the next morning. The journey continued in silence until I paid and wished him goodnight. Luckily my son had been staying at his dad's for the weekend and therefore there were no awkward questions to answer, which would have been the case if my parents had been babysitting.

After a fairly bad night's sleep, during which I finally decided that maybe he didn't fancy me after all, I got up feeling more confused than ever. We had been getting on really well and most men didn't usually turn down sex, did they?

I didn't expect to be asked out again after the events of that last date, so I was really surprised when he phoned and asked me out to the cinema.

"So, were you alright the next morning then after you got that awful pain?"

"Yes. It was really strange. I got up the next morning feeling fine. I'm really sorry. It felt serious at the time. Maybe I can make it up to you later?"

All thoughts of whether I should trust this man flew out of the window at midnight that night when round two began. This time we managed to get fully undressed and in bed. I was so turned on that I thought I might explode. It had just got to the point where we were about to actually have sex when he yelled out a swear word and moved away.

I couldn't even think of anything suitable to say so I just lay there waiting for an explanation.

"I've just pulled a muscle in my hip!" he winced in pain.

This was becoming a habit and I was beginning to wonder whether there was something wrong with him. He certainly looked as though he wanted to go through with it a few seconds earlier judging by what I had seen under the sheets.

After several false starts, we eventually managed to consummate the relationship a couple of weeks later. William had been staying at his dad's that weekend, meaning that I could stay over at Steve's house. I had gone out deciding that I would give him one last chance. If he complained of some pain part way through the big event that night, I would have had to have a rethink about where things were going. Luckily, everything went well and I woke up the next morning feeling happy and contented.

Now, six months later, I was glad that I had given him another chance. Even though he sometimes got ill or had unexplained pains at really inconvenient moments, I had known him long enough to know that he was committed to me and for some unfortunate reason just seemed to be going through a bad patch, health-wise.

"So. What did she say?" he had asked the next time I saw him after the girls' night at Lucy's. "You know, that medium or psychic or whatever she was that you saw."

"Well, err," I blushed, knowing that what I was about to say would probably sound totally ridiculous to this straightforward, one-of-the-lads sort of man.

He had only been half-looking at me as he asked the question, and began randomly scrolling through the Sky menu on the TV. The lack of direct eye contact made it easier to hide my embarrassment as I spoke.

"She reckoned that my grandma had come through to her and was telling her about why she had been adopted as a baby." I waited for some sort of recognition that he was listening. He slowly sat back and placed the remote control on the arm of the chair. He looked at me. I melted as I met his blue eyes with mine and felt rather vulnerable. I had no idea what he would think of what I was about to say.

"What did she say?"

So he was listening. There was no turning back.

"She said that my grandma's parents were witches and that their ancestors were witches too." There, I'd said it.

His mouth broke into a large grin and he laughed. "I hope it's not your ancestors cursing me with these accidents and illnesses I've had since I met you. What if they don't like me and are trying to scare me off?" his laughter indicated that he was joking. I had spent the ten days between Alice's reading and this weekend dreading Steve taking the whole thing seriously. I had built everything up in my mind until I had imagined him accusing me of being a witch and saying it was my fault that things seemed to keep happening to him.

Luckily he had laughed it off and had settled on Match of the Day. Normally I would have pointed out the unfairness of him coming back to my house and putting whatever he wanted on my TV, but it had given me the chance to sit and think. My mind wandered back to the illnesses and injuries he'd had since we met. He had put his back out only a few weeks after our first date. He had been queuing in the early morning traffic on his way to work when some buffoon, who was busy changing their CD, failed to notice that the cars in front had actually stopped. Strangely, the twenty-something male driver of the Clio had managed to get away with just broken headlights, but Steve had ended up being stretchered to hospital after his back spasmed to such an extent that he couldn't even get out of the car. Now, six months later, his back was still likely to go at the most inconvenient moments. I thought about those times when I had waited for him to come round on a Friday evening. Friday had always been a problem night for getting a babysitter for William, so we had tended to watch a DVD and open a few cans, or get a takeaway after William had gone to bed. I wondered how many times I had started flirting with him the moment the DVD had finished, or part way through if the storyline had been rubbish, hoping that he'd get the message. I wasn't very subtle, especially if the film was boring. I had lost count of the number of times that he'd started to get up from his seat, where he'd been sitting for the last two hours, but had winced in pain as his back gave out again and all thoughts of seduction had to be substituted with me playing nursemaid. Add to that two bouts of sickness and diarrhoea and three throat infections over the six months.

Steve worked behind the scenes in IT for a large bank. At night he liked to chill out with a beer and watch sport. He was an ordinary, down-to-earth man who lived in the real world. *Maybe he just needed to look after himself a bit better and get more exercise or something*, I thought to myself, wondering why he was ill so often.

My thoughts came back to the present time as the clock's digital numbers told me that yet another ten minutes had passed that morning. I woke William on my way to the bathroom. Steve hadn't stayed over, so there was just me and my eight-year-old son for breakfast. I looked in on him again as I crossed the landing in my fluffy dressing gown and pink slippers. He'd gone back to sleep, as usual.

"William, get up, it's school. Get washed and dressed!" I commanded impatiently, forgetting the fact that we now had to rush was because it was I who had pressed the snooze alarm twice and then daydreamed.

Luckily, my part-time job meant that I could drop William off at school and then go straight to work. So, as long as we were out of the house by half past eight, everything ran to schedule. At twenty past eight we had finished our breakfast, and we were just about to clean our teeth before getting ready to set off when I noticed a bright blue car across the road. My pulse immediately started to race. I looked out of my front room window and saw that woman again. She had obviously got up very early, especially to pay me a visit.

"What's wrong Mum?" William asked. He couldn't have helped but notice the way in which my voice went shaky as I ordered him to hurry up and get his shoes on.

"Nothing, let's just get going."

As I reversed off the drive, the woman in the blue car actually reversed to let me get off my drive and I noticed with horror that she was following me. I turned into the cul-de-sac next to William's school and, sure enough, she turned in too. I got out of the car and held William's hand tight. My initial thought to ignore her soon changed as she wound down her window and I was forced to walk past her car which was parked inches behind mine.

"What are you doing? Why are you following me?" I asked, clutching William's hand even tighter.

"You're having an affair with my husband, Ted." She looked me straight in the eye and accused me.

I couldn't believe it. I looked at this woman who was difficult to age, but would struggle to pass for under fifty-five.

"I'm not, honestly. There's only one man in my life and he's not your husband. He's not called Ted and he's never been married!" I wasn't sure why I had felt the need to supply all this information, but I wondered whether she was implying that Steve was actually her husband.

William started to cry.

"Look, you've made him cry now." The old cow actually had the nerve to make out it was my fault that my son had been frightened and made to cry on his way to school, on what should have been a normal, Wednesday morning. She must have got up very early to dress in her smart jacket and apply her make-up, in her attempt to look her best as she confronted the other woman.

"How dare you follow me around, accusing me of things I know nothing about and upsetting my child? I've already told the police about you. I'm going to let them know about this as soon as I've dropped him off." I grabbed William's hand and quickly ran through the school gates, which were luckily the pedestrians-only entrance. I had to explain to the teacher why we were late, yet again, when we had actually left on time, for once.

I wondered whether she actually believed me as I said that there had obviously been a case of mistaken identity and that we were followed to school by some crazy pensioner.

I phoned the police, quoting the incident number which had previously been issued, before continuing on my way to work. Luckily, my job with the local, free newspaper was hectic enough to take my mind off what had happened and the constant ringing of the phone left me with no time to dwell.

That evening, once William and I had eaten and he was busy playing with friends next door, I phoned Steve.

"Hi, I know you're coming round in a bit, but I need to tell you something."

"Okay. I'm just having my tea, is it quick?"

"I'll go into more detail when you get here, but that woman in the blue car actually followed me to school this morning."

"What?" he sounded genuinely shocked. "Did you confront her?"

"Yes. Listen. I'll tell you the whole story when you get here, okay?"

"Okay. See you later." He had proved not to be one for long telephone conversations and the realisation of what this woman was accusing me of seemed suddenly inappropriate to just drop into the conversation when he was about to eat. I had intended getting the whole story off my chest and had made myself feel worse by only having a brief conversation. What if Steve didn't believe that I wasn't having an affair? I hadn't thought of that earlier. What if someone was spreading rumours about me around the village?

My head was spinning by the time Steve arrived at eight o'clock. I waited until William was safely tucked up in bed before I gave full details of that morning's events.

He ran his hands through his dark, wavy hair, clearly annoyed. "What did the police say?" he asked.

"That they'd call round later and ask me to give them some further details."

"She needs stopping. The woman's not right in the head!"

I sat down, relieved that it was her that he was mad at and not me. Thank goodness he thought the concept of me knocking off some other man, presumably old enough to be my dad, was outrageous.

Just as I was managing to put the whole incident to the back of my mind, with the help of half a bottle of Shiraz and an episode of 'Shameless', there was a knock at the door. I jumped, spilling drops of red wine onto my favourite jeans.

"Who the hell is that at this time of night?" Steve wanted to know. "If it's her, I'll give her a piece of my mind!"

It was the local police officer. After apologising for the lateness of his call, he sat down, carefully avoiding the alcoholic wet patches, and took out his notebook. I told him the full story about how this woman had been parking outside my house for months but then, that morning, she had followed me to my son's school. I pointed out to him several times that I wasn't having any sort of affair with this woman's husband and that I had no idea why she had chosen me to accuse. I noticed with annoyance that he didn't seem to be interested in writing this part of my story down. I supposed he just wanted the facts about this woman's behaviour rather than what was happening in my love life, but I felt annoyed that anyone might think that I would be interested in anyone other than Steve.

"Did you happen to notice the number plate of the car?" he enquired.

Did I know the number plate? It was etched permanently on my mind! I thought about all those times I had seen the same make of car in the same shade of blue and had felt a stab of anxiety until I checked the number plate. There seemed to be so many of them around but only one thing on one of them identified the driver as being her. The number plate.

I supplied the details and he went on his way, promising to trace who the car belonged to and to have a word with her. He would get back to me with the results.

As soon as the door was closed, I went through to the kitchen and began scrubbing at my jeans with the dishcloth in the hope that the wine hadn't stained too much. I hadn't realised quite how much fury I was taking out on my clothing until Steve suggested that I stopped rubbing unless I wanted a hole in them.

I lay awake that night listening to Steve's breathing, furious at this woman's accusations.

The following evening, William was staying over at his dad's house and I had arranged a girls' get together at a quiet local pub. I felt that I had to tell them about this mad woman.

After a five minute walk from my house, I stepped over the grass verge and into the car park just as Lucy was trying to reverse her green Fiesta between two parked cars. Becky frowned as she got out of the passenger seat, her black dress rubbing against the door of the next car as she tried in vain to breathe herself in. Lucy never had to think about whether she had room to actually get out of the car, once she had squeezed it in between two larger vehicles. Becky wouldn't dare instruct her to move the car to a different parking space so that she could actually get out without using her clothing as a cleaning cloth.

I walked over to greet them whilst Becky frantically dusted herself down.

"Is Lizzie coming?" I asked as we headed towards the double doors of the Yellow Lion.

"Yes. She said she'd make her own way here because Pete's working late."

Lizzie had a ten-month-old daughter called Millie and had recently gone back to work part-time following her maternity leave from Debenhams. Pete worked as some sort of Manager for an IT company and often didn't get in until half past seven. This must have made things really hard on Lizzie, who was no doubt tired after her job which involved standing up most of the day, followed by picking Millie up from the nursery, feeding her, getting her to bed and then starting on the preparations for the adult evening meal. I was glad that William had reached school age.

"I'm not sure I could go through all that baby stuff again," I announced. "It's bad enough getting William ready in a morning. My days of fighting with a toddler to put his clothes on are over!"

"Does Steve want kids?" Lucy looked at me, scanning my face for a response.

"I don't know. We don't even live in the same house yet!" The question seemed a bit strange to me since Steve and I had only been together six months. We were both thirty-nine, so not all that young, and our sex life seemed to be cursed. Whether or not Steve wanted kids was something that had never been discussed and that I had never given a second thought.

The conversation was put on hold as we approached the bar and Becky got out her purse.

As we thanked her for getting in the first round and Lucy showed her surprise that I'd ordered Guinness, we looked around for a suitable place to sit and chat. Since most of the pub was actually empty, apart from a single pensioner leaning on the bar and telling the landlord stories about his wife's arthritis, then the two lads in their late teens sorting through their change for a fifty pence piece for the pool table, most of the seats were considered suitable for our group. I eventually persuaded the others to go to an alcove which was far enough away from the bar that the staff wouldn't hear every word of what we had to say but which was still visible from the door so that Lizzie would find us.

Becky was just questioning me on why I didn't want the bar staff to hear when Lizzie arrived. Her long, black top clung to the leftover pregnancy bump which it was probably meant to disguise, but she had mostly got her figure back.

"Those jeans look good on you," Lucy informed her, which was true but probably needed pointing out to Lizzie who looked as though she needed some compliments. Her usually cheerful face looked harassed and pale. Dark circles framed her blue eyes.

"I only slept about three hours last night," she announced in response to our concerned faces. "Millie kept waking up wanting a cuddle."

After we'd bored Becky with the difficulties of sleep deprivation for fifteen minutes, she decided that a change of subject was required.

"Anyway, Claire, what's this about some woman stalking you?"

I felt my pulse start to get faster and that slightly sick, stressed feeling that I got every time I saw or thought about that woman in the blue car, which was how I was referring to her at the moment.

"Well," I started, wondering whether to go into the full story or just supply a brief outline. "A few months ago, I was just getting ready to go out with Steve when I noticed this woman sitting in a car outside my house and just staring in at me through the front window."

"Weird!" Lucy announced, taking a sip of her Strongbow and moving forward in her seat.

"Anyway, I didn't think anything of it at the time because we were on our way out for the day."

I continued to tell my friends how she had regularly turned up at different times of the day including several times in the week when I had decided to have my lunch at home and also on some Saturday mornings. I finished with what had happened when she followed me to William's school and accused me of sleeping with her husband.

"What? Oh no, what did you say?" Becky put down her empty wine glass and looked shocked.

I retold the whole story of how I had told this woman she must have the wrong person and how William had ended up going to school in tears.

"What a deranged bitch!" Becky announced to raised eyebrows from Lizzie at the word 'bitch'.

"That was a bit much, saying that to you in front of William." Lizzie's concerned voice was in complete contrast to Becky's outraged one. "I hope she'll apologise when she finds out that she's made a mistake."

"It was a bit much saying it at all!" I announced, the fury rising within me again. "Why on earth would she think it was me? I've not been anywhere without either you lot or Steve. Why would I be interested in her husband?"

"Maybe her husband looks a bit like Steve and someone who only saw you from a distance with Steve made a mistake?" Lucy suggested.

"Or maybe I happened to be in the same pub as her husband once and said 'excuse me' to get past him or something and some paranoid idiot decided to make something out of it?" I added.

The truth was I really didn't know. I hadn't been anywhere with the man and had no idea how anyone could think we had been seen together. To be accused of something you hadn't done was bad enough, but to be continually followed and stared at was getting quite disturbing.

I offered to buy the next round of drinks and by the time I got back from the bar the topic of conversation had been changed to a debate on what the best age to have children was. I sat down, relieved, hoping to put the feelings which had been stirred up by talking about that lunatic woman to the back of my mind.

Chapter 3

I started to leap out of the armchair but yelled 'ouch' as that sharp pain shot across my hip joint again. I froze in a half-standing, half-sitting position for a couple of seconds before straightening myself up and walking over to the window ledge and picking up the cordless phone which had now stopped ringing. I dialled 1471 and was informed that my mum had just called. After a quick check of the time, I decided that I'd got half an hour to have a chat before William's bath time and keyed 3 to return the call.

"Hi, it's me. Sorry I didn't get to the phone in time. I was in the other room," I decided to tell her rather than mentioning my recently acquired dodgy hips. I managed to speak up quickly before she accused me of never answering the phone.

"How is Steve? Any better?" is what she actually said.

"Not really. Sometimes he seems to be getting better," I continued, "but he'll get up too quickly or pick something up at a funny angle and his back will go again."

"I'm sure it's his diet." My mum always thought of herself as the fount of all knowledge and came up with a reason for every scenario.

"Anyway, did I tell you about that funny thing that happened a few nights ago?"

"No, what funny thing?" I was glad that she'd changed the subject rather than have to listen to her advice all over again on what Steve ought to be doing.

"Well, as I was getting ready for bed, I dropped one of my earrings. I thought it had gone towards the radiator but I spent about fifteen minutes searching the bedroom carpet for it but couldn't find it anywhere."

"And that's funny because?"

"I've not got to the funny bit yet. Listen. Anyway, I mean funny peculiar, not funny ha ha," she informed me.

"Okay. Go on."

"Well, I was fast asleep when I was woken by someone patting me on the shoulder and then they put their hand around mine and squeezed it shut. I kept my eyes closed, thinking it was your dad at first, but then I wondered why there seemed to be something sharp sticking into my hand. I opened my eyes and my earring was there in the palm of my hand."

"Why would Dad do that in the middle of the night instead of just putting it on the dressing table?"

"He didn't. He was fast asleep the whole time. It took me ages to wake him up. You know what a deep sleeper your dad is." It was true. Car alarms, thunderstorms directly over the house and that minor earthquake that left several houses in Barnsley without a roof had failed to wake my dad up.

"Who put the earring in your hand then? Are you sure you didn't just find it before you got into bed and went to sleep holding it?"

"No. I was reading when I got in bed to take my mind off my annoyance at not being able to find the earring. I wouldn't have held the earring in my hand if I was reading; I would have put it down somewhere. No. Someone definitely put it in my hand in the night."

She had told me stories before about how deceased uncles and the like had visited her in the night and she reckoned that they only visited you if you weren't afraid. I had always been terrified of the thought of anything from the spirit world visiting me in the night and as I was growing up had desperately hoped that there were no such things. The psychic night at Lucy's had got me wondering. It was still all rather scary.

I noticed that it was half past eight and told her that I'd better get William ready for bed. I promised to either phone again soon to continue our conversation or call round later in the week.

After I'd finally got William to stay in his bedroom and made myself a cup of tea, I picked the laptop up and clicked on the Internet Explorer icon. This was becoming a bit of a predictable routine on the nights I wasn't seeing Steve. We'd decided not to live out of each other's pockets, agreeing that we needed nights when we did our own thing. Recently though, my own thing seemed to be going on the Internet and aimlessly looking at eBay or causes of prolonged back pain (and more recently hip pain). It was amazing how quickly it got to midnight and I would close down the laptop, feeling annoyed with myself for not doing something more productive with my time.

Tonight, though, I had something that I really wanted to find out about. I waited in frustration as the Internet seemed to take an age to get going. When eventually the relevant bits seemed to be displaying on the screen, I typed in 'witchcraft' and waited to discover what the search engine would come up with.

I read various descriptions of what a witch was, such as 'someone who practises magick' or 'someone who casts spells to act on another person'. Also, how these days there is the concept of a white witch who would only practise magick to help another person with their consent and how in the past many witches were hunted down for supposedly casting spells to act on others against their will. I also discovered that the word should be spelt 'magick' with a 'k' to differentiate it from the magic tricks that a magician on stage might do. I wondered what type of witches my ancestors had been, if they had been witches at all. Had they been wrongly accused? Had they been these 'white witches' who helped others, but had been chased out of the village by those who feared their apparent magical talents? There was obviously a lot more to this that I didn't understand.

I looked up 'witch trials', and discovered a list of people who had been killed for practising witchcraft. According to the list, the last person to be executed for being a witch was over two hundred years ago, although it mentioned that in reality it still went on in the early 1900s. The list showed the person's name, where they lived, what they had supposedly done, and how they had been killed. Entries such as hanged, beaten to death, or simply murdered were the most common. I tried another search. This account of what became of witches went on to state how they were never actually burned at the stake, but more likely tied to a stake and strangled, followed by the burning of the body.

This was gruesome and quite depressing. Supposing my great-grandparents had really been witches? I wasn't surprised that they had fled. It would have been the early 1900s but the idea of witchcraft would have still been taboo, I thought. And to have their daughter forcibly taken and not to know what had become of her? They must have spent the rest of their lives wondering whether she had been tortured and killed for being the daughter of a witch or whether she was being cared for and loved. I thought about what the psychic had said. She reckoned that they were all together again now and that they were happy.

So what about modern-day witches? Did they really exist? I wondered.

I made some more Internet searches and discovered that these days a whole load of people were modern-day witches. There seemed to be some sort of rule-of-three thing, which meant that unless a witch was really foolish, they would never do anything that would knowingly harm another due to the rule of three. This basically meant that if you wished something bad upon another person and it happened, then something three times as bad would happen back to you. This was why most modern-day spells ended with the words 'and it harm none,' so that the wish would only be granted if no one would be harmed because a witch wouldn't want to be guilty of causing harm to another.

I noticed as I looked up at the clock on the mantelpiece that midnight had long gone and that it was quarter past one. I went about my usual routine of checking that the doors were locked and that the gas hob was off. Even if I'd not used it that day, I checked each knob about three times due to my overactive imagination telling me that it might have turned itself on and was likely to pour gas into the kitchen which would then explode as I came down for a glass of water in the night, due to a spark from the light switch. I checked everything even more carefully that night, feeling that the spirits of some deceased witches might be annoyed with me for reading websites that gave an incorrect account of what their craft was all about. I left the landing light on, feeling safer with a strip of light coming under the door. Well, for about five minutes anyway, at which point I got up and turned it off again, thinking that it might be a fire hazard. It was much later when I finally got to sleep, as my mind raced with thoughts about what sort of witches my great-grandparents were and did this mean that I might be magical? Was it hereditary? Was there really such a thing as magic or even 'magick', or was this clairvoyant/psychic woman a fake and the whole thing imaginary? I then felt too scared to go to sleep, wondering whether I would be visited by spirits in the night who felt that I needed to be put straight on a few things.

That's where it all started, I suppose. The events that followed were to change my life forever.

I didn't tell anyone about my recent interest in witches at that time and decided not to mention anything else about what the psychic at Lucy's had said. It was a Wednesday teatime. William had already gone to his dad's to spend the night there and I wasn't seeing Steve until about half past eight. I was in on my own and decided to eat my bowl of spaghetti bolognese in front of the TV. I flicked through the Sky menu for several pages. Some sort of Psychic Channel caught my eye and I chose *Select*. The presenter invited the TV audience at home to phone and speak to one of the psychics working behind the scenes. Alternatively, you could send a text and choose whether to have it appear up on screen and the resident psychic would reply on air when it got to your turn, or you could have the answer sent directly to your own mobile, in private. I decided to send a text and have the reply sent to my mobile.

I was just wondering what to ask when the phone rang. I jumped like someone caught in the act of doing something that they shouldn't be doing. It was Steve.

"Hi, it's me. Not called at a bad time, have I?"

"Err, no. I was just eating my tea, but it's okay, I can talk." I muted the TV as I spoke, not wanting him to hear the TV presenter selling the services of the 'brilliantly gifted psychics who were waiting for your call'. I knew that he didn't like talking on the phone much, so there was no danger of my food going cold.

"I'll be round about half past eight," he continued (*yes, I knew that*, I thought). "Do you want me to get anything from the shops on the way?"

"Go on then, get a big bar of chocolate."

"Okay. See you later."

He could have just surprised me and turned up with the chocolate, like he often did, I thought.

I finished my bolognese and took the bowl through to the kitchen sink. I picked up my mobile again and typed in a question. "When will Steve's back be better?" I asked and then nervously keyed in the four-digit number and hit send. I left the phone on the kitchen table and decided to wash the pots while I waited for a response. I wondered whether they would actually reply and whether it would be good or bad news. *How could someone, even if they were genuinely gifted, know your destiny from a text message?* I wondered. *Maybe it was possible to know things about someone if you were face-to-face with them*, I thought, imagining someone interpreting some sort of vibes or aura that no one else could see. Text messages, however, were so impersonal.

I jumped as my phone bleeped. I ripped off my washing-up gloves, or tried to. Why did the left one always refuse to come off? I told myself to calm down. The message would still be there, however long it took me to get the sodding gloves off.

"With rest, he should be better soon my dear," the message read. I smiled to myself, forgetting any cynical thoughts that I may have been having a few minutes earlier.

I continued to wash the pots and wondered whether to ask anything else. At £1.50 per question and a further £1.50 per reply, I had already spent £3. My mobile phone bills were already double the thirty pound contract that I had signed up for. Two calls made via directory enquiries and VAT had soon helped to raise the balance even further.

I managed to control the urge to text again until about eight o' clock. "Why is some woman following me around in her car?" I asked.

Steve arrived a bit earlier than expected. The physic must have been busy or was having trouble answering my question because my phone had still not bleeped. I shoved it behind the cushion on the settee and sat down.

I engrossed myself in the DVD he had brought and shared the chocolate between the two of us. It was one of those DVDs showing all six episodes of series two of an ex-BBC comedy. After the first one ended, I decided to nip to the loo before we decided whether to watch the next one that night.

"I think you've got a text message," Steve announced, as I walked back into the living room. "It sounded like a phone bleeping anyway, and it's not mine," he informed me.

I took the phone from behind the cushion. I was glad that he was in the armchair and hadn't decided to dig out my phone and pass it to me. The screen was one of those which showed the first few words of the text message and who it was from before you even opened it.

I looked up at Steve and saw that he was engrossed in some trailer on the TV for a new series about football that was coming up. I opened the message. "This woman is very paranoid," it began. "She is worried that now she is getting older her husband will look elsewhere."

That was all it said. But then how much information did I expect from one text message? I hadn't told them anything about this woman accusing me of having an affair, and yet the psychic seemed to know that this was what it was about. *Was it a lucky guess or could someone really pick up on someone else's life through just a text message?* I wondered.

I deleted the message and put the phone back on the arm of the sofa. Steve looked at me as though he was waiting for me to say something. "It was Becky saying that they're thinking of arranging another girls' night out," I lied. Well it was part lie anyway. Becky had sent a message earlier asking which nights I would be free for a night out and, since I'd deleted the text message from the psychic, hers was now the last message showing again. Of course Steve would never have checked my phone anyway. He was one of the most trusting men I had met.

"When?"

"Don't know yet." This was true. No actual date had been confirmed yet for a night out.

"Has that woman been round again in her car?"

I jumped. Partly because only seconds earlier I'd been reading advice from a psychic I'd never met about this woman and partly because my stomach lurched every time I saw this woman or thought about her.

There was something very creepy about someone turning their car round outside your house and staring down your driveway to check whether you were at home. I assumed that this was what she was doing anyway. If she saw my car, then she probably assumed I was in and therefore not with her husband. What did she do on the days that my car wasn't there? Did she drive around the local area looking for me? Did she turn up at her husband's work to check that he was where he was supposed to be? I felt sick.

"Are you okay?" Steve looked concerned now.

"I'd rather not think about her unless I really have to. Just the thought of her makes me feel upset. It's really creepy, Steve."

"Phone the police again," was his advice.

"She's not actually getting out of her car and doing anything though, is she? Can they do anything about someone just turning their car round at the end of your road?" I doubted it very much.

Times like this made me start to love Steve just a bit more. Most men would think there's no smoke without fire and begin to wonder whether there was something going on between myself and this crazy woman's husband. Steve believed me and trusted me. I felt bad that I couldn't tell him what the text messages had said, both about his back pains and this woman. I thought again about my promise to myself to tell him everything. He had to like me for who I really was, even if I was someone who contacted psychics and was wondering whether my ancestors were witches.

Why is it that the more someone means to you, the more vulnerable you feel? I felt very vulnerable at this point. Someone was following me around, accusing me of something I hadn't done, and if my boyfriend decided to believe her I could lose him. I was also a bit scared now that it seemed that psychic people, witches, and spirits from beyond the grave might really exist. I had previously thought that they were only things that happened in stories. But now I wasn't too sure.

Chapter 4

It must have been a Friday, because I had finished work at lunchtime and had changed into my jeans and black jumper before spending a couple of hours doing boring tasks, such as cleaning the bathroom and sorting through the pile of letters which kept having to be moved from the dining room table every time we wanted to eat or a visitor came round. Part of me thought that really you should just be who you are and shouldn't assume that visitors were making judgments about you because you had piles of letters cluttering up your house and your breakfast pots hadn't been washed. Life wasn't like that though, was it? People did make judgments and assumptions.

The living room only got a very quick vacuum because I noticed that it was nearly three o'clock and William's school finished at ten past.

I shoved the vacuum cleaner into the already-full understairs cupboard, flinging a couple of worktops back onto the ironing pile, and shut the door quickly.

After grabbing my trainers I perched on the stairs to tie the laces. This seemed easier today, so maybe whatever had been wrong with my hips recently was getting better, I hoped.

It was only a five-minute walk to William's school, but another five minutes could easily be added on before I got to the outside door of his classroom, due to the number of pushchairs in the yard which had to be outmanoeuvred.

William eventually appeared, looking around to check whether I was on time today. He thrust a worryingly heavy sandwich bag and coat in my general direction which I seemed to have accepted without even realising and then he darted off up the grass bank next to the playground.

The heavy sandwich bag was usually an indicator that he had left most of his lunch and would try to grab crisps and biscuits out of the cupboard as soon as he got home. This would then be followed by a bad mood which I assumed was caused by not eating all day and then eating loads of sugary foods.

I was brought out of my analysis of William's eating habits versus mood swings by the realisation (a couple of seconds too late) that he was sliding down the grass bank on his knees in his new school trousers.

"Oh William, why do you have to do that?" I demanded to know. *It's a pity they didn't have to wear shorts for school like in my dad's day*, I thought. Skin seemed to get grass-stained a lot less than trousers.

I managed to grab the back of his school sweatshirt just in time before he attempted to head up the bank again for round two. "William, stop that now! Firstly, it's a waste of money having to buy new trousers all the time, and secondly it's really difficult getting the exact shade of grey that you like in your size!" It was true. He refused to wear the slightly lighter grey that some kids' clothing shops stocked in their school range. William would only wear the more fashionable charcoal grey. *Most kids must be the same though,* I pondered, since the charcoal grey trousers in all but age three to four and fifteen to sixteen had usually sold out unless you managed to go to the shop on the day that the clothes were actually being put out on the shelves! By some fluke, I had managed that last time and had stocked up on three new pairs to replace the last couple that had spent three out of six months with ever-growing holes in the knees surrounded by ever-darkening green stains.

On the way home, the raised voices of other harassed parents somewhere behind me soothed my fears that it wasn't just my child that didn't listen. Almost as soon as he had taken his shoes and coat off, and before he could raid the chocolate biscuit tin, or rummage through the freezer for ice cream, I thrust a banana in his hand and dug the almost full drink bottle out of his school bag and thrust that into his other hand. I guiltily switched the TV on, knowing that he'd plonk himself in front of it. I'd tried sitting down with him a few times in the past with the intention of having a mother-and-son chat about what sort of day he'd had, but he'd just frowned and said nothing had happened. After thinking about how I felt when I first got in from work, though, I could see where he was coming from. The first thing I always did was to get a coffee and a couple of biscuits and usually wanted to be on my own for at least as long as it took to get to the bottom of the mug of coffee. I was working on the assumption that he was the same and just wanted leaving alone for a bit. I knew he'd let me know if there was anything he wanted, or anything he wanted to talk to me about.

I sighed at the biscuit crumbs gathering on the floor and picked up the pile of clean bedding and towels which had been dumped on the back of the settee the night before. After I'd gone upstairs and stuffed them into the cupboard, I flung myself down onto the bed, hoping for a few minutes' relaxation time. I looked up at the recently-painted, pale blue walls and congratulated myself on finding a border and curtains which matched my colour scheme so well. My bedroom was one of the few uncluttered places in the house. It was my own little sanctuary where I could go to get lost in my own thoughts. I thought about Steve, his sparkly blue eyes and the way a bit of his hair curled down over his forehead. Then there was that cheeky grin he gave after cracking some joke. I imagined him standing there in front of me, tall and broad shouldered. I felt my pulse quicken and smiled to myself. He was probably the most attractive bloke I'd been out with and we got on really well. I'd always settled for the good personality and average looks in the past, assuming that all the best-looking men either wouldn't look at me or they would have an attitude problem. Steve didn't seem to have that arrogance which often went with good looks, though; he was jokey and funny and enjoyed a bit of banter.

The sound of a car going past outside cut into my happy thoughts and I felt my pulse quicken in a more anxious way. It was a red Ford Fiesta. I let out a slow breath of relief. I hadn't seen the woman in the blue car for a few weeks. I wondered whether this meant that she'd actually discovered her husband with someone and had finally managed to have it out with the correct person or maybe she'd driven round at times when I hadn't been at home. I felt my anger building up inside me. Every time she drove past and stared towards the house, I was being accused of something that I wasn't doing. I felt powerless. How could I get her to leave me alone?

"Mum?" William's shouts prevented me from being able to ponder the subject any further. "Mum?" he shouted again.

I went back downstairs to be met by a large plastic sheet with roads and car parks printed on it, the two-dimensional people and shops lying flat at the sides of the roads. "Will you play cars with me, Mum?" I picked up a battered, grey, miniature Volkswagen Beetle and started moving it along the road. I tried really hard to engross myself in this two-dimensional town centre, stopping my car at the traffic lights and parking up outside the shops. It was difficult. Dressing up dolls in home-made skirts and tops might have been more fun for me. I had spent hours with my sister making dolls' clothes which we would then sell with pretend money to each other as our Sindy dolls went on their spending sprees. Those were the days. I leant over and ruffled William's hair affectionately, feeling slightly guilty that I wasn't fully engaging myself in his car game. As I reached over, something caught my eye. I stood up and walked toward the window. William followed.

"Is it that woman again, Mum?"

Involving William in this whole annoying situation wasn't really what I wanted, but since she'd followed us to school that day I'd had to explain that it was a lady who'd got things very wrong and was worrying about things that weren't happening. William never forgot a car and informed me, "Yes. That was her number plate."

I tried to get back into the game with William. He seemed to forget about our local stalker a lot faster than me and was soon making roaring engine and screeching brake noises. I wandered into the kitchen, flicked on the kettle and picked up my mobile phone. 4:10, the digital clock told me. I scrolled down to the text icon on my phone screen and began to compose a message to Steve to inform him that the crazy woman had paid me, or at least my street, a visit. Given that it was a cul-de-sac and she didn't get out of the car, she must have driven and turned round at the end of the road for no other reason than to check on me. It's not as though she drove past on her way to somewhere else and I was worrying over nothing.

Steve replied just as I was putting the milk into my coffee.

"Are you going to let the police know?" was his solution.

"No, there's no point," I replied. "Will you be coming round tonight?"

"See you about eight thirty," was the reply.

I turned the dial on the front of the cooker, ready to grill William's chicken nuggets and potato waffles. After promising myself that tomorrow he'd get a proper wholesome dinner, I plugged the laptop in and opened it on the kitchen table. The wireless Internet connection now meant that I could browse and cook at the same time. I checked on William and noticed that he was engrossed in an episode of *Top Gear*, which he'd probably seen three times already but it still seemed to keep his attention.

I was eager to continue my research into witchcraft and wondered whether there were many witches out there today. I was informed that there were thousands out there in this country although in some countries it was still illegal to be a witch. I went into one website where a young witch who called herself Crystal sold all sorts of spells online but warned that spells should not be performed on others without their permission as this contravened the Wiccan code of practice. I wondered what it was like to cast a spell and imagined making the crazy stalker woman see sense or Steve being restored to the healthy state he was apparently in a few years ago. I realised to my disappointment that I would be casting spells on others against their will if I did that. I imagined the conversation with Steve.

"Hello darling, I've just got hold of a spell to heal your dodgy back. Is it okay with you if I try it out later?" I cringed as I imagined the scenario.

The smell of burning brought me back to reality. I grabbed the oven gloves and pulled out the grill pan. Black chicken nuggets. Luckily, there were plenty more in the packet and I started again, this time keeping a regular check on how my cooking (if you could call it that) was progressing.

The next few hours passed without incident. William went to bed without too much fuss and I was heading back downstairs at twenty past eight. I had left my mobile phone on the window ledge at the bottom of the stairs. Out of habit I picked it up to check whether I'd had any messages. I thought about how we were all much less needy before mobile phones were invented. Now people felt forgotten if they didn't receive texts on a regular basis from their friends updating them on their current situation. Despite the conversation I'd had with myself a few days earlier when I had told myself to stop this texting-the-psychics craze, I decided that one more question wouldn't hurt.

"Am I in the correct job?" I asked. As soon as I had hit *Send*, I wondered why I had bothered. What would I do if they suggested a different career path? Jack everything in tomorrow in search of my true vocation? It was one thing asking for advice from a friend, but to pay to ask and then receive an answer to a question you could have worked out for yourself was a waste of money, surely; but then so was getting drunk and then sicking up all you'd spent your money on a few hours later. I justified my actions to myself by thinking that all leisure activities cost money with nothing to show and that sending and receiving these interactive text messages only cost as much as buying a drink or two in the pub.

The doorbell rang and I quickly stuffed my phone behind the photograph on the window ledge before letting Steve in.

"How are you today?" I asked, hoping he was going to say that he was feeling really fit and ready for action.

"Same as usual really. My back's still aching a bit and I think I've pulled a muscle or something in my thigh."

I tried to hide my disappointment at the prospect of yet another night with limited sexual repertoire. I then felt bad for having such thoughts. *Relationships were about much more than sex after all, weren't they?* I asked myself. I suppose I just felt jealous. I knew that he'd had a really varied sex life with his previous girlfriend. Not that he went on about her all the time or anything. One of those programmes about sex came on late one night and he started laughing about one of them, saying that he'd tried that and they'd both fallen over. His string of injuries and strains since we had met meant that we'd never been able to try out any of the exciting antics shown on such programmes. It wasn't that we didn't want to; our bodies just seemed to prevent it. I wondered what it would have been like if I had met him in my twenties? But then thirty-nine wasn't that old, was it? Life was so unfair. Was my desire building up purely because I couldn't have what I wanted, or was I just more attracted to him than anyone I'd ever met?

I thought again about how silly it was to be jealous of his previous girlfriends. After all, he had finished with them because they just weren't right. I had been married before and Steve had to look at a walking reminder of my past love life every time he saw William, didn't he? Yet he didn't seem jealous or bothered. He always seemed so logical when it came to his feelings about things. I told myself that I ought to be more like that. Things that had happened in the past couldn't be changed, could they?

I was brought out of my inner dialogue by Steve announcing that my mobile phone had beeped.

"I'll check it later," I announced, trying to sound as casual as possible.

About fifteen minutes later, after getting up to go to the bathroom, I grabbed my phone from behind the photograph and took it upstairs with me. I quickly read the message from behind the safety of the locked bathroom door. *"You will do well in your current job although you would do well helping others with psychic work if you had the correct training,"* the text informed me.

Okay. So I was obviously interested in all this psychic stuff or I wouldn't have seen the clairvoyant at Lucy's or started asking them for advice, but become one of them? *Could someone become psychic with training*, I wondered, *or were people born like it?* I thought about Steve sitting downstairs. He was so down-to-earth. He'd think I'd lost the plot. I decided that I'd better go downstairs and act normally, or at least normal for me.

"Is everything okay?" was the first question he asked as I sat myself back down on the sofa.

"Yes. Why do you ask?" I tried again to sound casual. Why did I feel guilty?

I wondered whether I was getting a bit obsessed with this whole thing. The logical part of my brain told me to stop and just get on with my life. The other half of my brain decided that I just had to know whether all the answers to everything were already out there, predetermined. I lay awake that night after Steve had fallen asleep. The latest painkillers he was on seemed to knock him out the minute his head hit the pillow. Two a.m. I couldn't stop thinking about the suggestion that I could be one of those psychic people who helped others.

There had been those couple of times when I was a teenager when I'd been daydreaming. Well, not exactly daydreaming. It had been a bit weird. I hadn't deliberately been thinking about anything. I was just waiting for the toast to pop up in the kitchen when a picture of me with a ginger cat sitting on my knee came into my head. I had thought how strange this was, since I had never had a cat and neither had my parents, since they didn't even like cats. I had forgotten all about this until a few months later when I went to the house of my first ever boyfriend. I sat on the sofa in his parents' house, wondering what a fifteen-year-old girl should say to the parents of her boyfriend, when a ginger cat came and sat on my knee. I looked around and the whole room suddenly seemed familiar, even though I had never been there before.

It hadn't happened before then and I hadn't given it much thought since, until now. I wondered whether everyone occasionally had dreams or saw things which later came true or whether it was a special gift. I decided that maybe I would ask my friends.

The mobile phone bill arrived a week later. My usual £30 monthly tariff, which included a very generous texting package, was exceeded by a further £24. I quickly scanned the pages of my itemised bill until I came to the interactive text message listings. There were eight sent at £1.50 per text and eight received, also at £1.50 each. I wondered whether these people I had been texting were in fact just glorified agony aunts who were good at suggesting the answers to vulnerable people's problems. But then I thought about the ginger cat again. Oh I didn't know! The only thing I did know was that I had spent £24 to be told things that I could have worked out for myself. £24 which could have been spent on some new clothes for William. Whatever the truth was, the texts had to stop. I had decided.

Chapter 5

Over the next couple of weeks, I spent most of the moments of spare time I had on the Internet, searching for information on whether people could really be psychic. I really felt the need to know whether the psychic I saw at Lucy's was for real or just very clever at making things up. Even more importantly, I wondered whether I could be psychic or was the whole ginger cat premonition just a coincidence?

After what must have added up to about twelve hours of my precious spare time spent surfing the web, it seemed that there were two opinions out there. Firstly, that all psychics were frauds, and secondly, that everyone is born with psychic abilities, but most are not taught how to use them and therefore, the ability becomes lost.

Since I couldn't find any evidence to prove facts either one way or the other, I tried to recapture the sort of mood I had been in on the day I had had the cat vision. I couldn't. The more I tried to relax, I either ended up thinking about the ginger cat or my mind wandered onto what I needed to buy for tea. I decided that the best course of action would be to leave things for a while, thinking to myself that if I was meant to know the answer, then I would do in good time.

I really should have taken my own advice and just got on with my life at that stage, leaving psychic advice out of it, but it was like a pimple that demanded to be burst.

It started off like any other Thursday. Steve had stayed over and I had eaten breakfast with him at quarter past seven. I got up from the kitchen table and was spooning coffee into two mugs when Steve asked the question that I really didn't want bothering with at that time in the morning.

"So. Have you seen that woman in the car again?"

"No. Oh Steve, why did you have to bring that up?"

I wasn't even ready to think about day-to-day stuff like getting William up or deciding what to wear. Thinking about that deranged loon wasn't something I wanted to do when I was wearing my snuggly dressing gown and slippers.

It had been a couple of weeks since she had last bothered me with her visit to my street. Now thoughts of her had been brought to my consciousness again and, once there, were difficult to erase.

On my way to work, I decided that my 1980s compilation CD might be the best antidote to the stalker's venom. I was enjoying Madonna's "Like a Virgin" and was just getting into full swing with practising my vocal technique when the pelican crossing displayed a red light. I stopped singing mid-phrase, conscious that the pensioner crossing the road might not appreciate my idea of entertainment.

The amber light had started to flash and I looked towards the oncoming traffic, hoping that they were approaching slowly and had noticed that the old man hadn't finished crossing. The relief that the car on the other side of the road had stopped was soon replaced by a feeling of panic as I came face-to-face with the woman in the blue car. She stared right at me. I tried to engross myself in watching the pedestrian but I could feel her gaze upon me.

The second the old bloke stepped onto the kerb, I was off. I looked in my mirror. There were several cars behind me, so I thought that even if she managed to find somewhere to do a U-turn and try to follow me, there would be so many cars between us that hopefully she would lose me. I wondered where she had been at that time in the morning. Was she heading back towards home from the direction of town? Had she followed her husband to work and was on her way back home? Had she just paid a visit to another suspect before heading back towards my house to camp there for a while? Did she spend all day driving round the area, checking up on a whole bunch of suspects, hoping that eventually she would catch one of them out? I took the turning for Chesterfield and, to my horror, noticed her car only three behind mine. I felt a sort of dizziness come over me and the palms of my hands began to sweat. I tried to get the logical part of my brain to function and tell me to stop being so sensitive. I had done nothing wrong and this was just a stupid old woman wasting her petrol. However, my basic human instincts had taken over at the perceived threat to my existence (even if it was just a mistaken loony in a car). I turned left into the next housing estate. I didn't want her following me to work. I had no idea what I was doing, or where I was going. I would probably be late for work and the thought occurred to me that I would end up at the end of a cul-de-sac, backed into a corner. I saw my chance to escape. I saw a side road next to a primary school. I parked my car outside, got out of the car as quickly as possible and ran in through the gates. I noticed quite a large group of chatting mums coming in the opposite direction who must have just dropped their kids off at school. I put my head down and walked round them before going in through the main school doors. My intention had been to wait a few seconds and then come out again, hopefully in the middle of another group of parents.

"Can I help you?" I looked up and noticed a friendly woman in her fifties smiling at me from behind a partly open glass screen. I had to think quickly.

"Err, I wondered whether there were any vacancies for teaching assistants in the school at the moment?" I replied, wondering how I had managed to be so creative, so quickly.

"Actually, there is one," she informed me. "Let me get you an information pack."

She rummaged amongst various piles of paperwork and then carefully folded a set of papers into an A4 envelope. As she passed them to me she smiled and enquired whether I would like to arrange to look round the school. I informed her that I would phone to arrange an appointment as I didn't have my diary with me at the moment. I looked at my watch as I left the school. 9.15.

I was definitely going to be late for work now. On the plus side though, my stalker's car was nowhere to be seen and I managed to continue my journey to work without further stress.

Work was really busy that day. One person, Mark, had phoned in sick, but whether he really had a stomach bug or whether it was the thought of irate clients phoning him all day wanting to know why he'd cocked up their advertisements was debateable. This, of course, meant that I had to deal with the angry customers which then meant that my own work was getting further and further behind schedule. The silver lining to this cloud was that I didn't have time to think about her, the nutter who seemed to still be checking up on my life.

On the way home I had to call for petrol and decided that a bar of chocolate and magazine might help calm me down from the hectic day. I justified the chocolate on the basis that Steve and I were going out for a meal later that evening for his birthday and I'd have to go a whole extra two hours without food. I looked through the rows of magazines. My eyes were drawn towards one entitled *Spiritual Destiny*. I took this from the shelf and flicked through the pages. I noticed an article on how to meditate and discover inner psychic abilities, another about how a woman turned to her Guardian Angel to get her on the correct life path, and a reader's story of a ghost which visited her every night. At one time, I would have smiled and put this back on the shelf, thinking that it wasn't for people like me, who would rather not think about the possibility of spirits and ghosts. I decided that I would buy it for research purposes and handed over a five pound note wondering whether the middle-aged man at the counter thought I was one of those weird, 'away with the fairies' types.

Later on that evening, William had eaten his sausages and mash and was engrossed in an episode of *Scooby-Doo*. There was still about half an hour before my mum was due to come round to babysit, so I decided to flick though the magazine for ten minutes before getting ready to go out. There were three pages of advertisements for psychics, some of whom claimed to be able to give a reply to a text message within five minutes with guaranteed accuracy. I decided to put them to the test. If I texted three of them the same question and they all came up with the same answer, then there was a good chance that these were genuine psychics. If they all came up with different answers, at least two of them were frauds but at least I would know for definite that I had been wasting my money and had been conned over the last few weeks. I typed my question: "Should I confront the woman in the blue car or ignore her?" I sent the question to someone calling herself Cassandra, claiming to have had twenty years' experience at helping others with her proven abilities. Next I sent the same question to a man called Craig who claimed to be psychic born from a long line of psychics, then a woman called Sadie who claimed to have excellent skills with tarot cards. For something to do while I waited for them to reply, I went upstairs to have a shower.

I emerged from the bathroom at 7:01 (according to the digital alarm clock in my bedroom). The first thing I did was to pick up my mobile phone from the middle of the bed and check for messages. My heartbeat quickened slightly as I looked at the "two messages received" on the screen. I opened the first one and was disappointed to see that it was my mum saying that she was just setting off and would be there soon. The second message was from a four-digit number and I opened it quickly knowing that four-digit numbers were usually from interactive text services, such as TV competitions or anything else that cost a lot more than the usual tariff for text messaging. It read as follows:

"Ignore her, my dear. The woman is very confused at the moment. Any confrontation will not go well at this time. Things will sort themselves out in time." Sadie

Sensible advice, I thought to myself, although it didn't really take someone with psychic ability to suggest this course of action. Any friend could have advised me to just leave it. Maybe I should have just confided in my friends in the first place; however I didn't want one of them to innocently mention it to someone else in conversation and then rumours start spreading. My friends were well meaning and tried to be loyal, but also liked talking, and if it slipped out that someone was accusing me of having a fling with her husband, the gossip might reach less friendly quarters.

I decided to get ready to go out and forget about the whole thing until later. I picked out the black jeans and stripy top. They looked relatively smart, due to being new, but not dressed up enough to look wrong next to the jeans and shirt that Steve would undoubtedly wear, since smart trousers and jackets were not his thing. William was still engrossed in the third of back-to-back episodes of *Scooby-Doo* when I went downstairs and I felt bad at being an inattentive parent. Any guilt soon disappeared when I started talking to tell him that his nan would be here soon and he shushed me, saying that it had just got to the good bit.

William was lucky that my mum arrived at half past seven, just as the episode finished. They could both give each other their full attention. (Mum could show William which sweets she had brought and he could give her his full attention.)

I gave William a hug and told him to be good. I was picking Steve up since I wasn't bothered about drinking on a week night anyway, whereas it was only right that he should be allowed to down a few pints on his birthday. I turned the headlights on, thinking to myself that in a few weeks it would still be light at this time of night, especially once we put the clocks forward.

We arrived at the restaurant at eight o'clock and commented that we probably needn't have booked since there was only one other couple there. I had only ever been to the Horse and Coach at the weekend when booking was essential to avoid waiting forty-five minutes for a table. It had always been worth the wait though; the menu was extensive and the food always arrived well presented and tasting good. I ordered the chargrilled chicken with salad and Steve ordered steak and chips. The waitress had just walked away with our order when my mobile phone audibly vibrated in my bag. I took it out and checked the screen. It informed me that a text message had arrived. I pressed the key to open the message and noticed that it was the second of the replies to the questions I sent out earlier. I decided to read it later and stuffed the phone back into my bag. Steve had an enquiring look on his face, expecting me to explain who it was from. "It was just my mum saying that William had been good and had his bath," I lied, hoping that my face didn't betray me. I wasn't sure why I'd lied. I could have at least said that it was a reply from a friend about a question I'd asked her earlier, which would at least be sort of true.

The buzzing phone was soon forgotten and we enjoyed the food, commenting how young a group of girls looked who had just walked in and were probably celebrating a twenty first birthday or something. At twenty-one I had thought I was so grown up, but I felt so much older and wiser now. We were just tucking into a huge bowl of chocolate fudge cake which we were sharing between us when my phone vibrated again. I inwardly chastised myself for not turning off the vibrate option before coming out. I ignored it.

"Are you gonna see who it's from?"

"No, it'll be nothing important. If it was Mum and something had happened she'd ring. Do you want another drink?" I enquired, quickly changing the subject. Steve looked a bit surprised at first since I didn't offer to buy the drinks very often.

"Are you feeling okay?" he laughed. "It's not like you to offer to part with your money!"

"Well it is your birthday, so I thought I'd make an exception," I laughed. "I'm going to the loo anyway so I'll bring you a lager on the way back."

On the way back, I couldn't help getting my phone out of my bag and stopped in the corridor between the toilets and the bar to read the advice I hoped I'd been sent.

"It would be best to leave things to sort themselves out. She will discover the truth in due course." Craig

Similar advice to Sadie, I thought. I quickly closed that message and opened the one from Cassandra.

"The reason for her behaviour will become apparent in the next six months."

Wow, that's a bit more interesting, I thought as my heartbeat seemed to speed up a bit. I looked up and realised that Steve was no longer at our table. I jumped as I felt a tap on the back and turned round to discover myself face-to-face with Steve. I quickly closed my text message inbox and scrolled to the option to delete all.

"I was wondering where my drink had got to!" Steve joked, although the slightly suspicious look on his face made me feel the need to offer an explanation for the fact that I hadn't even got to the bar yet.

"I bumped into an old school friend in the toilets. Sorry, I'll get the drinks now."

I quickly looked from our table to where I had been reading my text messages a few minutes ago, wondering whether he had seen me on my phone. The restaurant was busier than earlier and I hoped that someone might have been blocking his view. *This was silly. Why had I lied? Everyone was always checking text messages these days. Why hadn't I just said that I'd had some text messages from a friend?* Thinking on my feet had never been my strong point, so the fact that I'd managed it at that school this morning was probably the only time it would happen for another three years. It wasn't even as though I was doing anything wrong. *Others might chastise me for wasting my money on interactive text messages, but it wasn't exactly wrong was it?* I told myself.

Conversation was strained as we took our drinks back to the table. Steve was quiet, his facial expression difficult to read. He clearly wasn't happy. I didn't know what to say. I asked for the bill from a smiling, twenty-something, blonde waitress who asked if we had enjoyed our meals. "Yes thanks," I replied, trying to lighten the gloomy atmosphere that seemed to be surrounding our table.

Steve put on each of the CDs in my car, trying to find something to eradicate the silence. Kylie, Christina Aguilera and Evanescence were not to his taste and he turned it off in a huff and looked out of the window.

The more I tried to think of small talk to make in the car, the less I felt able to speak. I daren't even ask Steve what was wrong because I expected him to ask who all the text messages were from. I knew I'd be too embarrassed to admit that I'd been texting some random strangers who claimed to be psychic and that I'd be more likely to dig myself deeper into my own mess.

I rummaged around the depths of my Tardis-like handbag for my keys, which I promptly dropped onto the floor outside the front door of my house. I didn't knock when I got back from a night out and wait for my mum, or whoever was babysitting, to let me in due to the likelihood of waking William up. My mum was just watching the end of some film, so Steve and I plonked ourselves down on opposite ends of the settee. I was just wondering how long it would be before it would be safe to speak, when Mum announced that it was due to end in a few minutes. After waiting patiently for the all-clear (no one ever dared to speak when Mum was in the middle of a good bit in a film), she stood up and started to gather up her various belongings including her magazine, handbag and cardigan.

"Oh, by the way, I let William off from having his bath. He said he'd washed his hair last night and he was in the middle of watching something that ended at half past eight. He's been a good boy."

Shit, shit, shit ... I looked at a dirty patch on the carpet, unable to make eye contact with either my mum or Steve. I busied myself with seeing Mum out of the house, standing at the door waving until she was out of sight in her Ford Fiesta.

Steve was waiting for me. He had that look on his face that only a man can get when he's seriously pissed off. Most women would have exploded in anger, burst into tears or sulked until asked for an explanation but I always thought that an angry man was much scarier. The deadpan, stony silence. The frown where normally there was a flirtatious twinkle in his eye.

"So. Is your mother suffering from short-term memory loss or did she just say that William didn't have a bath?"

I became interested in the dirty patch on the carpet again. The clock ticked on the mantelpiece. Mum must have turned the TV off, out of habit.

"Who was texting you earlier, if it wasn't your mum?"

I felt myself go red and all communication between my brain and mouth seemed to have been severed.

"I thought so. I should have expected it. It all adds up."

"No, you've got it wrong, I ..."

"Don't tell any more lies, Claire," Steve cut in. "Your reluctance to report this woman who's been following you about, secret text messages, lies ..."

"I didn't report that woman because I hoped she'd just go away. She's got it all wrong and I'm sure she'll find out eventually whether her husband is up to anything."

"Why would she choose you then out of all the women in the village?"

"I don't know," I tried to raise my voice, but the lump in my throat and runny nose just made me sound pathetic. "I thought you trusted me. I'm not up to anything."

"I'm going home. I don't know what to think but I do know that you've just lied to me so how many other lies have you told?"

"You can't drive, you've been drinking!" I informed him, not wanting a drink-drive conviction on my hands.

"I've only had two, I'll be fine," he announced, turning on his heels and heading for the door.

I let him go. I couldn't think of anything to say that would stop him. I watched him drive down the road and then I came back into the house and sat on the settee. Was that it then? Was my relationship with Steve only meant to last six months? Should I just let him go like that? I couldn't. It was bad enough that some stranger was accusing me of things I hadn't done, but for Steve to think I was up to something as well was too much to bear. I went around the house, checking that doors were locked and appliances were turned off in the kitchen and tried to avoid thinking about what had just happened. I went upstairs and looked in on William. He looked so peaceful when he was asleep. After visiting the bathroom, I got myself ready for bed. I was trying hard to tell myself that there was nothing else I could do that night and I'd talk to him tomorrow once I'd had a chance to think what to say. I lay awake most of the night wondering what I was going to say to make everything alright, but I couldn't. Should I just let the dust settle for a few days and then get in touch? What if those few days were enough time for him to go out with the lads and hook up with some tart in an attempt to try and convince himself he'd moved on? I needed to get this misunderstanding sorted out as soon as possible.

By the time the morning came round I decided that the best course of action would be to have a chat with one of my friends. My instincts told me that Lizzie was the best person to talk to on this occasion. I picked up my mobile and sent her a message.

"I need to have a chat with you as soon as possible, when are you free?"

Seconds later, the landline started to ring. I picked up the handset in my bedroom and recognised Lizzie's voice immediately, "Claire, what's wrong?" her gentle but concerned Sheffield accent enquired.

"I can't tell you the full story now 'cos I've got to get William up for school," I glanced at the digital display on my radio alarm clock and took in the 7:42, "but I think I might have just messed everything up between me and Steve."

The tears started to well up in my eyes again and I glanced over at my cheval mirror to see a swollen-eyed, blotchy-faced mess looking back at me with the remains of last night's eye make-up decorating her face.

"What happened?"

"It's a long story."

I wondered what Lizzie would say about the whole stupid situation I'd got myself into. Would she advise me to just walk away and say that if Steve didn't believe me it was his problem or would she tell me it was all my fault for not being open with him? I couldn't imagine her saying either of those things. She wasn't one of those to make judgements about how people should behave. I hoped she'd have some wise words of advice.

"I'll pop round tonight after Millie has gone to bed."

"Are you sure? Has Pete got plans for tonight?"

I suddenly felt guilty about getting her to come out at a time when she'd no doubt be glad of a rest after cooking tea and getting a rather active toddler off to bed.

"Of course I'm sure. Pete's watching some football thing on TV at eight and I'll only be tempted to talk all the way through it when I get bored. I could do with a girly chat after being in the house all day."

"Thanks, Lizzie. Can you come at eight then?"

"Yes, see you later."

Chapter 6

I'm not sure whether throwing a sicky that day was really the best course of action since I had the whole day to myself to dwell on what I could have done differently. All I wanted was for Steve to believe that I hadn't been seeing that woman's husband and that I hadn't been receiving text messages from another man. I picked up my mobile phone and started a text message,

"I am not seeing that woman's husband, please let me explain who the text messages were from."

I had hit send before really thinking whether it was a good idea or not. I looked at the screen waiting for a reply. Nothing. I tried to keep myself busy with doing some housework but found myself wandering over to look at my mobile phone screen every ten minutes or so, just on the off chance that he'd replied. So much for modern technology. It was helping me to make a right mess of my life at the moment. Maybe I should have gone into work, but given that at quarter to one my eyelids were still swollen and red and ditto my nose, it proved that staying at home was the only way to avoid questions or concerned looks.

Steve still hadn't replied at ten to eight and I tucked William into bed, trying to pretend for his sake that all was business as usual. It wasn't easy and I ended up apologising for snapping at him when he asked for a glass of water. As I came down the stairs, I noticed Lizzie parking her car and I quickly ran to open the door before her knocks brought my curious son back down the stairs. We would never get the confidential chat that I needed if William thought that he'd missed a visitor.

I put my fingers to my lips to indicate not to talk until we were safely in the living room. She followed silently, gently closing the doors behind her in the well-practised way that only a parent would do. She waited for me to sit down at one end of the settee before plonking herself down on the other.

"New jeans Lizzie?" I enquired, noticing that she seemed to have lost a few pounds since the last time I saw her and also that she'd had a few streaks put into her hair.

"Yes and a new hairdo, do you like it?"

"Yes, I was just about to comment."

"I thought it was time to make an effort after all these months of putting Millie first and going around looking like a minger."

"I don't think anyone would ever say that about you."

"Well you got your figure back straight away after having William and you were back in your size ten jeans the next day!"

"No, I wasn't. I ordered some from the catalogue in the same style but in a twelve."

We laughed for a few seconds. Having one of my friends to talk to was already cheering me up.

"Would you like a drink?" I was about to offer wine but knew that she wouldn't want that because she was driving.

"Yes I'll have tea please."

I nipped through to the kitchen and put tea bags into two mugs. I didn't fancy hitting the wine if my friend was having tea. I imagined myself getting increasingly maudlin as the alcohol took effect and knew tea and biscuits were definitely a more sensible option.

Lizzie came through as I poured the water. "What's happened then, Claire?"

I finished making the tea and then passed one to her. "I don't know where to start, it's all so embarrassing."

She sat down at the kitchen table. "I won't judge, I promise. I'm here to help."

I put my mug onto one of the mats that had been left out from earlier and sat down next to her.

"Okay. Well, to cut a long story short, Steve thinks I'm having an affair."

"What?" She paused a couple of seconds, and then said, "What has made him think that? I thought he agreed with you that the woman in the car was just some paranoid old bat!"

I had forgotten for a minute that I'd told my friends about that last time we were out at the pub and was taken by surprise.

She must have taken my look of surprise for guilt. "You're not, are you?"

"No, of course not! If I didn't want to see Steve any more I would have just finished things, not started seeing someone else as well."

She must have picked up on the hurt in my voice that she could even suspect me, "I didn't really think you would, but I thought I'd just check in case you'd acted out of character."

After a pause she went on. "What has made Steve start to suspect things then?"

I felt myself blush and I took another sip of my tea as I thought what to say. "I've sent a lot of text messages lately and not said who they were to."

"Well, that's no crime. Does he announce who he's sending his text messages to every time?"

"No, but my phone kept buzzing when we were out last night."

"Well, everyone has phones buzzing these days."

"I must have looked guilty though. I suppose I'd better tell you but you're gonna think I'm a bit of a nutter. Do you promise not to laugh?"

"I'm intrigued now, go on."

"I was texting some psychics," ... there ... I'd said it.

"Who? I mean, where did you get their numbers from?" She sounded more interested than accusatory so I went on.

"From a magazine ... yes, I know you think they're all frauds. I texted three thinking that if they all gave similar answers then there might be something in it."

"Did they?"

I told her the details of how the messages had come through and what they had said, adding that one had indicated that all would become clear in the next six months.

"So you were too embarrassed to tell Steve who these messages were from, but surely one instance of some unexplained text messages doesn't suggest an affair?"

"I've been texting psychics for weeks now, ever since we went to Lucy's. He must have noticed that I kept leaving the room to check my text messages, or I must have looked guilty or something. Then there was my reluctance to report that woman. He put two and two together and came up with five."

"Are you going to tell him what you've just told me?"

"He'll think I'm away with the fairies though, Lizzie."

"Would you rather he thought you were honest and away with the fairies or someone who runs off with older ladies' husbands?"

"When you put it like that ... if he's dumped me anyway I'd rather know he dumped me for being weird than for cheating on him, especially since the being weird bit is true," I laughed. I was so lucky to have Lizzie as a friend.

"Did their advice help?"

I paused for a few seconds before realising what she meant. "Oh, the psychics? Not really. I could have given myself that advice really."

"What made you contact them then?"

"It was after that night at Lucy's."

"Oh yeah. You never did really say what had happened."

I decided that since I was already spilling the beans without her reacting badly, I might as well go on. I told her about how the psychic at Lucy's had suggested that my ancestors were witches and how I'd spent hours on the Internet finding out all about what happened to those practising witchcraft and about modern-day witches.

"Is being a witch hereditary or do you just choose to be one?"

"That's what I was trying to find out."

"Do people really cast spells?"

"It looks like it. There were loads of spell books for sale, even on eBay!"

"Do they actually work, though, or are people making money out of desperate people who'll try anything?"

"I don't know. I did think of trying one to make Steve better but I thought better of it. Especially since there was some rule about not practising magick on others unless they have asked you to."

"Do you really believe in all that stuff then? It sounds as though you've researched it thoroughly."

"I'm just curious, that's all."

"You could cast a spell to get Steve back or make that woman go away," Lizzie laughed. She was joking.

"I think I might as well tell him the truth. At least he might just think I'm silly rather than a two-timing liar."

I diverted the conversation away from casting spells. After spending hours reading up on it, I was beginning to wonder whether it really was possible to cast spells that worked. Not that I'd any intention of meddling with that sort of thing. What if they really did work and a spell to make that woman go away actually made her have a nasty accident? It would all be my fault. What if I magicked Steve back, only to find that he wasn't right for me after all but then I couldn't get him to go?

"Hello, anyone there?" Lizzie waved her hands in front of my face.

"Oh, sorry. I was just wondering what to do."

"Tell him the truth. He has to like you for who you really are. You need to stop texting those people though Claire. I bet you can work the answer out for yourself without their help. I'm always there as well if you need to talk something through."

"You're right. Thanks."

"I'd better go now. Millie will probably have me up at half past six."

I looked at the clock and was surprised to see that it was half past ten.

That was it then. I would talk to Steve.

****

I woke up on Saturday morning to the sound of my bedroom door brushing against the carpet and was greeted by William in his Spiderman pyjamas. I sat up in bed and gave him a hug. I ruffled his hair affectionately.

"Guess what, we've got teacakes for breakfast. Let's go and get them toasted."

"Yeah," he smiled and headed down to the stairs.

"I'll just be a minute, William."

I headed into the bathroom. I realised that it was the first time I had slept right through the night in weeks. My chat with Lizzie had really helped. I told myself that I ought to confide in my friends more often, rather than worrying about things. Now that I'd made a decision on my next course of action I felt much calmer. I sat with William at the table as we ate our breakfast then spent half an hour on the PlayStation with him, still wearing my dressing gown. I realised that it was quite a while since I'd let myself relax this much. I felt guilty as I thought about how much time I'd spent on the computer finding out about this witch business when I should have been spending time with my son. I decided that from now on I would make more of an effort to be a good mum and get back to reality.

I realised, with a sense of regret that today was one of the Saturdays that William was going to his dad's. He usually stayed with his dad on alternate weekends. I was really enjoying the car rally game on the PlayStation but told him that he'd have to go and get dressed because his dad would be here in twenty minutes.

I helped him to get his jeans and T-shirt out of the wardrobe and had a quick shower. I had just managed to get dressed when the doorbell rang. William had already answered it by the time I was heading down the stairs, hair still wet.

Greg glanced through towards the living room, probably wondering where Steve was. He'd had to get used to another man being there when he came to pick William up. Even though we'd split up a long time before I had started seeing Steve, Greg had looked uneasy for the first couple of months of coming to the house and seeing another man there who had obviously stayed over. I don't think Steve particularly enjoyed the situation either. He hadn't got an ex-wife or children which meant that anyone from his past could be left well and truly there.

Sometimes I had felt jealous of the women Steve had been out with, even though it was completely irrational. Rather than settling down at a young age like I had, he'd been out with quite a few women over the years and even though some of them were relatively long term girlfriends, he'd never felt the need to commit to any of them. I had thought that he'd felt differently about me due to the things he'd said, often without realising it. We had only been together about two months when I was talking about how my grandma had gone really forgetful from being about seventy, right up to the time she had died, over twenty years later. He had laughed and said, "Oh, so that's what I've got to look forward to is it? You losing your marbles when you get old?"

On another occasion he had mentioned something about us travelling around Europe together when we retired! Since I was only thirty nine at the time, I could only surmise that he was imagining us growing old together. I had just smiled, trying not to read too much into it. I'd been with one man for years and was still coming to terms with the fact that I was now a divorcee. I wasn't going to rush into another marriage or anything. I couldn't deny the fact though that things had felt right with Steve. We had got on really well from the start, sharing a similar sense of humour and always feeling at ease in each other's company. Then, adding to that the attraction that we both felt for each other, the chemistry had felt just right. I realised that I should have just told him who I was texting. He probably would have just laughed. He enjoyed taking the mickey out of some of my 'silly little ways' as he called it. It was all done in good-humoured banter and I gave as good as I got, joking about his inability to multitask and obsession with anti-bacterial spray.

Once William had gone with Greg, I decided that I had to smarten myself up and get round to Steve's to put things right. Since he didn't like talking on the phone, there was no point phoning him. I would just go and talk face-to-face.

I dug my favourite jeans out of the ironing-basket, or rather, Steve's favourite jeans because they clung in all the right places. I got them ironed then went upstairs and was pleased to see the new, bright pink top which really seemed to suit my complexion. I put on some waterproof mascara, just in case I got a bit emotional. I wouldn't look very attractive with panda eyes. Just a tiny spray of the fragrance that Steve bought me for Christmas and I was ready to set off.

I was on a mission. Nothing or no one was going to stop me sorting things out with Steve. Even the woman in the blue car couldn't stop me today, or so I thought. I was annoyed with myself for even letting her get into my thoughts. It was eleven o'clock on a Saturday morning. I thought about how she used to regularly turn up at this time on a Saturday but hadn't done for the last few weeks.

I tried to put her out of my mind and concentrate on the current situation with Steve. I got into my car and set off down the road. I turned the corner and there she was, just on her way towards me.

"Oh, not now!" I said out loud to myself. I hadn't wanted anything to destroy my confidence at this moment. I needed my wits about me. For some reason, this woman had the ability to make my stress levels rise in seconds.

I tried to ignore her and carried on up the road, but a glance in my rear-view mirror told me that she was doing a U-turn and following me. I carried on towards Steve's, hoping that I'd lose her. It was about five miles to Steve's. It crossed my mind that if she followed me, at least she would see that I wasn't going somewhere to meet her husband, but on the other hand, did I really want her to find out where Steve lived?

I pulled up in the bus lay-by. I'd had enough of this lunatic ruining my life. If it hadn't been for her, I wouldn't have been texting those psychics for advice on Thursday night and Steve would still be with me.

She pulled up behind me. I got out of the car and without thinking what I was going to do or say, found myself striding towards her car. She wound down her window and glared at me.

"Why are you following me?" I demanded, trying to keep the shakiness out of my voice.

"You know why. You're on your way to see my husband, Ted."

"I don't even know anyone called Ted and if he's the same age as you, he must be pushing sixty! I have a good looking, thirty-nine-year-old man of my own. Why would I be interested in yours?"

"Because you're after his money, they always are," she crooned.

"Listen. I don't know who your husband is so please stop following me. You're harassing me and I'll phone the police if you don't stop!"

I hadn't realised how much I'd raised my voice until a woman in her fifties walking her dog turned round, taking in the situation with a frown.

I lowered my voice slightly, "I'm on my way to Steve's. Now follow me if you like but you'll be wasting your time and your petrol!"

I turned and marched back towards my car. Once inside I locked the doors to protect myself from that lunatic. I carried on with my journey and was surprised to see her turn right at the end of the road as I turned left.

I had just about stopped trembling as I turned onto Steve's road. I couldn't see any parking spaces at first. When these terraced houses were built about a hundred years ago, the need for parking spaces wasn't an issue. I eventually found a space about six houses down from Steve's. I took a deep breath, checked my appearance in the mirror on the back of the sun visor and got out of the car. I had only taken a few steps when I saw Steve's front door open. As he turned to lock the door, I started to run.

"Hey, come here," I heard a voice demand from behind me. I turned round assuming that they couldn't mean me.

"Yes, you!"

I stopped, wondering why a thirty-something bloke would be shouting me.

"You've parked outside my house and I've got an elderly relative coming round soon. Would you move your car please?"

"Can you give me just a minute, it's important."

"No, look, they're here now, you'll have to move it now."

As I got back inside my car, the tears welling up in my eyes, I saw Steve get in his car and head down the road in the opposite direction. I thought of following him but then decided that it was a bad idea. I had no idea where he was going and I was in too much of a state to have the sort of rational discussion that I had planned. He'd no doubt be going out with his mates tonight so I'd have to try again at teatime.

Chapter 7

I spent the afternoon sorting through my CD collection. I hadn't actually collected that many over the years but I decided to play my favourite track from each CD in the hope that it would cheer me up and give me something to think about other than Steve. It worked for a while as the tracks from the 80s CDs reminded me of events from school. 'Don't You Want Me' by The Human League brought thoughts of the youth club that some parents from our school had started up. For fifty pence a week we could listen to music, play table tennis, play games on the Atari or just hang out. On the days when we weren't at the youth club we still played on the Atari or listened to music but it was usually in one of our bedrooms. When none of our parents felt like having teenagers hanging around in their house, we would just stand around at the end of the road talking. 'Do You Really Want to Hurt Me' by Culture Club reminded me of the boy I was going out with when I was fourteen. He didn't like Culture Club, but the song was doing well in the charts at that time and somehow my brain had linked this music to this person. Maybe I used to listen to it at home before I met him or something? This also seemed to involve a lot of hanging around on streets although there were never just the two of us. I can only ever remember going out on double dates at that time, probably because the boy I was seeing was so shy that he wouldn't have known what to say to me if there had been just the two of us. Come to think of it, he only ever took hold of my hand if the other couple were holding hands and only ever kissed me if the other couple were kissing. I hadn't thought of this before. 'What Is Love?' by Howard Jones reminded me of the boy I was going out with when I was sixteen. More kissing practice, indoors this time and just the two of us.

Many of the tracks which might have reminded me of my ex-husband, Greg, were now at Greg's house. When we split up and divided our belongings, I was disappointed to realise that he had bought most of the CDs during our marriage and I had been happy to listen to whatever he had bought.

The afternoon progressed like that. Each relationship being analysed in turn until I got to the CDs I had bought since meeting Steve. I decided that I couldn't face any more relationship analysis that day and just shoved them back in the rack. I looked at the time. Four o'clock. I wondered whether it would be a good idea to drive to Steve's on the off-chance that he was calling back home to get changed before going out again at night, or whether I should phone and let him know that I was calling round. I decided to phone.

I was about to hang up when a very business-like Steve answered. "Hello?"

I remembered that he didn't have caller display and therefore wouldn't know who to expect on the other end of the line.

"It's me. Claire," I announced even though I felt sure that after only a couple of days, he would still be able to recognise my voice.

"Oh," was all he said in reply.

"Listen, we need to talk," I winced at the cliché.

"Do we?" His tone was very matter-of-fact and didn't exactly give me any encouragement to continue.

"I called round earlier, but you were just on your way out. I don't think you saw me," I explained. I hoped he hadn't seen me and had just ignored me anyway. I decided to put that thought out of my head.

"Mark and Ian are coming round in a bit so tonight's no good."

"Listen, I am not having an affair with that stupid woman's husband or anyone else for that matter," I blurted out.

Since he clearly wasn't going to see me that night, I started putting forward my case over the phone, even though earlier I had told myself that I wouldn't do that. There was a sigh at the other end of the phone and then silence. "Are you still there?" I said to break the silence more than anything. I hated that, when men just didn't say anything. *Why did they do that?* I wondered.

"I wasn't texting any secret admirers either," I continued, despite the lack of acknowledgement from Steve, or any signs that he was still listening. "I was just a bit embarrassed about who the texts were from, that's all."

That hadn't sounded right at all. I was making a complete mess of this. I had at least expected him to ask who I had been texting or receiving texts from, but the disinterested silence caused me to lose any confidence that I might have had left.

"If you're not interested to find out the truth then I suppose there's nothing more to say."

I hung up. I was angry with myself for my teenage-like reaction, but my emotions were getting the better of me. I flung myself down onto the settee. I was too angry with myself to cry. I was too angry at Steve. He could have at least been interested enough to hear my side of the story.

I phoned Lizzie's number. I really needed to hear a friendly voice after what had just happened. No reply. I sent her a text message. "Hi Liz, I could do with a chat. When are you at home?"

"We're at my mum's in Manchester, staying overnight. I'll phone when we get back," came the reply.

Great. I didn't have the energy to try another friend since that would involve telling the whole story from scratch.

I flicked through the TV menu on Sky but couldn't decide what to watch. I eventually settled on the music channels and after scrolling though a few, stopped at *The*

Killers live performance of *'Mr. Brightside'*. Memories of the concert I had gone to with Steve only a couple of months before came flooding back and any anger I had been feeling was replaced by a sense of loss and the tears started to roll down my face. I told myself that maybe this was only meant to be a short relationship and that everything would seem better in a few weeks' time. I decided that the only thing to do would be to just get on with my life. I cried myself to sleep that night thinking that once I had got him out of my system, then the rest of my life could begin.

The weeks passed by with work and William keeping me busy until eight o'clock each night. The hours between eight and eleven thirty were the ones where I had time to dwell and wonder whether things would have turned out differently if I had never texted those psychics or if I had just told Steve from the start instead of letting him think the worse. I had managed six weeks without succumbing to this habit. Every time I was tempted, I reminded myself that the future would unfold in its own good time and I just had to be patient.

****

I turned over in bed and rubbed my eyes. I panicked for a couple of seconds when I noticed the eight fifteen displayed on the clock and then sighed, rolling over onto my back in relief as I remembered that it was Bank Holiday Monday, or May Day as some people still called it. There wasn't any sound from William's room, but then I'd let him stay up late the night before to watch the *Shrek*

2 DVD that he had persuaded me to put on at quarter to eight.

I was glad that he hadn't come through to disturb me yet. The dream I had just had was a bit strange and I wanted time to just stay put for a while and think about it. The dream must have been set in the past, although I had no idea how my imagination had managed to think up the clothing and housing in such detail. I lived in a small cottage and was sweeping the floor with a broom. It was one of those old-fashioned ones that always seem to be in use in children's fairy stories with lots of birch twigs tied to a long wooden handle. I was wearing a long, fitted dress which seemed to be made of grey cotton with an apron over the top, presumably to keep the dress clean whilst I was doing my chores. There was a large fireplace, although the fire wasn't lit. Sun streamed through the small windows. The room was quite warm so it must have been summer. I opened the door to see a man approaching on horseback. He dismounted and tied the horse to the wooden fence which surrounded my cottage. He patted the horse on its back and it began to chew at the long grass which grew at the other side of my fence. The cottage was surrounded by fields with a dirt track leading to more houses. The man opened the gate and started to walk towards me. He was quite tall and fairly slim. Unruly brown curls hung around his face, and as he smiled my heart skipped a beat. We were lovers and he had come to visit me. I looked closer at his face and realised that it was Steve, except he was dressed like one of the men out of a Jane Austen novel.

Seconds later the dream had switched to another scene. I was walking through a large market place. I had a basket in my hand and was heading towards a stall packed with potatoes. I was suddenly confronted by a woman. She had fair hair and blue eyes and was probably a couple of inches taller than me. She would have been attractive if an angry scowl hadn't transformed her face.

"Leave him alone, I met him first, he's mine," she hissed.

She held eye contact for long enough to make me feel intimidated and then turned her back on me and strolled away. I stood as though glued to the spot. It was the woman who was following me around in the blue car.

As I lay there, I thought it strange that my imagination, or subconscious, or whatever it was that provided your brain with dreams during your sleep, had decided to set the story in the distant past. Sometimes I had dreamed about places I had worked at ten years ago, or about people I had known when I was at school, but I couldn't ever remember having a dream about people I knew now being set a couple of hundred years ago. Maybe this was just my mind's way of sorting out recent events, but nevertheless, it was unusual.

I actually went to bed early the next night, hoping that the dream would continue, but it didn't.

The following Saturday, Lucy had arranged a get together for the girls at her house, since her husband, Nick, was having a night out with some of his mates. It was a while since we had all been together and once the wine started to flow, so did the stories. Becky had started seeing a man called Dave who was a divorcee with teenage girls. Apparently, they had met on a work-related course and had just clicked. Becky seemed so excited about him. I had never seen her like this before. Lucy was her usual self, dashing around putting garlic bread in the oven and checking that everyone's wine glasses were topped up. I had passed the word around before we got together that Steve and I were no longer a couple. They must have felt unsure of whether to bring up the subject or not. No mention had been made of my circumstances at all and I busied myself with asking Lizzie about Millie. After a while Becky and Lucy went through to the sitting room and dug out an old Abba CD. Lizzie took the opportunity to ask me how I was getting on without Steve. I told her how I had just been trying to keep myself busy, hoping that time would help me to get over the break-up.

"I was doing okay until the dream I had the other night ..." I started to say.

"I like analysing dreams," Lucy joined in as she came back into the kitchen.

Becky poked her head round the door and realised that a story was about to unfold. I told the three of them the story.

"Maybe it's your brain's way of helping you to work out what went wrong with Steve," Becky suggested.

"What if your subconscious is telling you to put everything in the past and move forward which is why you saw Steve and this woman as being in the past," Lizzie added.

"Interesting theory," I said. "It's made me start thinking about that woman again though. If it wasn't for her, Steve wouldn't be suspecting me of things I hadn't done."

"It takes a while to get over a relationship properly," Becky advised. "Just give yourself time."

"It's the way in which things ended between us that's causing me the problem. If we'd decided we weren't right for each other, then I'd be able to accept it and move on, but this whole thing with this woman makes me feel as though there's some unfinished business. I can't move on until I know why she's been following me. Steve and I were getting on so well. I need him to know the truth!"

"He sounds a bit accident prone to me," Becky chipped in.

"Well, yes, it has been a bit frustrating," I admitted.

"Yes, how did you manage with him always injuring himself?" Lucy winked.

I rolled my eyes in mock exasperation, then smiled. "I feel so calm when he's around. I feel as though I can just be me."

"If it's meant to be, things will sort themselves out." Lucy tried to add some words of wisdom.

"It's weird, I feel as though I've always known him. I'd only seen him a couple of times when I thought to myself how he was just like the person I'd always imagined myself ending up with. I wonder if the dream was true?

Do you think we knew each other in a former life or something?"

"Do you believe in all that then?" Becky laughed. "How can the same person be born again?"

"Who knows anything?" Lizzie added. "I mean, maybe we just have one chance or maybe we are reincarnated loads of times."

"That psychic, Alice who we saw, does past-life regressions," Lucy reminded us.

"Yes, actually, most of what she told me was about the past."

I repeated what I'd told Lizzie a few weeks earlier about my ancestors.

"Shall we book her again?" Lucy suggested. "Maybe she can throw some light on the situation with this woman who keeps following you.

"I'm not sure," Becky frowned.

"I'll give it a go," Lizzie looked at me waiting for my response.

"Oh, why not."

****

It was three months later before Alice could fit us in. Becky didn't come this time saying that she didn't believe in all that stuff.

Lizzie, Lucy and I waited nervously. We had decided to have the readings at my house this time since William was at his dad's and we'd have the house to ourselves.

Lizzie went in first and came out twenty minutes later saying that Alice had told her she'd have a son in eight months' time.

"Have you been trying for another one?" Lucy asked.

"Well, actually, yes, for the last six months, but nothing seems to be happening. If I do a test now and I'm not pregnant, I'm going to be even more disappointed since she's just built my hopes up," Lizzie sighed.

Lucy patted her on the shoulder and went in to take her turn with Alice. I thought to myself that if Lizzie did turn out to be pregnant, then maybe it showed that there was some truth in what Alice would tell me today. I really hoped Lizzie was pregnant again. I'd had no idea she'd been trying for another baby and she looked so anxious now, wondering whether she was in fact pregnant again.

"Oh, I don't know if you want to know, but I saw Steve's Sister in Asda the other day," Lizzie informed me.

"Oh," was all I could think of to say in reply.

"I had a chat with her for a few minutes," she added.

"Really?" I was surprised since Lizzie had only met her once before when we'd been out for a few drinks in town.

"I asked her if he'd met anyone else."

"You didn't!" Now I was really shocked. Lizzie was normally so tactful and one of those people who always said the right thing.

"She said he's hardly been out since you two split up. She said he got some girl's phone number and was going to go out on a date when he fell down the stairs and broke his leg."

"I wouldn't wish that on him."

I wasn't ready to hear that he'd started seeing someone else and was relieved that he wasn't, but I'd have rather thought that it was because he was missing me than because some accident had prevented it.

Lucy came out of the sitting room looking slightly shocked. She told me that she'd tell me her news later and that I should go straight through.

"Hello, Claire," Alice smiled as I sat down nervously on the sofa. She studied my face for a few seconds and then looked upwards with a thoughtful expression on her face as though she was in the process of receiving some very interesting information.

"There's a woman whose name starts with 'G'."

"Err, I don't know."

"Older than you, I don't think you know her very well but there's a strong link between you and her."

I was puzzled. I couldn't think of anyone I knew whose name started with 'G'.

"Glenda or Glyniss, that sort of name." She looked at me waiting for some sort of acknowledgement; I didn't give any. I was starting to feel rather disappointed.

"Okay, maybe you'll realise later who she is. Let's see. You feel that someone is following you and accusing you of something you haven't done."

"Yes, that's true," I replied, nervously.

"This woman has a real fascination with you. She is almost obsessed in fact."

"She's really scaring me actually. I was hoping that you'd be able to tell me why she's following me around," I admitted.

"Ah, she's the woman whose name starts with a 'G'. Right let me focus on her for a minute then and try to find out more."

This was more like it. I felt my pulse start to race.

"Oh I see." She looked slightly worried. "It looks as though you and her knew each other in a former life and there's some unfinished business. I can't tell you today exactly what it's about but it's to do with a man. She was jealous of a man you were dating and later married."

"But why is she following me around now?"

"Something in her mind is linking you with her husband, but she's got it wrong. It was a man in her previous life that she hoped to marry but he chose you instead."

I thought about the dream I'd had. Both she and Steve were in it and she'd told me to keep away from Steve. I was too flabbergasted to speak.

"There's a man who keeps having accidents and injuries." She paused as if waiting for me to acknowledge this.

"Yes."

I waited to hear more but she informed me that there wasn't anything else for me today. I got the feeling that she was holding something back, but if she was, she had no intention of spilling the beans today.

After leaving the room, I told Lucy and Lizzie what Alice had said.

"What, you mean you knew that nutter in the car in a previous life and Steve as well?" Lucy was getting quite excited about the news.

"You had a dream about that as well, didn't you, Claire?" Lizzie's mouth hung open. "Do you think you're a bit psychic, Claire?"

I was beginning to wonder. I told them about the premonition I'd had involving me sitting stroking a ginger cat which actually came true.

"Yeah, why are we paying Alice twenty quid a time when you could do it?" Lucy joked.

"What did she tell you Lucy?" I tried to change the subject. I needed time on my own later to think about what had just happened.

"She said she saw a change of career for me later this year. She said an unexpected opportunity would occur, something I'd never thought of doing before."

I was about to bring up what she'd said about Lizzie being pregnant but decided to leave it. If Lizzie was pregnant, I knew she'd let us know once she'd done a test to confirm it.

If I'd been at someone else's house, I would have made my excuses and left at this stage. I needed thinking time. I was too shocked at what I'd heard tonight to be sociable any more.

"Are you alright, Claire?" Lucy asked.

"A lot's happened. I just need some time to take everything in."

We both looked at Lizzie, she was about to pour herself another glass of wine from what remained of the Australian red, but thought better of it. She handed the bottle to me.

"I think I'd better be heading home. I'll be in touch."

I smiled at her to acknowledge that I knew what she meant. I knew that she'd be off to get a pregnancy test as soon as the shops opened and that the next time I heard from her she'd know, one way or the other.

I divided the remaining red wine between Lucy's glass and mine. We chatted for about twenty minutes about what possible career change could be in store for her at which point the conversation started to get really silly as we came up with the most unlikely vocations.

"Just think, when you're working five nights a week at the local pole-dancing club, you'll have lovely, toned abdominal muscles."

"She said an unexpected opportunity. If it was something like that, I don't think Alice would have been able to keep a straight face."

We both fell about laughing. "I wonder what she would say to someone if she really saw them doing something like that in the future?"

"She'd probably say they'd be doing something unexpected."

We laughed until the tears started to stream down our faces. I hadn't laughed so much in months. Lucy eventually departed at half past twelve. Luckily, I'd drunk enough wine to knock me out as soon as my head hit the pillow, meaning I could leave having to think about anything for now.

Chapter 8

It was his dark, shoulder-length hair that I noticed first. I had always found slightly longer hair in men attractive and willed him to turn round, hoping that his face didn't disappoint. I took in the broadness of his shoulders in the dark grey, fitted jacket and his confident walk. The clothes reminded me of those from two hundred years ago, maybe three hundred, but I wasn't worried that people didn't dress like that these days. It all seemed perfectly natural. He ran and then hurdled over a couple of fences. In doing so, a small, white piece of cloth fell out of his pocket, probably a handkerchief. As he bent to pick it up, he turned to face me and I got a look at his face for a few seconds. He was a young man of around eighteen to twenty. I wished that I was closer but didn't want the poor man to think that I was following him.

He continued down a track through some open fields until he came to a village. I looked closely at the detail in the thatched roof of the first cottage and then noticed that he was knocking on the door of a small terraced house further down the narrow track. He went inside the house and was greeted by a middle-aged couple. The older man was dressed in a shirt that had probably once been white with a dark grey waist coat. His trousers were calf-length and were tucked into thick socks which, like the shirt, had greyed with wear. He led the young man into a small but inviting room and asked if he'd like anything to drink. The older man then left the room and two women entered. The first was a middle-aged woman who I assumed was the wife of the man who had gone to organise the tea. She had her greying hair scraped back into a bun and a once-white apron over her beige dress. She removed the apron upon seeing the young man and turned to the younger woman who I seemed to know was her daughter. The girl, or on closer inspection, young woman was in her late twenties. Her face showed that she hadn't been weighed down by the same worries that caused her parents to look old before their time. They looked as though they had worked really hard all their lives. These were not well off people. Their tanned, lined faces showed that they spent a lot of time outdoors. The young woman had a paler complexion. I got the feeling that she spent more time indoors although this didn't make sense to me.

I looked more closely at the young man and my heart skipped a beat as I realised that it was my Steve. I looked at the woman again and felt a jealous panic as I realised that it was her again; the woman whose name starts with G.

The older woman turned to the door and was handed a tray holding a pot of tea, some small cakes and some plates, cups and saucers. I thought it odd at first that the girl of around sixteen who had brought the tea was then invited to sit with everyone else, but after noticing the resemblance between her and the woman in her late twenties, I realised that they must be sisters and that this family were too poor to employ any type of maid. The 'Steve' that I could see was much better dressed than the other people in the room and I wondered what his business with this family was. I tried to listen in on the conversation, but annoyingly the woman whom I shall call G for the time being, seemed to be getting up from her seat and asking her parents something.

"Yes, that's a good idea, a walk will do you good," her father said.

The teenage girl got up from her seat but was glared at by her older sister who then turned towards Steve and indicated that he was to accompany her. Steve and G left the room and the girl was excused. I was then able to listen in on the conversation between the older couple.

"He's the first young man to take an interest in our Rachel since Robert broke off the engagement last year," the older woman announced.

I was puzzled for a few seconds who Rachel was, but then realised that this was G from the past and she must have been called something else in her former life.

The man continued, "It's a pity he's not older. His age makes him much more suitable for Beth."

"Well, you've seen what Rachel's like. Poor Beth isn't getting a look in. As soon as Edward arrives, Rachel sends Beth off on some pointless errand so that he gets to spend as little time with her as possible."

"Yes, the way Rachel flirts with Edward is a bit too obvious for my liking," the man frowned.

Edward? My Steve used to be called Edward? I asked myself.

The older man continued, "I think we should take Rachel out more and introduce her to men of a more suitable age. It's just not the done thing for a man of nineteen to marry a woman of twenty-eight."

"Marriage?" the rising pitch of the woman's voice showed her surprise. "Who said anything about marriage? Men of nineteen aren't ready for marriage! I was thinking more that Rachel is getting so besotted with Edward that she's not likely to look elsewhere for a suitable match. If we can get Rachel to look at men in their thirties, then a friendship might blossom between Edward and Beth, and in a few years' time, who knows?"

"You've got it all worked out, haven't you?"

"Well we need to get them married off. We're not producing enough on the farm to feed four adults."

Rachel and Edward (who had the faces of younger versions of Steve and G) were walking down a path which ran alongside a stream. The long grass at the other side of the path moved gently in the summer breeze and the trees boasted a pretty pink blossom.

"So, how are things with your parents?" Edward enquired politely.

"Oh, they don't mind us coming out together, or at least they haven't said anything about the age difference."

Rachel linked her arm through Edward's as she made this announcement.

"No, I didn't mean that." Edward removed her arm from his, a surprised blush creeping up his face. "I mean how are they managing after the bad harvest last autumn?"

"Oh, we've all had to tighten our belts, so to speak."

I opened my eyes, annoyed that the dream had been stopped at this point. I tried to get back to sleep for about fifteen minutes but I was so busy analysing what I had just seen that sleep just wasn't going to happen.

I looked at the clock. It was only five a.m., so I grabbed my towelling dressing gown and headed downstairs to sit at the kitchen table with a glass of water. Unanswered questions filled my mind about what happened next. Did Rachel's dad warn her against trying to flirt with someone nine years her junior, or had her parents successfully set her up with someone her own age? Did Edward later marry Beth? Why did Rachel's fiancé break off the engagement?

I finished the water and went back upstairs. I felt annoyed that I still couldn't get back to sleep. William was at Greg's for the weekend, which meant that I should be having a lie-in on a Sunday morning. Also, I really wanted to continue the dream.

That afternoon, I went for a walk in the park. It was early November and I was regretting my decision to go out without a coat, thinking that the thick pink cardigan which I was holding together across my chest would have been more suitable for late September. I kicked a pile of brown leaves, again regretting my decision as water splashed onto the top of my foot, reminding me that I should only do this when wearing boots in case there was a puddle under the leaves.

I wondered whether I had really known Steve and this lunatic G in a previous life, or whether it was just my vivid imagination making up stories during my sleep. After all, the two of them were on my mind a lot lately. I knew I wouldn't be able to stop thinking about the woman in the blue car until I could prove to her that I had nothing to do with her husband and was innocent of her accusations. In an ideal world, this woman would admit that she'd made a mistake and I'd take her round to Steve's house to tell him. Or at least that was what happened in those American movies anyway. The truth would all come out in the end, everyone would be sorry, the couple would be reunited and live happily ever after ... or did they? We all assumed that they lived happily ever after, but the story always ended at the point where the girl got the man she wanted. The stories of messy divorces and fights over child custody were always in a different movie.

"Hi, Claire!" I felt myself jump as a familiar voice brought me out of my thoughts.

"Oh, Lizzie, sorry, I was miles away. Hi, Pete," I smiled as I ruffled Millie's hair.

As I looked down at Millie, I noticed a slight bulge under Lizzie's jumper where her pregnancy was starting to show.

Lizzie had told me of her pregnancy a few weeks earlier via text message but had told me not to let on to Pete that I knew. He thought they should wait until she was at least twelve weeks pregnant before they told anyone.

"Is William at his dad's then?" Pete asked.

"Oh, I thought I'd forgotten someone!" I laughed. "Yes, he'll be back in time for his bath later. William, that is!"

"Has Lizzie told you that she's pregnant?" Pete smiled.

"Err ..." I looked at Lizzie who quickly smiled and nodded. "Yes, she told me a couple of days ago," I fibbed, unsure of when I was supposed to have been informed.

"How are you feeling?" I enquired of Lizzie.

"I'm much better now. I was sick most mornings and sometimes in the evenings for about eight weeks after I found out I was pregnant but it's not as bad now. I still feel a bit queasy when I get tired though."

"I remember that well. I used to get up in the middle of the night to go to the loo to be sick. Oh, well. It soon passes and you get a lovely little one like this," I smiled, ruffling Millie's hair again.

"What does Millie think about it?"

"We've told her that she'll be getting a baby brother or sister and that he or she is being made in Mummy's tummy," Pete said as he gently patted Lizzie's very slight baby bump.

"How are you anyway?" Lizzie's friendly concern showing on her face.

"I'm okay."

I could have told her that I hadn't seen Steve for a few weeks now. I could have poured my heart out about how I was beginning to reluctantly tell myself that it might really be over, but this didn't seem appropriate in the company of her husband and daughter. Small talk was always more appropriate in these situations.

"We'll have to get together for a drink or something soon," Lizzie smiled. "There's some girly gossip due I think."

"Yes, I think you're right. I'll text round to check whether all the girls can make it to mine next time William's at his dad's."

"Is that in a couple of weeks' time?"

"Yes."

"I think that's okay for me," Lizzie said, looking at Pete.

"I think so. I've not made plans," Pete confirmed.

As I walked along the cul-de-sac, I could already see Lucy and Becky through the gaps in the venetian blinds in Becky's kitchen window. Becky's house was a relatively new house, only being built in the mid-1990s. The kitchen was at the front of the house and the yellow glow from the window was warm and inviting on this cold autumn evening. Becky had said to arrive between seven thirty and eight. It was ten to eight when I got off the seventy-three bus that had dropped me a five minute walk from Willow Close, where Becky lived. The original idea had been to gather at my house, but Becky had invited us all to her place before I'd had a chance to invite everyone to mine. We hadn't seen Becky for quite a few months now, since she hadn't been there when we saw the psychic, Alice, a few months earlier. We had, however, been in touch via telephone and text message so she knew about Lizzie's pregnancy.

Becky waved at me as I approached the driveway and was holding the front door open for me as I walked sideways between the wall and black Ford Focus.

"Got a new car, Becky?"

"I've had it about a month. I thought I'd treat myself."

"Oh, yeah. You got promoted at work. How's the job going?"

"Good, thanks. I have to stay a bit later these days but I suppose I'm getting paid for the extra responsibility."

I took off my brown fake-leather boots and placed them at the bottom of the stairs next to a pair of black boots. I guessed these were Lucy's due to them being too small to be Becky's. There was also a pair of trainers which looked more like something that Lizzie would wear. I wondered for a brief moment what it would be like to have all your income to spend on yourself and to be able to accept any promotions or additional working hours without having to think about childcare arrangements or costs. I quickly stopped this train of thought by reminding myself that I'd always wanted children and would have been quite depressed if I'd got to my late thirties and hadn't had any kids. Becky didn't seem to mind though. She appeared to be perfectly content with herself and the way her life had gone so far.

"It seems ages since I saw you, Becky. Are you still seeing that bloke?"

"Yes. Dave. He was talking about us moving in together, but I think it's too early."

"Well, if you're not sure ..."

"No, it's not that. It feels right but it's only been a few months. I think it needs to stand the test of time before we risk selling one of our houses and then finding out we've made a mistake."

"Hi, Claire," Lucy came into the entranceway and handed me a glass of white wine. "Here, I've poured you one already."

"Thanks, Lucy."

Lizzie was standing, deciding which crisps to have with her glass of lemonade.

"Oh, Claire, while I remember, I can give you a lift back later so you don't need to book a taxi."

"Thanks, Lizzie," I smiled, grateful to be getting a ride home later with a friend rather than a stranger. I hated getting taxis, especially if I was on my own or the last one getting out.

"That's okay. I've already told Lucy that I'll drop her off later as well."

"Has anyone got any exciting news then?"

"Not really," sighed Lucy. "They've just announced that they're going to have to make some of us redundant at our place but they haven't said who yet."

"That must be a bit stressful ... waiting to find out," Becky stated.

"I'll just have to hope that if it's me there'll be another opportunity coming up. Alice said there would be."

"Who's Alice? Someone at work?" asked Becky.

"No. That psychic I saw with Claire and Lizzie a few weeks ago. You know, the one you saw with us earlier in the year but wouldn't see again. You don't believe in that sort of stuff, do you?"

"No. I think you're born and then you make decisions which affect what happens during your lifetime and then you die. End of. These psychics seem to reckon that it's all planned out. You know, fate."

"Well, she said Lizzie was pregnant and it turned out that she was."

"Yes, and it looks as though Claire might be a bit psychic as well," chipped in Lucy.

I wished she hadn't said that. The always logical Becky would think that I'd lost the plot if I explained. She took a sip of her wine and simply raised an eyebrow in response.

Lucy continued, "She's been dreaming about events that happened in a former life. Steve and the woman from the blue car were there."

"I'm not sure Becky wants to hear about that Lucy," I mumbled, before taking a large slug of my wine and grabbing a handful of crisps.

"Oh, go on. Tell us. I'm interested." Lizzie's enthusiasm outweighed Becky's scepticism at that moment and I told them about the dreams.

"It might be that they're both on your mind a lot at the moment and it's your brain's way of trying to sort out what's happening while you're asleep," suggested Becky. "After all, it's that woman's fault that Steve left; you're bound to feel as though there's some unfinished business."

"It's not entirely her fault. I couldn't bring myself to tell Steve about all the so-called mystics that I'd been texting, so he thought I must be having an affair after all."

"What were you texting them about?" asked Becky.

"Well, the woman in the blue car."

"I rest my case. If it wasn't for her ..."

"What's she called?" Lizzie looked up from where she'd been busily emptying a plate of Pringles. "Didn't you say her name began with a G?"

"Yes, but that's only because Alice said that her name began with a G. I don't know anything for definite about what she's called."

"It's not Glenda Jones, is it? I think she had a blue car. One of those small one-litre type things."

"Who's Glenda Jones?"

"When you're all ready for that lift home, I'll show you where she lives and you can tell me if it's the right car."

"Can we go and see now?" I asked. "I can't wait until later."

"Yes. Okay," Lizzie nodded towards Becky. "Becky can come too!"

We quickly downed our drinks, had quick visits to the loo, then started to get our coats and shoes on.

"Is it far?" Becky asked. "You shouldn't be driving backwards and forwards in your condition."

"No, it's not far from here. Really. In fact it's just on the main road near the Princess Pub where she lives, this Glenda woman."

"Okay then."

So that was settled. The four of us got into Lizzie's car and set off in search of Glenda's house in the hope that there would be a car on the drive that matched the one owned by the woman who had been making my life a misery.

We turned right at the end of Willow Close onto Rose Avenue. The housing estate had all been built over a three-year period and had been finished about twelve years ago. The mixture of two-, three-, and four-bedroomed houses were typical of those which sprang up in the mid-1990s and had since become worth four times what they were originally bought for. I took in the white-framed UPVC fake Georgian windows, white UPVC front doors which all matched, regardless of whether you lived on Willow Close, Rose Avenue or Bramley Drive. We turned left and I realised that we were no longer on the estate but on a wider, main road where Victorian semi-detached houses stood well back from the cracked pavements which had been lifted by the roots of well-established trees.

"It's just down here," Lizzie told us. "I can't believe that I didn't think of this sooner, Claire."

"It might not be her. After all, there are quite a few women out there with names starting with G and blue is a pretty common colour for a car," I said, trying not to build my hopes up. After all, what were the chances?

We passed the front of a large pub. I looked at the sign. The Princess. Lizzie had said that Glenda lived near this pub. I scanned the nearby houses, aware that my heartbeat had quickened. Lizzie pulled up outside the second house after the pub. I looked down the driveway but couldn't see any cars.

"Her car's not there!" I sighed, failing to keep the disappointment from my voice.

"Is that it? Look. There, across the road!" Lucy pointed with excitement.

I looked across the road and there it was; the same blue car that I had dreaded seeing for what must have been about a year. I had memorised the number plate after the second time she had turned up outside my house and had quoted it to the police. *So this was where she lived, just a five-minute drive from Becky's*, I thought to myself.

"So, it's Glenda Jones, then," stated Lizzie.

"What made you suddenly think of her then?" asked Becky.

"Her husband, Ted did some decorating for us a while ago. He must be in his mid-fifties," Lizzie told us. "I couldn't find my cheque book on the day that he and his mate, Bill, finished the work. Pete was at work so I took a cheque round that evening."

"Must be doing well with the decorating business if they can afford to live round here!" commented Lucy.

"I think he said they'd always lived round here and had paid about nine thousand for this house in the 1970s," Lizzie told Lucy.

"Did you see his wife Lizzie?" I asked desperate to find out more.

"Yes. She was very suspicious. She was eyeing me up and down the whole time I was there. She didn't say much. She just stood there next to Ted watching me write out the cheque."

"What's this Ted like?" Becky asked.

"He was very chatty and friendly when he was doing the decorating," Lizzie told us. "He told me stories about his grandchildren,"

"Was he a flirty type?" asked Lucy.

"No. That's just it," said Lizzie. "He was one of those fatherly types, the sort you'd feel comfortable with because he reminded you of your dad."

"I thought you said this woman was in her sixties?" Lucy questioned me.

"Yes. Well she looked it."

"Maybe he's ten years younger than her or something and she's worried that, now she's in her sixties, he'll go looking for something younger?" Becky suggested.

"She did seem very suspicious when I was there but she's got no need really. Ted was always talking about holidays they'd had together and there was never any hint of any unhappiness between them."

"Still ... it must be difficult if you marry a man a lot younger. Is Ted good-looking?" Lucy asked.

"He might have been once but he just looked like an average fifty-something bloke with middle-aged spread and thinning hair from what I remember. I wouldn't have fancied him," Lizzie informed us.

Any effects of the wine I'd had were wearing off by the time Lizzie dropped me back home later that evening. I poured myself a glass from the half empty bottle of white Zinfandel which had been in the fridge from the night before. I must have dozed off on the sofa because I was woken up by the feeling of something cold and wet on my leg. I looked down and sleepily took in the fact that the glass which I was still holding in my right hand was tilting to one side and what must have been about a quarter of a glass of wine had just poured onto my jeans and was soaking through onto my thigh.

I took off my jeans and walked through to the kitchen. I flung them into the washing machine so I didn't forget to put them in with the dark wash the next morning. I went up to bed and slept quite well for a change.

Chapter 9

I sat up suddenly in bed. Who was that phoning at half past eight on a Sunday morning?

"Hi, Claire, it's me, Lucy." Lucy sounded fully awake.

I coughed but still sounded a bit croaky as I replied, "Hi, Lucy. Are you okay?"

"Yes. I woke up and couldn't get back to sleep. I had an idea."

"Oh," was all I could think of to say. I wasn't very enthusiastic about anything first thing on a Sunday morning.

"Yes. I was thinking about that Glenda woman."

I started to feel a bit more awake but was still annoyed at being phoned at this time on a Sunday but tried not to show it.

"I think that one of us should go round there and put her straight, now that we know where she lives."

"Oh, I don't know, Lucy. If I go round she might take my knowledge of where she lives as proof that there's something going on."

"I'll go. She needs putting straight, Claire."

"I don't know, Lucy. She might start following you around as well then!"

"I don't care. She's an idiot."

"When will you go round?" I asked, not really believing that she'd go through with it. Once she'd had breakfast and thought things through, I felt sure that she'd change her mind.

"Later."

"I don't know, Lucy. I'll have a think about it and I'll phone you this afternoon when I'm a bit more awake. Okay?"

"Okay," she replied, although I wasn't sure that she was really listening.

Lucy and Nick had been together nineteen years. They had met when Lucy was only twenty and she had become pregnant when they had been together about a year. Surprisingly, their relationship and marriage, which took place when Lucy was about six months pregnant had stood the test of time. Their eighteen-year-old daughter, Sadie had recently left for university in Newcastle. Nick was often out on Saturdays or Sundays playing golf. I assumed that this was one of those Sundays and that Lucy wanted to give herself something constructive to do now that her only child had flown the nest.

I put the kettle on and put a heaped spoonful of instant coffee into a mug. I put the last two slices of brown bread into the toaster and waited. I wanted to put a stop to this woman's lunatic ideas once and for all but had decided to follow logic for a change and leave things. Even those psychics that I had texted had said that all would become clear in about six months. That must be quite soon. I half wished I hadn't told my friends now. I imagined Lucy knocking at Glenda's door. No. It wasn't going to happen. Lucy wouldn't go through with it.

****

It was just after twelve when the doorbell rang. I put down the romance novel that I had been engrossed in for the last half an hour and glanced at the half cup of cold coffee.

I opened the door and was greeted by a very excited Lucy. Before I could speak, her eyes lit up as she announced, slightly out of breath as though she'd been running, "I've done it!"

"What?"

"I've just been round to Glenda's house and had it out with her."

"You're joking!" was all I could think of to say, although I knew that she wasn't joking.

I gestured that she should come in, too flabbergasted to speak. I shut the door behind her. I took her through to the living room and sat down in the armchair. Lucy perched on the arm of the settee.

"I've come straight here," she announced.

"What happened then?"

"I knocked on the door at about eleven and a man answered."

"Oh. What did you do then?"

"I said that I was a friend of Glenda's and wondered if she was in."

"Right."

I couldn't imagine how she would have got round that one. Surely Glenda would have come to the door and said that she didn't recognise Lucy?

"He said that she'd just called round to the corner shop and that he would have invited me in to wait but he was just on his way out ... Anyway," she continued, "I walked very slowly to the end of the road and a few minutes later, this Ted bloke drove past me in a white van. He even waved."

I raised my eyebrows, still unable to think of anything appropriate to say.

"I was about to cross the road to go back to my car when I spotted a blue car coming down the road from the opposite end. I watched and sure enough, it turned onto the driveway which Ted had just left."

Lucy had my full attention now. I sat up straight. Lucy leaped up from the arm of the settee and stood in front of me.

"I waited a few minutes until she'd had time to go inside and then I walked slowly back up the road and knocked on the door," continued Lucy. "She answered and looked a bit confused. I think she thought I was selling something. Anyway, I said that she didn't know me but I was there on behalf of a friend and I was worried about something. I told her that a close friend of mine had been followed around by her for over a year and that it had to stop. She tried to shut the door in my face at this point but I stopped it just in time. I told her that she'd got it wrong."

"I don't suppose she believed you, but thanks for trying," I smiled.

"No, there's more," Lucy continued. "She told me that she'd been informed by a reliable source that her husband was seeing someone else who lived nearby. She told me that it had taken her months to track down someone by the name of Claire who fitted the description that she'd been given and she was sure that it was you. I asked her who this source was. She wouldn't say, so I asked her when this person had seen you and Ted together. She wouldn't tell me that either."

"Well, her so-called reliable source needs a good talking to then, don't they!" I was furious now. Not with Lucy but with this gossip that had put the idea in Glenda's head in the first place. "We'll have to find out who gave her this information and make them take it back."

"Take it back?" the beginnings of a giggle were starting to show at the corners of Lucy's smile. Admittedly, it did sound rather childish.

"You know what I mean. Get this *reliable source* to admit to Glenda that she'd made a mistake and before we can do that, we need to find out who told Glenda this pack of lies!"

I got up and paced across the carpet before placing my head in my hands on the mantelpiece. I exhaled a sigh of frustration before turning to face Lucy. "Why would someone lie about me and spread malicious rumours. I've lost Steve and if the rumours spread any further, the whole village is going to have me labelled as some slag that runs off with other women's husbands." I couldn't hold back the tears any longer, so I turned and headed for the kitchen to hide my embarrassment.

Without saying a word, Lucy came through, gave me a friendly hug and pat on the back before handing me a piece of kitchen roll. She turned to where the kettle stood empty and started filling it at the kitchen sink.

"Let's have a nice cup of tea and have a think what we should do," she said in that calming way she had of speaking.

By the time the teas were poured and we were back, in the sitting room, I had had time to calm down and think straight once again.

"We can either do nothing and hope that she somehow finds out that it wasn't me after all, or go round there, all guns blazing, and demand to know who told her."

"Maybe we could do a bit of detective work and keep an eye on this Ted to find out whether he is seeing anyone else?" Lucy suggested.

"I don't think we'll have time to do that. Anyway, it only takes Glenda to see us following Ted around, or turning up at the same locations as him, and she'll be even more convinced that there's something going on!" I pointed out.

We got to the bottom of our cups of tea long before all the possible courses of action had been discussed. There was no dignified solution, other than to wait it out and hope that the truth would emerge in the end.

However, the truth started to emerge sooner than I had expected. Becky phoned me on Monday night, just as I was serving up tea. I was going to ignore the phone, which started ringing just as William came through into the sitting room. He'd eventually shown up after my third time of calling him down from his bedroom to tell him that tea was ready. William had answered the phone before I had reached the end of my command to ignore it.

"Mum, it's for you," he announced, handing me the cordless phone.

"Go and sit down at the table," I whispered, pointing through to the dining kitchen as though he didn't know where it was.

"Hello," I spoke into the handset as I followed William and started to serve oven chips onto his plate.

"Hi, Claire. It's me, Becky," Becky announced with an unusual tone of urgency in her voice.

"How's it going?" I asked wondering what the news was, since Becky usually made arrangements via text message.

"I've just driven past that Glenda woman's house on my way home from work and you'll never guess what!"

"What?" I asked, giving the expected response.

"I saw her opening the door to that psychic woman that we saw at Lucy's."

"Are you sure it was her?" I couldn't imagine anyone like Glenda having Alice round to do a reading.

"I wasn't sure at first so I turned round and went back. I'm sure that the car outside was the one which Alice had when she saw us at Lucy's."

"I didn't really notice what sort of car Alice had," I replied.

"On that night we saw Alice at Lucy's, I left before the rest of you, if you remember. I had a right job getting my car out because Lizzie had parked right behind me and the car in front was one which I didn't recognise. It was a gold Peugeot. By the time I'd got my car out, I'd seen enough of it to remember it and it was the same car outside Glenda's just now.

"Right, so Glenda sees psychics as well," I said. "Thanks for letting me know, but I'm just serving tea so I'd better go!"

"Don't you get it?" Becky asked, unusually excited for the level-headed businesswoman.

"What do you mean?" I asked, still confused. It was interesting that Glenda also saw Alice, and rather surprising, but Becky seemed to be implying that there was much more to it than that.

"What if Alice is the one who's told Glenda that Ted's seeing someone else?"

"Oh!" I hadn't imagined anything like that.

I checked on William to see him busily dipping a piece of sausage into a pool of tomato ketchup and walked back into the sitting room.

"Come to think of it, she, Alice that is, had a bit of a strange look on her face last time I saw her and she told me that someone whose name began with G was causing me some problems."

"I think it's that Alice who's causing you all the problems, Claire," Becky stated in that business-like tone of hers. "She's told Glenda that her husband is having an affair with you, then told you that this Glenda woman has got it wrong. I think she's telling people contradicting information just to keep herself in business. I told you it was all a load of rubbish," Becky reminded me.

It wasn't until later that evening, after I'd pushed my food round my plate, washed up, and got William ready for bed in a sort of daze, that I remembered that I'd written down what Alice had told me on the two times that I had seen her.

I ran upstairs and rummaged through the pile of handbags at the back of my wardrobe.

"What are you doing, Mummy?" William shouted from the next bedroom.

"It's okay, I'm just looking for something. You get to sleep." I eventually dug out the notebook in which I'd jotted down what Alice had said. It had been Alice who suggested that I did this after the first time I spoke to her saying that I might want to refer back to it at a later date.

Woman whose name starts with G, it said. *She's got it wrong. There was someone she was hoping to marry in a former life who married me instead.*

My hands trembled. I thought about the dreams I'd been having. My Steve couldn't have married this Glenda woman in a past life. He must have married me. Maybe this was why it had felt so right with Steve, even though I had only known him a few months. Maybe I had known him in a former life. Maybe he was my soulmate? If only I could get Alice to tell Glenda that she'd got it wrong and tell her what I thought I knew?

****

All Becky's suggestions about Alice just stirring things up to create business were put to the back of my mind at this point. I sat down on the edge of my bed for a few minutes to gather my thoughts. Rain started to blow against the window. I looked at the digital alarm clock. Eight thirty-three. If Steve was my *Mr Right*, then why did everything go so wrong? It wasn't as though we'd been together for years and then split up. It had only been a few months. I just felt as though there was a whole load of unfinished business. The succession of illnesses and accidents that he'd had since we had met meant that the physical side of our relationship had been a bit hit and miss, but this proved that there was more to it than physical attraction. I did find him really attractive and would have quite happily enticed him upstairs every time I'd had the opportunity. But, regardless of all that, we got on really well. We shared the same sense of humour and seemed to know what the other was going to say. Sometimes I'd think something but decide not to say it and then he'd go and say the exact thing that I'd been thinking. It just felt right and I felt as though the chain of events caused by Glenda's accusations had meant that we hadn't been given the opportunity to find out whether our relationship would stand the test of time. I supposed that a lot of relationships that felt right finished anyway for reasons due to circumstances: for example, an eighteen-year-old girl was going away to university in Leeds and her boyfriend was going to London; or a couple who'd been together for years, separated because he wanted kids and she didn't. *Maybe it was all down to chance and circumstances*, I pondered.

My mind wandered like this for quite a while until I became aware that my back was aching from sitting in the same position for a long time and a draught had given me a bit of a stiff neck. I looked in at William on the way back downstairs. He was fast asleep.

Why did I have to go and develop an obsession with texting those psychics? I asked myself. Any doubts Steve may have had were made stronger when he realised that I was receiving rather a lot of text messages and seemed embarrassed that they had come through when I was in his company.

I sat down at the kitchen table and rested my head in my hands. "Please let Steve find out the truth!" I asked, hoping that some higher being was listening.

Chapter 10

It was the last Saturday before Christmas and all the girls had arranged to have a night out at the local pubs in the suburb in the south-east of Sheffield where we had grown up. From previous nights out, we knew that many of those we were at school with still lived in the area and we were sure to bump into others who we knew. It was only five miles from where I now lived and even nearer to where Lizzie lived, meaning cheap taxi fares. The drinks were much cheaper than in town too. At the time of arranging this night out, I had told them that I had decided not to talk about Steve or this Glenda business. I had decided that the whole thing would sort itself out if or when it was meant to and I intended to enjoy myself.

For the first twenty minutes or so, the conversation seemed to centre on Becky's love life. We all agreed that we were really pleased that she had met someone and teased her about the way in which she smiled and blushed at the mention of his name. This Dave bloke had somehow managed to melt the heart of our career-minded friend and had her finishing work early on a Friday so that she could get ready to go out for a meal or even a romantic weekend away. Previously, if we had arranged any nights out on a Friday, she would have turned up late, still in her work clothes, saying she'd grabbed a burger on her way and hadn't had time to call home.

Lizzie's pregnancy was going well and stories of morning sickness, and needing to go to bed early due to feeling tired were received with understanding nods from me and sympathetic smiles from Becky.

The conversation had gradually deteriorated from sensible, grown-up talk to silly giggles with each round of drinks, until Lizzie announced that she was going home. Her car was parked across the road and I watched my sober friend cross the road and get into her car from the pavement outside the Crown. Knowing that she was safely on her way home, I realised that I recognised one of the smokers who were littering the pavement.

"Hi, Jill. Not seen you for years!" I announced, taking in her skimpy top and three-quarter-length jeans.

As she turned to stub out her cigarette on the nearby table, I couldn't help noticing the red band of her bra which crossed her back and wondered whether she was cold wearing a backless top in December. I looked down at her black sling-backs, noting that it was the height of the heels that were making her so much taller than me.

"I thought you'd had a late growth spurt or something then, Jill. You were only a bit taller than me at school. How do you walk in those things?"

"Oh, you get used to it. What are you doing anyway?"

I told her about my job at the local newspaper.

"What are you doing?" I was curious to know whether she'd actually managed to get anywhere with the modelling career that she was always going on about in the fifth year at school.

"I work part-time at Fringe."

"Part-time?" was all I could think of to say. Fringe was a small hairdressing salon just down the road from where we were now standing.

"Yeah, I'm at home with my youngest. He's not at school yet."

"Youngest?"

"Yeah. He's four. My daughter is twenty-three."

"Oh," was all I could think of to say. She must have been pregnant when we took our 'O' levels as they were in those days. She had always had a string of boyfriends all the way through school. I had no idea who she was dating in the fifth year and I could hardly ask who the father was, even though I was desperate to know. I made my excuses and turned to go back inside. In front of me, a group of men around my age were just making their way into the Crown.

"What time are last orders here, Steve?" I thought I heard a familiar voice say. I didn't recognise the man with his back to me, who then turned to hold the door open, but as he moved to the side to let me through, I saw Steve and John heading for the bar. John and his girlfriend Alex had been out with Steve and me on a couple of occasions.

I looked around for my friends and noticed Lucy and Becky chatting to a mixed group of men and women, who on closer inspection I recognised as Richard Stevens from our year at school, one of his mates whose name I couldn't remember, Richard's younger sister, Kerry, and a couple of other women who must have been Kerry's friends.

"Claire, you remember Richard and Philip, don't you, from school?" Lucy looked from me to the two men for signs of recognition. "And Kerry?"

"Yes, what are you up to these days?" Richard had lost most of his hair and that which remained had been shaved close. His face still looked the same but with the lines expected of someone in their late thirties who had smiled and laughed a lot. Philip had filled out rather a lot round the middle and wore black-rimmed glasses, probably designer. He stood at around five foot eight and looked short and stocky next to his friend who was tall and lean. He had a confident air about him and I wasn't surprised when he told me that he was the manager of a large department store in town. Richard told me that he worked at a large chain of stores which sold computers. He was based at the local retail park. As he spoke, I tried to concentrate on what he was saying, but I couldn't help noticing Steve pushing his way through the crowds behind Richard and Philip. I glanced over Philip's shoulder just as Steve turned and looked me in the eye before turning and heading towards the gents'.

"How are you these days?" I enquired of Kerry in an attempt to show my interest in the group in front of me and blank thoughts of Steve out of my mind.

"Great. I've got two children, both girls, aged eight and ten," she informed me.

"I've just got one. He's at his dad's this weekend."

"Oh. Divorced are you? Me too." Kerry gave me an understanding nod.

"Most of us are!" Richard announced and started to discuss the amount of child maintenance that he was paying his ex-wife. "I wouldn't mind but it was her who chose to leave and move in with someone else and now they're well off and I'm scraping together a living selling laptops!"

We continued to catch up with the events of the last twenty or so years during which time a couple of rounds of drinks were bought and consumed.

I hadn't noticed Steve and his mates leave the pub, but as the bell announced last orders, I glanced over to where they had been standing and noticed two older couples saying their goodnights to each other in an otherwise empty corner.

"Let's go outside and see if we can grab a taxi," Lucy suggested.

Luckily, it was only a few minutes later that we were flagging down a black cab and instructing the driver of our destinations.

As the taxi did a U-turn in the road and headed back down the hill, I noticed Steve and Jill, hand in hand, flagging down another taxi. Then, when our taxi stopped at the lights, I turned to see Steve playfully slapping Jill on the bottom as she stepped inside their taxi. My heart sank. Lucy chirped on about how good it was to see people from school and how it was funny that they sort of looked the same but a lot older, and she wondered whether we looked as old as that to other people. I wondered whether she'd seen Steve get into the taxi with Jill and was just trying to divert my attention by talking about something else, or whether I was the only one who'd noticed Steve going home with that tart.

"It'll all turn out alright in the end. You'll see." Lucy patted my arm in an attempt to reassure me. "It'll just take time. You've got your friends around you."

Lucy got out of the taxi first and passed me a five pound note as her contribution to the fare. "Text me when you get home," she said.

Instead of falling straight to sleep that night, which was what usually would have happened after a night out with my friends, I tortured myself with images of Steve and Jill together. For a minute I tried to tell myself that maybe he was just helping her to get a taxi or perhaps she lived near him. The way they were holding hands and flirting with each other, and especially that slap on the bottom, had suggested something less innocent though. I imagined them together in Steve's bed and felt my heart rate increasing with both anger and jealousy. All the time he had been with me he'd had injuries and illnesses, but he had looked fighting fit tonight and Jill was most likely getting the benefit of it. It wasn't fair. He could've at least found himself a nice girl that his mum would approve of instead of that tart who had a reputation at school. But why should I care? Even if we had been together in a previous life, it didn't mean it had to work out this time. Maybe I was destined to be with someone else. I chastised myself for being so ridiculous. What was I doing? Couples broke up all the time and didn't analyse everything the way that I was doing. They cried for a bit and then moved on. I told myself to get over it. Greg and I had been together a long time and got married, while other people had had lots of short-term relationships and were only just settling down now. I had got divorced and met Steve. Maybe it was my turn to have my share of short-term relationships and break-ups? Maybe it would be a while before I was destined to find my Mr Right. Maybe I needed to get to sleep and just stop thinking about it!

I woke up just after six with a banging headache and went downstairs for some headache tablets. I was halfway back up the stairs when I realised that there was no way that those headache tablets were going to be staying down and ran to the bathroom to be sick. I eventually climbed back into bed where I spent a few more hours feeling far too ill to think about the events of the previous night. I was surprised when I woke again and saw that it was one o'clock. I wrapped my dressing gown around me, and spent the afternoon skipping aimlessly through various channels on TV before eventually deciding to get showered and dressed and pull myself together.

Greg brought William back at half past six and I spent an hour and a half trying to be enthusiastic about a game of Mouse Trap, followed by Connect Four, before running William's bath.

Once William eventually settled after two chapters of *Charlie and the Chocolate Factory*, I ironed an outfit for work and got my packed lunch ready. William would be spending the next day at my mum's because schools had broken up for Christmas. I had to work another two days before my Christmas holidays started. I really disliked getting everything ready on a Sunday night because it marked the end of the weekend and the remains of a hangover were not helping.

I wasn't looking forward to Christmas without a man in my life. There would be one less place set at my mum and dad's dinner table this Christmas. We'd had a really good time last year with Mum, Dad, my sister, her husband and two children. Card games had followed dinner with William being particularly excited at winning Chase the Ace (with my help of course).

Christmas Day this year soon came round. William and I had been taking turns to open our presents that Santa had left under the tree since half past seven. At half past eight there was a knock on the door. William ran to see who it was and had answered the door before I had finished telling him to let me get it.

"Daddy!" William's cries announced the arrival of Greg before he appeared at the doorway to the sitting room. I quickly pulled my white towelling dressing gown closer together at the front and brushed my fingers through my hair. I hadn't been expecting visitors at this time in the morning and was annoyed that Greg had turned up without warning, even if he was William's dad and it was Christmas Day!

"I didn't know you were coming!" was all that I could think of to say, not wanting to let my annoyance show in front of William.

"I was opening my presents with Sarah and I felt bad that I wasn't watching William open his. One of the best things about being a parent is watching them open their Christmas presents, isn't it?" Greg said as he kneeled down next to where William was ripping the paper off a large box.

I could have said, *"You should have thought about that before abandoning me and your son for another woman,"* but I kept this thought to myself and found myself offering him a cup of tea or coffee.

"Coffee, please," was Greg's reply.

"How are Sarah's kids?" I asked.

"Great, they were up at six opening their presents so they'd finished by seven. I'm glad I got here before William had finished opening his." He started to remove a red shiny parcel from the carrier bag he'd brought with him and added it to the pile. "Oh, look what I've found, William," he grinned. "Another one!"

William frantically tore off the wrapping to reveal a PlayStation 3. I couldn't decide whether to be furious with Greg or pleased for William. Greg hadn't consulted me about what to buy and had assumed that it would be alright to buy an expensive present which made all the others look insignificant in comparison. William stopped opening the others and began searching through the box for the leads.

"Let's plug it in, Daddy, and have a game," William suggested, his eyes lighting up.

Greg was about to help him when I thought I'd better stop both of them in their tracks.

"Hang on a minute, you haven't finished opening your other presents yet. You can't play with any of them until they've all been opened. Those are the rules."

Greg moved back away from the box, realising that he'd got a bit carried away. We both watched William open the rest of his presents without much talking.

"Can we play on the PlayStation 3 now, Mum?" William asked.

"I could do with a shower first," I said, knowing that I'd have a battle getting William to let me have a shower before he set up the games console. I was hoping that my announcement of wanting a shower would send Greg packing.

"I'll set it up for him while you have a shower if you like?" Greg offered.

Although the thought of leaving my ex-husband downstairs in my house while I had a shower wasn't really something I wanted to happen, I knew that the alternatives were that I either sat there in my dressing gown for another hour while the two of them played on the new PlayStation or, if I managed to get rid of Greg, William would try to set it up by himself while I was in the shower and probably break something or electrocute himself. I could think of no alternative other than leaving the two of them together whilst I went upstairs and had a shower.

I came downstairs to see the two of them engrossed in some sort of car racing game. As soon as that race seemed to be over, I told William that he needed to get dressed and ready to go to his grandma and grandad's house.

"Ah, but we need to do one more race to have tried out all the different circuits, Mummy."

"Okay. One more race and then that's it!"

"Okay, Mummy," William said as he scrolled down the menu and selected the racing circuit.

As soon as that was finished I asked him to put it away and suggested taking it to show Grandad.

Greg finally went back to his new family and left us to get organised for our Christmas dinner at my mum and dad's house.

We eventually got there, and as William walked past the kitchen towards the sitting room where my dad was handing out various alcoholic drinks, my mum caught sight of the PlayStation 3 box. Her questioning look was answered with one word from me. "Greg!"

"Oh," was her one word answer.

After I had accepted a glass of white wine from my dad and he had assured William that they would play on the PlayStation 3 after dinner, I went through to the kitchen.

"Happy Christmas, Mum." I hugged her. "I've put your presents under the tree to open after dinner."

"Did William like the set of board games I bought him?" my mum asked. "I thought it looked really good. It includes snakes and ladders, ludo and all sorts."

I wasn't sure what to say, but my mum seemed to read my thoughts before I'd had chance to formulate a reply. "I don't suppose he gave it much attention once he'd seen that," my mum said, nodding towards the sitting room. "I thought you'd decided not to let him get hooked on those video games and wanted him to at least try out some more traditional games which used the brain first."

"Greg just bought it and turned up with it. I didn't know anything about it until William opened it!"

Mum rolled her eyes. "How are you anyway? I knew that Steve wasn't right for you. Don't worry, you'll meet Mr. Right one of these days. Just concentrate on looking after William for now."

Trust Mum to always have an opinion on everything. I ignored her comment and started to set the table, knowing that the best cutlery always came out on Christmas Day. I checked the top drawer of the dresser and, sure enough, there it was in the presentation boxes which it came in forty-odd years ago when they got it as a wedding present. I thought about my cutlery at home. Various sets were all mixed up together in one drawer, including the cheap set which I bought when Greg and I first set up home together, other odd knives and forks that Mum had given me, plus some of the more expensive set which Greg's mum and dad had bought us. This had been divided between us when we split up.

"Where's Steve?" Jake, my sister's youngest piped up, just as we were all sitting down to dinner.

"Oh, he's gone to have dinner with his mummy," my sister quickly replied.

"They've split up," William announced.

"Anyone for roast potatoes?" my dad asked, trying to change the subject.

"What does that mean?" Jake asked, too young to pick up on the hint.

"They've fallen out," William supplied the answer.

"Oh."

I was glad that the children decided to leave that line of conversation there and concentrate on the food.

Steve's name wasn't mentioned again that day by anyone. The rest of the afternoon and early evening were spent drinking and playing on William's new game. We left at eight o'clock when the children started to get tired and fall out with each other.

Chapter 11

I looked down at the flowers. I was clutching the stalks tightly in my right hand. I examined the pale cream and blue petals and wondered what type of flowers they were and whose wedding it was. The bride had her back to me, her fair hair fastened up tightly and decorated with flowers which matched the ones I held. Sunlight lit up the stained glass windows to the right of the isle where I walked slowly behind the bride. I glanced at the congregation for signs of familiar faces. *Why was I here?* I wondered. As I got near to the front of the church, I glanced to the left and was surprised to see Steve sitting there in a suit and looking smarter than I'd ever seen him. It was then that the realisation dawned on me that this was actually Edward from my dreams. It was strange how, even though I knew I was dreaming, I didn't wake up but found myself taking a seat next to Edward just as the bride turned round and handed me her flowers to hold. It was Rachel, the woman who Glenda used to be in a former life. I felt my pulse quicken. So who was she marrying? I felt relief that Edward was sitting next to me and not standing next to her.

As Rachel and the groom turned to face each other, I decided that he must have been in his mid-thirties. He had kind brown eyes and the way he looked at Rachel told me that he adored her. Due to Rachel having her back to me I couldn't see her facial expression, so I continued to look at the man as they both said their wedding vows. He never took his eyes off the bride. I was so pleased that she had found love, especially because this meant that Glenda hadn't been married to Steve in a former life.

I became aware of my left hand feeling warm and being held. I looked down to see my fingers entwined with Edward's. It felt just the same as when Steve had held my hand. I looked into his face and he smiled at me. My heart melted and I didn't want the moment to end.

I became aware of the service being over and being told to stand for the bride and groom, who were now turning to leave the church. Glenda, or rather Rachel, smiled at her new husband, but the smile soon faded as she turned and saw me with Steve, or rather Edward. The colour rose to her cheeks and a look of jealousy entered her eyes. She started to walk a little faster, ignoring various members of the congregation who were hoping to wish her well as she walked past with her husband.

"Mum," I became aware of a shout and realised that I was being gently patted on the arm. I opened my eyes and, after taking a few seconds to focus, realised that William was trying to wake me up. "Mum, you were talking in your sleep."

I looked at the clock. It was only half past five in the morning but the birds had already started to sing their morning song.

"I'm okay, William. I was just having a dream."

William climbed in bed next to me and asked whether it was time to get up yet.

"Not yet, sweetheart," I said, as I ruffled his hair. "Try to get back to sleep."

I continued to stroke the back of my son's head as I thought about the events of the dream that had just played out in front of me.

If Glenda was jealous of me in a former life when she was Rachel and Steve was Edward, did that have any link to why Glenda was following me around now, accusing me of having an affair with Ted? If so, why?

I lay awake for some time thinking about how much more complicated life seemed to have got over the last eighteen months or so. It was summer again and I still hadn't really solved the mystery of why Glenda had been following me. Having said that, I hadn't tried to. I had been determined to forget the weird dreams, Glenda, and Steve, and look forward to the future. I had tried to let logic take over for once by telling myself that there was no way that I would be able to get over Steve if I kept thinking about him. I had started reading murder mystery novels before I went to bed, hoping that I would fall asleep thinking about something that wouldn't remind me of any of the events of the previous year.

I wasn't sure what had triggered another of those dreams. Was it the stress of recent events that had caused me to start inventing these stories in my sleep? Was this my way of trying to make sense of everything that had happened by linking it all together in some way? Or did I really have some ability to see events from a previous life? Should I seek specialist help to find out whether I had some psychic ability, or should I just try harder to think about something else?

I couldn't think about anything else though. If the dreams were true and Glenda, *or Rachel as she was*, was happily married to whoever this man was in the dream and I seemed to be getting close to Steve (*previously Edward*), then why did there seem to be some unfinished business in *this* life? Then an awful thought dawned on me. What if I had an affair with her husband in a previous life, the one in the dream? He had seemed so devoted to Rachel in the dream and I had seemed so happy with Edward though, that this scenario didn't seem likely. I thought about what Alice had said about the woman whose name starts with G. She said that she'd got it wrong.

That was it, I thought. *There was only one thing for it. I had to get back in touch with Alice and get to the bottom of this.*

I tossed and turned until seven, then tried to make myself feel human with a shower, followed by strong coffee. I was particularly impatient with William. I hadn't had much sleep, my head was all over the place and, as soon as I'd dropped him off at school, I had planned on phoning Alice to make an appointment to have another reading with her. Since I usually only just had time to drop William off and get to work, I was trying to hurry him along to create an extra five minutes. Why is it though that the more you try to rush children, the longer they take? Why hadn't I just got William up earlier since I had been awake for hours anyway?

Once William had been safely left at school, I started to walk as fast as I could towards the car.

"Oh, glad I've caught you," I turned to see a large but neatly dressed woman smiling at me. I tried to place her and decided that she had two daughters, one a year younger and one a year older than William. I'd passed her in the schoolyard a few times but never really had anything to do with her before.

"Hi, I'm Jessica and Amy's mum. You're William's mum, aren't you?"

"Yes," I replied, wondering why she seemed to have been looking for me in particular.

"I'm on the school fundraising committee and have been given the task of organising the summer fair this year. Someone told me that you've helped out in the past with one of the stalls and I wondered whether you might be able to help this year?"

"I might be able to, but I'm in a bit of a rush now. What date is it?"

"It's a Friday evening, 9th July."

"I think so," I said. "Can I have a word with you one day after school to sort out the details?" I asked, hoping that she wouldn't keep me any longer but wanting to appear polite and helpful at the same time.

"Yes, I'll talk to you nearer the time."

"Okay. Bye." I tried to keep my voice light and airy, hoping that my impatience wasn't apparent.

I glanced at my watch. Nine o'clock. I now only had fifteen minutes to get to work and it took fifteen minutes. I'd have to phone Alice at lunchtime instead.

It turned out to be a particularly busy day at work and I had to grab a sandwich to eat at my desk rather than having the walk which I had planned. This meant that any personal phone calls would be out of the question since they would be overheard by at least six others.

I got to the privacy of my car after work and scrolled down my contacts list, only to discover that I didn't have Alice's number saved anyway! I rummaged through my handbag, feeling sure that it was scribbled on a bit of paper somewhere. Shit. I didn't have her number. I knew that Lucy would know it. She was more organised than me and would have written it down in an alphabetical address book. I tended to write things down on the backs of envelopes and then, when the pile of envelopes got too big I would throw away the ones I didn't need any more and stuff the others into a drawer.

I didn't want to tell any of my friends that I was planning on seeing Alice again, since I'd told them all that I was trying to forget the whole business and get back to normal. I didn't want to look like someone who was going back on her word and have to listen to them advising me to let sleeping dogs lie.

"What are you doing, Mummy?" William made me jump, as he came up behind me later in the kitchen where I was emptying piles of old envelopes and leaflets out of one of the drawers. "Are you tidying out the drawers?" he asked. "You said that my drawers needed tidying out in the school holidays."

"I'm just looking for something, William,"

"Who's Alice?" the question made me jump.

"I know how to spell Alice. There's a girl called Alice in my class at school," he announced as he handed me a pink leaflet advertising aerobics classes at the local sports centre. I turned it over, and, sure enough, the name *Alice* was scrawled on the back and a phone number.

"Thanks, William. This is what I was looking for!" I gave him a hug.

"Are you going to phone her?"

"In a bit," I informed him.

"Who is she?"

"Oh, just a friend," I told him. "Oh look, its six o'clock, are you going to watch *The Simpsons*?"

"Yes, Mummy, but will you watch it with me?"

"In a minute, I'm just going to make a phone call," I pushed him gently towards the sofa.

"Can't you phone in the adverts?"

"Oh, okay!" I gave in, hoping that the adverts were interesting ones today so that he didn't follow me around, listening to the phone conversation. In a morning, when it was time for school, I regularly had to tear him away from some exciting TV advertisement.

I grabbed my moment twelve minutes later as William became engrossed in an advert for some very expensive car which boasted all the latest gadgets.

I nervously typed the numbers into the handset of the phone and waited as it rang. After about twelve rings I heard a familiar voice but then my heart sank as I realised that it was an answering machine.

"Hello, this is Alice Walker. Sorry, but I can't take your call at the moment. Please leave a message after the tone."

"Hi. I had a reading with you a while ago and wondered whether I could arrange to see you again."

I left my name and number then hung up. I immediately wondered whether it had been a mistake to leave a message for her to phone back. I didn't want her to phone when I had visitors. I wanted to deal with this whole thing in secret from now on.

Two weeks passed and she still didn't return my call. Maybe she knew how much trouble she'd caused. Maybe she knew that I was angry with her. I tried again but got the same answerphone message.

Chapter 12

"Come on William, you already tried on four pairs of trousers and I'm not buying any more than two. Which ones do you want?"

Most of the time my son hated the idea of clothes shopping but once you actually got him into the shop he decided that he wanted to try on everything because he liked having new things to show his friends. He was only nine, but fashion already seemed to matter.

After eventually choosing some wide-legged jeans and combat-style trousers, we queued for ten minutes behind a young boy of about three, who was either very bored or very naughty, or both. He kept pulling the gift vouchers and jewellery from the nearby displays and throwing them onto the floor. "Stop it!" his harassed looking mother commanded. Well I say commanded, but she didn't really sound as though she meant it and just left the pile of merchandise where the child had thrown it on the floor and didn't ask him to pick it up either.

"He's naughty, isn't he, Mummy?" William announced, followed by the young mother turning and giving William a *Shut up, or else!* look. When she had turned round again, I held my finger up to my mouth and shook my head to indicate to William that he shouldn't voice his opinion at the moment. I just wanted to get out of there without conflict.

When we eventually got out of the shop and the woman with the young brat in tow had disappeared amongst the crowds, I thought I'd better have a word with the sulking William.

"Sorry, William, but I thought that that lady was going to get cross with us," I tried to explain.

"She should have got cross with her little boy, Mummy. You would have made me pick those things up. Why can other children do naughty things and not me?"

"Other children can't do naughty things, I'm sure his mummy is telling him off now!" I tried to reassure William, whilst out of the corner of my eye I saw them in the queue for an ice cream.

"Why didn't you tell him off?"

I was trying to think what to say to that one, when I saw Steve coming towards us with a very attractive blonde, probably still in her twenties. They smiled and laughed easily in each other's company. Steve pretended he hadn't seen us as he approached and looked the other way but William had already spotted him.

"Steve, Steve!" William called.

Steve looked awkward.

"Hello, Steve, who is your friend?" William addressed Steve directly.

"Err ..."

"I'm Joanne," the young woman spoke to William. "What's your name?"

"William," William informed her.

I smiled awkwardly and glanced at my watch. "Oh, look at the time. We need to get back before the traffic gets busy."

"United are away today," the pretty blonde announced, "so the traffic won't be too bad."

I assumed that she didn't know that she was being friendly with one of Steve's ex-girlfriends. Either that or she wasn't the jealous type, or maybe just knew that her looks were superior.

"I'm John's sister by the way," Joanne smiled. "You know, John Bryan, one of Steve's friends."

I nodded, not sure what I was supposed to say in response to this. Why did I need to know that Steve was seeing the much younger sister of one of his friends?

"Steve's the best man at John's wedding and my boyfriend is going to be one of the ushers. He was meant to come with Steve today to pick up his suit but he had to work, so he sent me with Steve instead."

Boyfriend? I tried not to let the relief show on my face. I had thought I was getting over Steve and moving on, but clearly not if I got jealous when I saw him with another woman.

I noticed a watch on the floor. It was the one I bought Steve for his last birthday.

"I think you've dropped your watch," I informed Steve, automatically bending to pick it up.

As I put the watch into his hand I felt the tips of my finger brush against the palm of his hand. I suddenly felt a bit dizzy. I was just taking a deep breath and composing myself when Steve suddenly put a hand to his lower abdomen as the colour seemed to drain from his face.

"Are you alright?" Joanne asked.

"Yes, it's just a bit of a ..." But then Steve's words were cut short as he bent over double this time, clearly in agony.

"Is Steve hurt, Mummy?"

"Yes, I think so!"

"Where does it hurt?" I asked, now addressing Steve, although I could see him clutching his abdomen.

He pointed to the lower right-hand side of his abdomen again.

"Should we call an ambulance?" Joanne asked, looking at me, her confidence of a few minutes ago being replaced by girlish uncertainty.

Steve let out another groan.

"Yes, I think we should."

I led Steve to a nearby bench and sent Joanne in the direction of the first aid point to get help. I phoned for an ambulance. I instinctively put an arm round his shoulder. I felt dizzy again and Steve groaned in pain once more.

At that point a woman in her early thirties and wearing a green uniform came up to us and asked whether an ambulance had been called. Next she started talking into her radio to inform the managers of the shopping mall of our location.

Quite a crowd had gathered by now and I was glad when two ambulance men told them to move away as they came through with a wheelchair.

We quickly decided that it would be too distressing to take William in the ambulance with Steve. Joanne didn't look as though she would be any use at staying with Steve or looking after William if I went in the ambulance, so we decided to stay behind and phone Steve's family after checking which hospital they were taking him to.

Later that night I had a phone call from Steve's mum to let me know that he'd had his appendix out and was making a good recovery from the operation. "I'm not sure what's happened to him this year," she continued.

"He used to be so fit and hardly had any time off school when he was a child."

I couldn't get to sleep that night. Even though I knew that Steve was going to be alright, the strange events of the day and, in fact, previous year kept going through my mind. If Steve had always been so well, why did he have to start getting ill as soon as he met me? It wasn't fair. I leapt out of bed, grabbed my dressing gown, and was halfway down the stairs before I realised just how wound up I had become. I stopped and sat on one of the stairs. This was ridiculous. He had seemed as though he really liked me. I tried to imagine what it must have been like from his point of view. He'd had a really bad year when he kept getting ill and then his girlfriend started getting mystery text messages and looking guilty about it.

I moved to the sitting room and decided to have a lie down on the sofa where I could have a think. There were loads of men out there after all. Maybe Steve just wasn't my *Mr. Right*. I just needed time to get over him and move on. I had thought that I was doing okay with the *moving on* situation but events in the shopping mall had been a major set-back. I then felt very guilty for having this thought. After all, appendicitis was quite a big set-back for Steve, wasn't it?

I must have drifted off to sleep with this question still out there, unanswered. The next thing I knew I was face-to-face across a big, old wooden kitchen table looking at Rachel.

"But I thought you loved Peter," I heard myself saying.

"Pete's been good to me and adores me, but how can I love him when my heart is elsewhere?"

"But you married him!" I heard myself saying.

"Well it was clear that Edward preferred you, and Mum and Dad preferred Edward to be with you as well. It doesn't mean that I've stopped loving him though."

The look in her eyes reminded me of the look that Glenda gave me when she accused me of having an affair with her husband. I wasn't sure whether it was jealousy or anger.

"Why are you looking at me like that? What have I done?"

"Well, look at you. You're younger and prettier than me and could probably have any man you wanted, but you had to have the one I wanted, didn't you? It's not fair. I hope everything goes wrong between you and Edward. If I can't have him then neither can you!" Rachel marched out of the kitchen, slamming the door behind her.

I walked over to the window noticing the darkness outside and jumped with shock as I saw Beth's reflection and not mine looking back at me. So I was Rachel's younger sister in the dream. Rachel's sister, Beth, had been paired up with Edward like their parents had wanted, and Rachel had been encouraged to marry someone of a more suitable age. Rachel had pretended to be happy with this arrangement, but clearly wasn't.

I managed to get in touch with Alice and actually speak to her in person a few days later, only for her to tell me that she wasn't taking any more bookings for that month, because she was going away for a holiday, but could probably fit me in some time around the middle of September.

I hesitated, not knowing what to say because I wanted answers now.

"Don't worry," she added. "You'll get the answers you want before then anyway!"

"Oh," was all I could think of to say. So much for my plan to give her a piece of my mind.

Chapter 13

I spent the next two weeks trying my best to block out recent events by keeping myself busy at all times. Whenever I was at home with William I suggested that we played games together. I was becoming quite proficient on the new PlayStation 3. The challenge of remembering how to use the control pad alone was enough to keep my mind away from Steve. Once William had gone to bed I consulted my 'to do' list and kept myself busy until my bedtime. I had cleaned out all the kitchen cupboards, shortened and re-hemmed the trousers I had bought about a month earlier for work, and had even dusted the venetian blinds in the conservatory.

Work was busy enough during the day to keep my mind away from Steve and the other events that I wanted to forget about. Two members of staff were away on holiday, meaning that the rest of us had their work to do as well as our own.

I had just put William to bed on the Sunday night and was wondering whether to punish myself with yet more chores, or give myself a night off and reward my efforts with some wine and TV, when the doorbell rang. I hoped that it would be Lucy or Lizzie, thinking that I was due some female company other than the stressed-out work colleagues I saw in the daytime. I glanced through the front room window first, just in case it was a door-to-door salesperson rude enough to think it acceptable to cold call on a Sunday evening.

I stared and felt my jaw drop, not believing what I saw. It was Steve. He was about to ring again when he noticed me looking through the window. I mouthed "just a minute," hoping that he wouldn't ring the bell again and disturb William.

The look of surprise must have still shown on my face as I opened the front door and just stood there, not knowing what to say and wondering why he had turned up on my doorstep.

"Can I come in?"

"Oh ... I ..." I really couldn't decide how to react. I hesitated, feeling annoyed that he was there after I had spent two weeks working myself into the ground in an attempt to pass the time without thinking about him. However, I couldn't help feeling intrigued at the reason for his unexpected visit.

"I need to talk to you. Something's happened," he continued stepping forward.

I moved out of the way to let him through and at the same time felt my pulse quicken. Something about the way he said "something's happened" told me that something really wasn't right.

He was in the living room standing in front of the fireplace before I could decide whether it was the anticipation of what he was about to tell me, or merely having Steve standing next to me in my own front room again, that had got me so flustered.

I took a deep breath and tried to calm myself before turning to face him.

"This is going to sound so weird, Claire, and I can't believe I'm about to say this, but ...." He paused as his voice started to dry up and he swallowed.

"What?" I felt the need to fill in the silence.

"Someone's put a curse on us, Claire."

I looked into Steve's eyes. He had always been the joker during our time together and seeing him look at me with such a serious expression, and saying something that was so unlike the Steve I knew was frightening me.

"What?"

"Have you noticed how every time we're together I get injured or ill, or something just crops up to stop us being together?"

"Yes, but Steve you're frightening me now," I replied, trying unsuccessfully to stop the tremble in my voice. "I thought the same thing, but come on, that sort of thing doesn't happen in real life does it?" I said, trying to convince myself because I really wanted what he had just said to go away and not be true. "You're winding me up aren't you?" I asked, hoping that he would break into laughter and tell me of the real reason for his visit.

"I wish I was, Claire, but ... well ... I suppose I'd better start from the beginning and tell you the whole story."

"Would you like a beer?"

"Yes, please, and I think you might want one too!" Steve answered, following me into the kitchen.

We sat opposite each other at the kitchen table and poured our beers in silence. Steve took a sip and cleared his throat before speaking.

"I've just got back from John's stag weekend."

"And ..." was all I could think of to say, as I wondered what on earth could have happened at the stag weekend to make him come straight to my house."

"Well, one of John's mates, Clarkey, is into visiting mediums and clairvoyants and booked one for us all to see as part of the stag weekend."

"That's a strange thing to do on a stag weekend!" I announced, trying to sound as though this wasn't something I was interested in and added a roll of the eyes.

"That's what I thought, and it took them quite a lot of persuading to get me in there, but that's when I got told that someone had put a curse on us."

"On both of us? Who?" I asked.

"Someone we both knew in a former life who was jealous of us put a curse on us. Apparently we were married in a former life, and this woman who was your sister was really jealous and put a curse on us so that if we ever tried to get together in a future life we would be prevented."

"Oh," my voice croaked, and I felt as though my heart was going to burst through my ribs it was beating so hard. "I think this might be true, Steve. You see I've been speaking to psychics as well, and in fact that's who I was sending text messages to."

"What? And you let me think you were seeing someone else rather than admit the truth?"

"I tried to tell you afterwards but you wouldn't listen. That woman in the blue car who kept turning up has got something to do with it as well. Oh, Steve, I've been going mad. So much has been happening, but I've not been able to talk about it because it all sounds so made up and unreal."

"Well, you might as well tell me now." Steve sipped his beer slowly as he waited to hear what had been happening.

"Remember that psychic, Alice, I saw with the girls round at Lucy's?"

"Yes, we had a laugh because she said your ancestors were witches ... oh," his expression changed as he realised that this had something to do with what had been happening.

"Well, she, Alice, that is, said that the woman in the blue car thought I was having an affair with her husband but that she, the woman in the blue car, that is, had got it wrong."

I sipped my drink before continuing. "There's something else though." I wondered whether I dared tell him about the dreams I'd been having, or whether this was just too much, too soon for someone who had only just been introduced to the idea that some people might be able to see into the past or future. I went on anyway.

"About the time that woman started following me around, I started having these weird dreams that seem to be set in the past about a hundred and fifty or two hundred years ago. I thought it was just my mind's way of making sense of things while I was asleep, but the thing is, you and the woman who's been following me around are in the dreams."

I continued to tell Steve the whole story about Glenda previously being called Rachel and how she had wanted to marry Edward, but Edward married Beth. I explained that I was Beth and he was Edward in the dreams.

"I still don't know for sure whether they are just normal dreams or whether I've developed some special ability to see into the past, but with you coming round and saying exactly the same thing, that we were married in a previous life, then maybe it's true!" I continued. "In fact I bet it was her, Rachel, who put a curse on us. She said something in the last dream I had about hoping everything between me and Edward would go wrong, and that if she couldn't have him, then she would make sure I couldn't either."

Steve looked slightly confused and stopped to have a think through what I had just said.

"So, I was Edward, you were Beth, the stalker woman was Rachel. She wanted to marry me but I married you instead, so she put a curse on us."

"Yes. I think so!" I nodded and smiled, pleased that he seemed to be on my side.

"But why would this Glenda woman follow you round in this life?"

"I don't know. I think she also saw Alice, you know, that psychic, who made her think that her husband was with someone else." I went on to tell Steve about Lucy's visit to Glenda and how Becky had seen Alice's car parked outside Glenda's house.

"So what are we going to do?" Steve asked, looking into the bottom of his empty glass.

"We could go and see Glenda and tell her what we know, but I don't know whether she would believe us. If she did, it might stop her following me around, but I don't know how we can get rid of this curse!"

"Why don't you go and see Alice again?" Steve suggested. "She might be able to tell you what to do."

"I tried to make an appointment, but she said she wasn't available until September and I'd know everything by then anyway."

"Phone her tomorrow and make an appointment anyway. You can always cancel if we work everything out before then. Anyway, I suppose I'd better go home soon and get an early night after all the drinking I've done this weekend." Steve finished off the last few dregs of his beer and stood up.

I glanced at the kitchen clock. Ten o'clock. I wondered for a split second whether to suggest that he stayed over but kept silent, not really sure where my relationship with Steve now stood.

"I'll phone a taxi," I said instead.

He picked up his bag as he headed towards the front door. I'd forgotten that he'd come to my house straight from a stag weekend and hadn't even been home yet.

"You must be worn out!" I said, unable to think what else to say.

"I've got work tomorrow, so I'd better get back and sort my stuff out, but whether I'll sleep or not is another matter!"

I leaned forward and gave him a quick, friendly peck on the cheek. He dropped his bag and winced in pain. I moved away, wondering what had happened.

"My back!"

I wasn't sure whether it was that sodding curse, or whether he just happened to have a bad back.

The taxi driver gave Steve on odd look as he walked out to the taxi, letting a woman carry his bag for him.

"He's pulled his back," I explained.

"Oh yeah?" the taxi driver gave me a knowing wink.

The alarm went off at seven the next morning and I hit the snooze button, needing time to come round before I got up. I felt as though I'd only just got to sleep but knew I had to get up anyway. I'd got to drop William off at my mum's and then do a day's work. I'd also got to find time to phone Alice. It was only two weeks until September now, but what if she had become booked up until October since I last spoke to her? I should have made an appointment when I had the chance.

"You look tired!" my mum commented as I got out of the car on her drive. She had come out to meet me and opened the back door giving William a hug.

"Bad night!" was all the explanation I felt like giving.

"You ought to get more exercise, that'll help you sleep," my mum felt the need, as always to offer her advice.

I handed over various bags containing William's toys.

"Oh, he won't need those. We're going out for the day," my mum announced. "We'll drop him back round at your house about seven."

"Okay." I gave William a quick hug and headed towards the car.

I pulled up outside work at eight forty-five and decided to give Alice's phone number a try.

"Hello!" Good. She was there. The soonest she could see me was the twentieth of September. I booked this date but felt disappointed, wondering how I could possibly wait a month.

Chapter 14

It was actually Steve's idea that we should go and see the clairvoyant that he had seen in Whitby at John's stag weekend. He unexpectedly turned up on my doorstep at eight thirty the following Saturday morning, saying that he'd woken up at six o'clock and the idea had just popped into his head.

"What about William?" I asked.

Before Steve could answer, William was standing behind me in his pyjamas.

"What about me? What's happening?" William looked up at us both, waiting for an explanation.

"Do you fancy a day out at the seaside?" Steve had already asked before I had a chance to think things through.

"Yeah," cheered William. He looked at his pyjamas and announced that he needed his shorts on. He ran upstairs to get dressed.

"So what happens if we drive all the way up there and we can't find this clairvoyant of yours?"

"I've got the details here," Steve said, producing a business card.

Angelica Green

Medium and Clairvoyant

Henrietta Street

Whitby

"She handed us all a card before we left. I looked in my jeans' pocket and it was still there," Steve informed me.

"She might not be there today!" I didn't fancy driving over a hundred miles for nothing.

"I phoned her at eight this morning and told her it was an emergency. She said it was fine. She would be there all day and that we should just call in when we got there."

So that was it. We set off in Steve's Ford Focus at ten past nine with a very excited child in the back and two very anxious adults in the front.

The start to the journey didn't bode very well. The first call was to get petrol. Every pump at the petrol station had a queue of at least two vehicles at it and an assistant was trying to "assist" someone with the "self-service" pump which claimed to be quicker because you could pay at the pump and save time. Unfortunately, the machine had decided to eat the debit card of the rather annoyed-looking man of fifty-something. Two more cars had pulled up behind before the drivers had realised their error and were now looking around wondering whether a reverse manoeuvre might be possible.

By the time we got to the front of our queue and had loaded Steve's car with fuel, another assistant had joined the twenty-something woman at the "self-service" pump leaving only one member of staff serving in the kiosk. Steve joined a queue of nine harassed looking customers waiting to pay.

We finally got away from the petrol station at twenty-five to ten.

"At least the journey seems to be going okay now," Steve uttered as we drove up the A1.

Before I could even urge him not to tempt fate, Steve had to brake suddenly to prevent us from hurtling into the wall of lorries which seemed to have suddenly formed in front of us. Luckily, the driver of the car behind managed to brake in time (just), stopping about six inches from Steve's rear bumper.

It was one of those situations where no one could see what the problem was and, to start with, we were sure that it would clear in a few minutes, but as the minutes passed by, drivers started to look from one car to another whilst anxiously biting their nails and straining their necks. After about fifteen minutes, the lorry which shouldn't have even been in the outside lane in the first place gradually started to edge forwards. Other traffic in the outside lane began to move with the occasional helpful driver letting someone from the middle lane in.

Luckily we were in the middle lane. If we'd been in the inside lane, goodness knows how long we would have been stuck there.

As we passed the tall lorries which had blocked our view of the cause of the hold-up, we looked to our left. Metal bars were strewn across the carriageway. The drivers of two of the lorries and the rather embarrassed driver of the wagon which had shed its load were trying to get the bars back onto the trailer. Flashing lights could be seen in the mirrors indicating that someone had eventually called the police.

Luckily we were on our way again and we arrived at Whitby without further incident. We found a parking space in the car park on Langbourne Road.

"Right! Let's get on with what we've come for, shall we?" said Steve, grabbing his jacket from the back seat.

"When are we having our dinner?" William asked. I glanced at my watch. It was after midday.

"Shall we get some lunch first, Steve, before all the cafés get really busy? William will get really mardy if he doesn't eat soon and so will I for that matter."

Steve's excitement at eventually arriving at Whitby was soon replaced by a look of disappointment.

"They sell sandwiches there," William pointed to the Co-op store. "Me and Dad got sandwiches, crisps and a drink for three pounds each once."

"What, your dad brought you to Whitby?" Steve asked.

"No, but there's a shop like this near Dad's house."

"It'll be quicker than waiting for our order in a café," I reasoned.

"Okay," agreed Steve.

By the time William had changed has mind twice about which sandwiches to have and three times about which drink he fancied today and we had joined a queue of twelve, it was twenty to one by the time we paid.

We ate our lunch sitting on, or rather leaning against, a stone wall which was splattered with seagull poo, surrounded with fishy smells and queues of people determined not to miss the one o'clock boat trip on the *Sarah Rose*.

"Boat trip?" enquired a tanned man with weathered skin of around sixty.

"Can we?" asked William.

"Maybe later," I tried to appease him as I gathered together all our empty sandwich and crisp packets and looked around for a bin.

"Right, let's get on with it then," Steve said, as he walked towards the bridge. "Come on, it's this way," he urged us on.

Ten minutes later a very puzzled William asked for the third time why we weren't going in any of the shops.

"Steve wants to show me something first," I tried to explain.

"How much further is it Steve?" I asked, as we pushed our way through the crowds.

It was turning into a very hot Saturday afternoon. If we had been here to slowly wander in and out of the shops like everyone else seemed to be doing, it might have been fun, but trying to get through a very crowded street which happened to be on a hill with a child as quickly as possible was no fun at all.

We came to the end of the shops and I stopped to look up at the Abbey.

"Are we going up all those steps?" asked William.

"Not just now," replied Steve. "We need to carry on round this corner."

"It's just a bit further along here," Steve continued, "in those terraced cottages there."

He stopped us outside a solid wooden door which had been painted black, although it looked as though a fresh coat of paint wouldn't go amiss. Flakes of paint could be seen on the doorstep and the door itself gave evidence of its previous colours of blue and dark green.

I looked at Steve and then William. "We can't all go in, can we!" I pointed out to Steve.

"Oh. I hadn't thought of that."

I looked beyond the houses to where the path seemed to lead towards a beach.

"One of us could take William for a walk down there while the other goes in to see her," I suggested.

"See who?" William asked.

"Oh. Someone your mum wants to meet. An old friend," Steve quickly improvised.

So that was it. I'd been volunteered as the one to see the clairvoyant whilst Steve and William went to get a better look at the views of Tate Hill Beach.

I watched Steve and William head towards the steps before giving the door knocker a firm knock.

I felt my throat dry up and my heart felt as though it would explode through my ribs. I waited about half a minute. Nothing. I knocked again and waited. Still no answer. I started to rummage through my bag in search of my mobile phone. Steve and William were too far away to shout by now. I had just started to explore underneath the lining of my bag where many things such as car keys had become hidden previously when I became aware of a voice.

"Hello."

I had expected an old lady and was surprised to see a woman around my age dressed in jeans and an orange-coloured tie-dyed top. Her long, light brown hair hung loose around her shoulders and her grey eyes looked calm and friendly.

"Was it your boyfriend who phoned this morning?" she asked in a calm, friendly tone.

"Err, yes. He was here last weekend."

"Steve?" she asked.

"Yes," I became aware of my heartbeat again and wondered whether she could hear it trying to beat through my chest.

"Come in. I'm just with another client. I won't be long. You can wait in here."

She opened the door to what looked like a small dining room. The first thing I noticed was how dark the room was. The curtains were almost fully drawn across the small window, probably to stop passers-by having a nosey into the room which overlooked the street. The table and chairs were of an old-fashioned, dark sort of wood, and a dresser stood at the far end of the room holding decorative plates. The room felt cold and had a slight musty, unused smell about it. I couldn't imagine eating my meals in here and wondered what the rest of the cottage was like.

I had just pulled out one of the chairs and sat down when I heard voices and then a door opening and closing. I waited a few more minutes, and then the door at the far end of the room next to the dresser opened and the woman who showed me into the house earlier was standing there.

"Sorry, I didn't introduce myself properly earlier," she said. "I'm Angelica Green. I was just passing on some very interesting news to someone when you arrived and I wanted to get back to them quickly before the moment had gone. My daughter usually shows clients in but she's gone out today."

I got up from my seat wondering what was going to happen next.

"It's okay, don't be nervous," she said, picking up on my uncertainty. "Come through and we'll try to find out if there's anything I can help you with."

I followed her through the doorway which she had come through and went into a room which must have been at the back of the house, although the blinds were drawn.

"It's easier to do this if I shut out all distractions," she explained, noticing me looking towards the window. She pointed to a brown leather sofa. "Take a seat," she instructed and then sat herself down in the armchair set at ninety degrees to the sofa.

"Right, let's just have a few moments of quiet, calming ourselves."

I tried to relax, although it wasn't easy when sitting in the house of a complete stranger who was probably going to tell me things about myself that I didn't even know. I wondered what Steve and William were doing.

"Steve couldn't come in with you, could he?" she said, but before I had a chance to answer she continued. "He's looking after a child. Don't worry about them, they'll be fine. The thing that's affecting you and Steve can't reach the child."

I hadn't even thought about this, but before I could try to understand my feelings about what she had just said, she went on:

"I'm glad you've come to see me. When I saw Steve last weekend I had the feeling that things weren't quite right with him. Something seems to be coming through from the past which is affecting him now. Someone said something which they didn't really mean and nothing would have come of it if you and Steve hadn't met. I think you're having trouble with an older woman." She waited and I wondered whether I was supposed to say something at this point.

"Yes," I answered, not wanting to say too much. I wanted to find out whether what she said matched up with what had been happening in my life and in my dreams. I wanted to find out whether I could really trust in this woman. It was important after everything that had happened.

"You and this woman were very close once but there was some jealousy over a man. I see you with the man that she wanted. She said that she hoped that things would go wrong for you. This woman had very strong magical powers although she didn't really believe in her own abilities. This is why you should always be very careful what you say or wish for because it might come true. You see, this woman accidentally put a curse on you and Steve.

Steve was the man you both wanted in a former life. The feelings she had were so strong that her words have carried through to this life, meaning that as soon as you and Steve met up the curse continued to work."

I found myself nodding in agreement.

"You already know this, don't you?" she asked.

I wasn't sure whether to let on, but found myself nodding anyway.

"Because you and this woman were sisters in a former life, there is still a connection between you in this life. The feelings of jealousy she had in her past life come back every time she sees you in this life, but she doesn't know why. She thinks you're guilty of things you haven't done."

"How do I put things right? How do I stop this curse?" I asked, although the words seemed to be coming from somewhere else. I had said them before I had even realised that I was speaking.

"There is more than one path you can take but all will lead to the same ending. You may need to try a few paths before you find the one which works for you."

I looked at her, hoping that she was going to elaborate. It was no good her telling me what the problem was and then leaving me without a solution. That would be like a doctor saying you had broken a leg and then just walking off.

"If I say too much, you'll get stuck trying to get to one particular solution and stop seeing what is right in front of you. You have several options. I'll hint at a couple of them to set you in the right direction and then I know the way forward will come to you. You and your sister both had special gifts in your former lives and still have them now. Make sure you only use your gifts for the good of others." She paused, and I wondered whether this was all she was going to say.

"One solution is to get this woman to take back the curse. This will be difficult for a number of reasons." She paused before continuing. "Another solution lies with your grandmother's things. I can see her old things in a dusty room, possibly an attic."

She stood up at this point and I looked at the clock. It was quarter past two. I wondered how much she charged. She showed me out of a different door which led into a corridor. At the end of it I could see what looked like the door I had come in through about an hour ago. She passed a piece of card to me which had some writing on.

"Please read this before you go. I'll leave you to see yourself out. Have a safe journey home."

She went back the way she had just come and left me alone in the hallway to read the card. It said:

I cannot ask for a fee for passing on what I see.

This gift was given to me so that I could help others rather than to make money.

You may make a voluntary donation if you feel that this is appropriate.

I rummaged through my bag and found my purse. I took out some money, wondering whether to knock on the door again so that I could give it to Angelica or whether I should just leave it somewhere. I looked around and noticed a small basket suspended by a piece of thin rope from a hook in the ceiling. It reminded me of the one my mum used to have in the bathroom with plants growing out of it. I looked inside and saw some money already in there. I added mine to it and hoped that she would find it.

As I went out onto the street I screwed up my eyes in the bright sunlight and stood for a few moments. People walked past going about their business. I felt as though I'd just come from another world and wondered whether it showed.

I made my way in the direction that Steve and William had taken earlier, hoping that they hadn't gone somewhere else. I walked past someone reading a newspaper on a bench and a mother trying to feed a sandwich to a toddler who was protesting at being strapped into a buggy. I looked down and noticed that the tide had started to come in. I wondered where they were. Then I spotted them. The *Sarah Rose* was just going out past the harbour and I could see Steve and William on it. I waved frantically, hoping that they would see me, but they didn't notice.

I wondered how long the boat trips were for, and whether I would have time to get to where we had seen the boats earlier on, so that I could meet them when they came back.

I dashed all the way back through the crowds, past all the little shops that I wanted to go in, back across the bridge, and found the place where the man had asked us if we wanted to go on the boat trip at one o'clock. Steve and William must have gone on the two o'clock trip.

"Did you get to see your friend?" William asked when eventually we were reunited.

"Oh. Yes," I answered.

"Did she have lots to say?" Steve asked. We both knew that we'd have to wait until much later on, probably when William had gone to bed before we could discuss what had been said.

"Yes. Loads."

"Let's make the most of Whitby since we've driven all this way," suggested Steve. "We'll talk later."

We spent another three hours in Whitby looking round the shops, walking along the beach and making a few sandcastles. We rounded the afternoon off with fish and chips. Luckily the traffic wasn't as bad on the way home as it had been on the way there. William was tired after his busy day out, so after a quick drink and biscuit he was easily persuaded to go to bed and quickly fell asleep. I ran through the story from beginning to end.

"So we either need to turn up at this woman's house or look through your grandma's old stuff for some sort of clue?"

"That's about it."

"I say we go round there first thing, to that Glenda woman's house."

"I'm not sure just turning up like that is a good idea," I said. "Imagine it. *You put a curse on us in a former life and we want you to take it back.*"

"It does sound a bit far-fetched, doesn't it?"

"Angelica said it would be difficult."

"If we don't try, we won't know."

"That's true."

"Where's your grandma's stuff? What happened to it after she died?" Steve asked.

"I think it was either shared between the family or thrown out," I said, remembering the carriage clock which was given to me, only to stop working after a few weeks."

"Which will be easier? Asking various members of your family to let you look through anything they might have which used to be your grandma's, or going to see this Glenda woman?"

I didn't know the answer to this. I imagined going to my mum and dad's and asking if they had anything of Grandma's in their loft that I could just look through. They would want to know why. I couldn't imagine my dad just getting out the ladders and bringing down anything they might have without asking any questions. What if the thing I was supposed to be looking for wasn't even at their house? Would I need to visit each of my uncles in turn and ask if I could look through their stuff?

"I don't know," was the only answer I could come up with.

Chapter 15

We talked well into the night, trying to decide which course of action to take. It had reached three o'clock when I suggested to Steve that maybe we should sleep on it. There was a moment of awkwardness at the mention of us sleeping in the same house before I told him that it would only take me a few minutes to make the spare bed up.

There was nothing more I wanted than to have him in bed with me to snuggle up to. My bed seemed even emptier than normal, knowing that he was in another bed just at the other side of the plasterboard wall. I kept reminding myself that if I went too close to him, the curse might take effect again and something bad might happen. I spent quite a few more hours awake, with my thoughts alternating between being terrified that there was some curse out there waiting to get us if we laid a finger on each other, and having feelings of lust. The fact that I was being prevented from going near the man that I really wanted in the next room made these feelings even stronger.

I felt as though I had only just drifted off when I was awoken by a faint knock on the bedroom door. My heart began to race, wondering whether it was William or Steve. Within seconds I was confronted by a child in Spiderman pyjamas. I was surprised to discover that it was half past eight.

"Mum, I think there's someone downstairs!" William whispered.

"It'll be Steve. He stayed here because we had a lot to talk about last night and it was too late for him to drive home." I felt myself flush even though I knew that an innocent child was unlikely to read anything into the situation.

I grabbed my dressing gown and made a quick visit to the bathroom before going downstairs. By the time I got to the kitchen, William was already asking Steve to help him make some toast.

"I can put my own jam on now, though," he said, as Steve pushed the lever down on the toaster.

The phone rang. It was Greg asking if he could take William out for a bit later that morning. He was going to the cat shelter and wondered whether William would like to help him choose a cat.

"Yeah. Fine," I answered. "What time are you planning on going?"

"About eleven if you can have him ready for then?"

"Okay," I answered.

"How would you like to help your daddy choose a new cat?" I asked William as I went back into the kitchen.

"Yeah. Today?" he asked.

"Yes. Later this morning," I informed him.

It was when William dashed upstairs to get changed fifteen minutes later, that Steve suggested that we should go and confront Glenda while William was with his dad.

"What, today?"

"Yeah. Strike when the iron's hot and all that!"

"Oh. What will we say?"

"There's probably no point in planning it out too much," he reasoned. "We'll play it by ear depending on how she reacts."

At twenty past eleven we were standing together looking up the driveway towards Glenda's front door. At twenty one minutes past Steve was knocking on the door as I felt more nervous than I could ever remember. What if Ted answered? But it was too late now. I could hear a key turning in the other side of the lock and the door slowly opened to reveal her. Glenda.

She trembled and looked from one to the other of us. Her mouth opened as though she was about to speak and then closed again in silence.

"We've found out some very important information that we think you should know," I found myself saying, wondering what on earth I was going to say next.

"We know why you feel jealous of Claire and it's not what you think," Steve continued.

"I think you've got a cheek coming round here. I wonder what lies she's been telling you?" Glenda gesticulated towards me as she addressed Steve.

"I found out the truth for myself," continued Steve. "Claire has done nothing wrong."

"Go on then, tell me!" Glenda demanded with a note of defiance in her voice.

"Is there anywhere we can talk in private rather than on the doorstep?" I asked, conscious of the next door neighbour starting to set the lawnmower up in his front garden.

"No. Here will do," she said, glaring at me whilst folding her arms and making me feel like a child who was trying to think up excuses to tell the teacher.

The lawnmower started up and I hoped that the noise would prevent the thirty-something man next door hearing anything.

I glanced across nervously and then looked at Steve. Steve took over.

"Do you believe that we've all been here before and get reincarnated?" Steve asked her.

I swallowed nervously. *Okay, get straight to the point*, I thought. *She'll think we're some weird religious fanatics.*

"What's that got to do with anything?" she asked. "I haven't got all day you know!"

"Have you ever seen a clairvoyant?" he asked her. How he could remain so calm and in control I had no idea. I felt myself going shaky and cold with nerves.

"Why do you want to know?" she demanded, glaring from one to the other of us.

"Okay. I'll say it," Steve went on. "Claire and I have both seen different clairvoyants who have both told us that you and Claire were sisters in a former life."

Glenda rolled her eyes in an attempt to look unaffected by this news.

"In a former life, you were jealous that Claire and I were together and you accidentally put a curse on us."

"Get out of here!" she hissed. "What are you insinuating, that I was some sort of a witch?"

"Well, actually yes, but you didn't know of your ability."

"You were a good person," I quickly added, hoping that if we let her know that we were on her side she might listen for a bit longer. "You just said something in anger that you didn't mean. You know, like *'if I can't have him then she can't either,'* or *'I hope something happens to stop them being together.'* The problem was that for some reason, through these words you accidentally put a curse on us, meaning that if we tried to be together bad things would happen."

"And I'm supposed to feel sorry for you, am I? After what you and Ted have been up to?" she started to raise her voice and I glanced across at the next door neighbour, hoping that he wouldn't turn his lawnmower off any time soon.

"Claire hasn't been up to anything with Ted!" Steve was also raising his voice now.

"Well someone told me she had!"

"Did that someone specifically say that I'd been with your husband?" I demanded.

"It was a clairvoyant if you must know," she said. "And since you are so convinced that the ones you saw were right, how can you stand there and tell me that the one who told me about you and Ted was lying?" Her breathing started to get faster and she went pale.

"Were her exact words that *Claire and your husband are having an affair* or did you just assume that this is what she meant?" I yelled. "Could it have been that *someone you really loved is with someone else?*" I demanded. She held onto the door frame and looked slightly unstable but I continued anyway while I had the upper hand. "Could she have been talking about me and Steve in a former life and not me and Ted in this life?" I shouted.

Glenda looked from one to the other of us. She was breathing rapidly. She tried to answer but couldn't get her breath. I waited.

"I ..." She fell backwards and collapsed just as Ted came through to find out what all the commotion had been about.

"What have you said to her? What have you done?" Ted asked us.

"Nothing!" I answered with tears in my eyes. "She's been accusing me of having an affair with you and I just came to set her straight!" I cried.

"What?" Ted bent down and put his arm under her neck. "What would make her think that?" He studied her face in a way that only someone deeply in love would look at someone else.

Before either of us had time to come up with an answer I felt someone gently moving me to the side. I looked round. It was the man from next door.

"What's happened?" he asked, looking from Ted to me and then Steve.

"Looks as though she's collapsed," replied Ted.

"Have you phoned for an ambulance?" the neighbour asked.

By way of a reply, Ted grabbed the phone. After waiting a few seconds he said, "Ambulance please."

I looked at Steve and felt the tears start to well up in my eyes. "What shall we do?" I mouthed. Steve shrugged.

"Who told her this?" Ted asked.

"I don't know," I replied. It didn't seem appropriate to go into the whole story now.

There was an awkward silence as Ted gently stroked Glenda's hair and the neighbour looked at me and Steve, probably wondering who we were and what we had said.

Eventually the ambulance arrived. The neighbour, Steve and I moved away from the door and stepped down onto the path to let the paramedics through. The neighbour looked at us disapprovingly and was probably hoping for an explanation.

"Right, there's not much we can do here," Steve spoke up and started to head towards the car. I followed, wondering whether we were still being watched. I didn't dare look round. Eventually as we pulled away in the car, I turned my head and looked out of the window. The man was walking back towards his house.

"Do you think she's had a heart attack?" My voice trembled as I asked Steve.

"I don't know. She didn't put her hand to her chest or anything. She just sort of passed out."

"Oh, Steve. If she dies it'll be my fault."

"She started this, Claire. In fact, if everything is true, she started this a long time ago."

"She was just jealous, she didn't mean any harm."

"Jealously is a very powerful emotion," Steve warned. "If it wasn't for her jealousy, none of this would have happened. In fact ..." He stopped, suddenly changing his mind about finishing the sentence.

"In fact what?" I asked.

"It doesn't matter."

I wondered whether his sentence was going to be *'in fact we'd still be together'*.

Steve parked the car on the road outside my house. I recognised the car which was already parked in front of us. I was just trying to work out who it belonged to when Becky stepped out of it and headed towards my front door. I wondered what she would think when she turned and saw me with Steve, which she was bound to do when no one answered the door.

We were halfway down the drive when she decided that I wasn't in and turned to go.

"Oh!" she jumped, then blushed as she realised that I was with Steve.

"Hi, Becky. What brings you here?" I asked, trying to break the awkwardness.

"I just had a bit of gossip, that's all," she replied. "I was on my way back from the shops," she continued, "when I saw an ambulance outside that Glenda woman's house."

"Yes, we know. We were there," I replied.

I wondered whether, in fact Becky had seen us there and had come to find out what was going on, or whether we would have been blocked from view by the ambulance.

"Shall I go so you two can have a chat?" Steve asked, looking from me to Becky and probably feeling awkward.

"No, it's okay," I smiled. "Here. Take the keys. You can get the kettle on."

"Are you two back together then?" Becky asked the expected question as soon as Steve was out of earshot.

"I don't think so. He believes me about not having an affair with Ted though. We were just talking to Glenda about her mistake when she collapsed."

"Oh. Things have obviously moved on since I last spoke to you!" there was a look of anticipation in Becky's face.

I could have quite easily poured out the whole story to Becky there and then as we stood on the driveway. I hadn't been in touch with any of my friends since Steve had turned up on my doorstep after his friend's stag weekend.

"Yes, quite a lot has happened!" I agreed. "We'll have to get together with the other girls soon so that I can bring you all up to date."

"Promise you'll tell us all the latest news?" Becky asked.

"Yes. If I haven't arranged something by Tuesday, give me a ring or send me a text to remind me."

"I'll arrange it today," Becky decided. "I'll text everyone to find out when they're free. You'd better reply by tonight!" Becky laughed.

"Do you want to come in for a cup of tea?" Steve called to Becky through the front room window.

"No, it's okay, thanks," Becky answered. "Dave and I have made plans to go out for a meal. I'd better get back really!"

"Okay! Bye!" called Steve as he closed the window.

"Right. I'll be off then," said Becky.

"Okay. I'll be in touch later," I replied.

Becky headed back towards her car, turning round and waving her mobile phone at me before opening the door.

Steve had made two mugs of tea and was sitting on the sofa by the time I got indoors.

"I thought I might as well make myself comfortable. I know what you girls are like when you get together."

"We haven't even started catching up on the gossip yet!" I laughed. "All we've said so far is that we'll arrange to go out so that we can talk!"

"Women!" Steve joked.

We sat down for a few minutes sipping our tea. The jokey atmosphere quickly subsided as the enormity of what had happened earlier started to sink in.

"I feel awful." I was the first to break the silence.

"I've told you already, it's not your fault. Stop beating yourself up!" Steve tried to reassure me.

"What if she had some underlying condition and the stress of us turning up like that has brought it on?"

"What about the stress she's put you through?" Steve reasoned.

"What if she dies?"

There was another lengthy silence. I wondered whether Steve was thinking the same as me. I felt so selfish and mean that I couldn't bring myself to say what was on my mind. After a couple of minutes which seemed a lot longer, Steve spoke up.

"It looks as though we need to go to plan B and look through your grandma's old things."

It occurred to me later that evening that, even if Glenda hadn't collapsed and we had managed to get her to listen to the whole of our story, we had no idea what she had to do to reverse the curse. We had rushed in without thinking things through properly. The consequence was that someone had collapsed unnecessarily.

Chapter 16

As I pushed open the heavy double doors, the heat, loud voices and music hit me. I took in the three-deep mass of twenty- and thirty-somethings which spanned the full width of the bar and immediately decided that the Red Lion had been a bad choice for our get-together. I had come out with the intention of having a good catch-up with my friends. I certainly hadn't planned on shouting out my news at the top of my voice over some crappy karaoke.

I spotted Lizzie amongst the crowds at the bar and wondered whether I could catch her eye and pass her some money through to get my drink. She'd probably been waiting a while, so I assumed a suggestion from me to go somewhere else wouldn't be appreciated at the moment and she probably wouldn't be able to hear it anyway. I looked around the pub and noticed Lucy and Becky already clutching straight half-pint glasses, both containing what looked like lager. I pushed my way through crowds of people who were lucky enough to have already been served and eventually reached them.

"We'd just got our drinks when Lizzie arrived," Lucy shouted into my left ear.

"She's at the bar, ask her to get yours," Becky shouted into my other ear.

I found my way back to where I'd seen Lizzie and called her name. Several blokes looked round, probably curious to find out who was shouting, since I assumed that none of them answered to the name of Lizzie. I shouted again but she still didn't respond.

"Which one's Lizzie love?" a thirty-something bloke asked.

"Is she fit?" his mate added, as a whole group of men started to laugh.

I was wondering whether to call her name again or ask one of them to attract her attention, when luckily she looked round. She looked pleased to see me and gestured for me to push my way through.

"I'm glad you're here," she said. "I've only got a twenty pound note and they haven't got the right change."

I rummaged through my bag and pulled out a heavy purse. I had been ready to set off half an hour earlier when I realised that I'd forgotten to go to the bank. I looked through my knicker drawer where I normally stored my loose change and discovered that I had enough money in the house anyway, although it would mean having a very heavy bag! I passed Lizzie a heap of change and asked her to get me a dry cider.

We fought our way back to Becky and Lucy, who were in the midst of taking turns to shout their turn in the conversation into the other's ear.

"So, what news have you got?" Lizzie shouted at my face, probably hoping that I could lip read.

"I've got loads to tell you but it's too loud in here," I shouted.

"Yeah. This karaoke thing wasn't here last time I came in," Lizzie shouted back.

"It gets the crowds in," I commented, realising that there was no point in trying to have a proper conversation in here.

All four of us listened (and cringed) in silence, as a balding man who must have been in his seventies crooned along to an Elton John number.

"Can we go somewhere else?" I mouthed.

The unanimous decision to quickly finish off our drinks in silence and head towards the door answered my question and we were soon out on the street.

"Well that's me with only fifty percent hearing left!" Lucy joked.

"Where are we going?" Lizzie asked.

"Crown?" Lucy suggested, followed by all of us turning and following her down the hill.

"Will we be able to talk in there?" I called from the back.

"Hope so!" Becky turned and replied. "Anyway," she continued, "you can start telling us now."

"What's this?" asked Lucy as she dashed back to be at my side. "Some gossip?"

"Steve went on a stag weekend a few weeks ago and a visit to a clairvoyant had been arranged," I began.

"Am I missing something? Are you and Steve back together?" Lizzie butted in.

"I hadn't seen him for ages and he just turned up on my doorstep telling me about this clairvoyant he'd seen."

"And?" Lucy prompted.

"Well, to cut a long story short, it turns out that we had a curse accidentally put on us in a former life and we need to work out how to remove it."

"Oh. My. God." Becky added to the conversation. "So Steve believes in all that stuff now as well, does he?"

"That's not all," I added. "We both drove all the way up to Whitby to have another reading."

"What did she say?" asked Lizzie.

We stopped as we reached the Crown.

"I'll get the drinks," said Lucy, "but don't tell them anything else until I get back from the bar," she added.

"We can't all stand in silence while we wait for our drinks!" Lizzie tutted before digging her mobile phone out of her bag and showing us some recent pictures of Millie and the baby.

"Was the birth straight forward then?" asked Becky.

"Not really," replied Lizzie. "I needed a caesarean because he was breech.

"What's he called?" I asked, feeling guilty that I'd forgotten. "Sorry, I'm rubbish at remembering names," I added by way of apology.

"Jake," Lizzie replied.

"Oh yes. I remember now," I smiled.

Lucy returned after about five minutes. We seated ourselves around a table in the corner and the previous conversation resumed.

I told them what Angelica had said during our visit to Whitby and went on to describe the visit Steve and I had paid to Glenda.

"So what's happening to her now then?" Lucy enquired.

"I don't know. I daren't go round and ask," I answered.

"So if she's the only one who can remove this curse, you're stuffed basically?" asked Lucy.

"Angelica said that there were other ways. She said something about my grandma's old things."

"Where are your grandma's old things?" asked Lizzie.

"I'm not sure," I sighed, "I suppose my mum and dad would know, but what do I say when they ask why I want to know and what I'm looking for?"

"What are you looking for?" Becky decided to join in the conversation.

"I don't know," I shrugged. "I think it's one of those situations when I'll know it when I see it!"

"Do you think you and Steve will get back together now that he knows that you were telling the truth?" Lucy asked.

"I don't know. I can't get near to him at the moment without something bad happening. Unless we sort this mess out there's no point."

"You'll have to think of something that your grandma used to have, like an old photo or something and ask your mum and dad if you can go round and look for it," suggested Lucy.

We were silent whilst all of us finished our drinks. I took my turn at the bar and when I returned, the conversation had moved onto Lizzie's baby and how much Lizzie had missed being able to have a proper night out with a few drinks. By the time we had discussed sleepless nights, Lucy's new job, and established that Becky was still happy with Dave, several more drinks had been consumed and last orders had been and gone.

We all got in one taxi and asked the driver to drop us all off in turn. The others each gave me a contribution to the fair once it became apparent that he was dropping me off last.

"That'll be twenty-one pounds please," he informed me, as he pulled across the shutter and held out his hand.

The others had each given me five pounds, meaning that I had another six to find. I still had a heap of pound coins which had fallen out of my purse and were rattling about in the bottom of my bag. I dug a few out and handed them over.

"Night, love," the taxi driver called in his Yorkshire accent.

"Night," I replied, as I eventually managed to close the door properly.

My mum and dad had been babysitting and must have both fallen asleep watching the TV. They woke as I opened the door to the front room. The weather was being forecast on Sky News.

"Oh. We must have nodded off," laughed my dad.

"I wonder how many times that same weather report has cycled round while we've been asleep?" laughed my mum as she got up from her seat.

"Good night out then?" asked my dad.

"Yes. Lizzie's baby's four months old now," I informed them.

"Bet she was glad for a night out then," Mum stated.

I wondered whether now was the time to ask where my grandma's stuff was. My dad excused himself and nipped upstairs to the bathroom.

"Err ... what happened to Grandma's things?" I asked my mum.

"Some are in our loft, some are at your Uncle Cliff's house and some stuff went to charity shops or the tip. Why?"

"Oh. I was just thinking about her and wondered if I could come round and have a look through some old photos," I said, quickly thinking of what Lucy had suggested.

"Your dad's scanned them all onto the computer," my mum informed me. "We could email them to you if you like," she added.

"What else have you got of Grandma's?" I asked, hoping for some clue which would help me to find what I needed.

"Oh all sorts," my mum added.

"Your grandma's stuff?" My dad joined in as he came back into the room. "There are loads of books. Would you like some of them?" he asked. "They're cluttering up the spare room," he added.

This was just the excuse I needed. "Oh, yes please," I said. "I love those old-fashioned novels," I lied. "Can I come round and look through them?"

"Of course you can!" Mum replied. "Take as many as you want! I want to be able to turn the spare bedroom into a sewing room."

"Okay. I'll call round soon," I told them.

We said our goodnights and they left.

About an hour later I woke up with a stiff neck and the dregs of a cup of instant hot chocolate spilt on my jeans. The TV was still on and I stared at it for a few moments, thinking that I ought to get up and go to bed, but really couldn't be bothered to move. I put the mug (which now contained dried on brown bubbles) onto the coffee table before turning and putting my feet up on the arm of the settee. I must have fallen back to sleep again.

The next thing I was aware of was seeing a young woman pull some bags out of the bottom of a big wardrobe made of dark wood. She sat on the floor and opened one of the bags and started to remove what looked like a thick, brown book. She heard footsteps on the stairs and quickly forced the book back into the bag and pushed the bags back into the wardrobe. Seconds later, an older woman, possibly her mother, opened the door and told the younger woman that dinner would be ready soon and she should go downstairs. The younger woman waited until she could hear the older woman going back down the stairs and then took a key out of a small pocket in her skirt. She put the key into a small lock on the wardrobe door and turned it, before putting it back into her pocket. She started to make her way down the stairs.

I woke up and looked at the clock from where I had been sleeping on the settee. Quarter to two. I got up and turned off the TV before checking that the doors were locked and things switched off. Luckily they were, I thought to myself, since any burglar would have been able to wander in as I slept on the settee having my strange dream. Why was it that dreams always ended just as you were getting to the interesting bit, or your alarm went off just as you were getting to the important bit? I wondered whether the women in the dream were people I was supposed to know. I didn't recognise them, although the wardrobe looked vaguely familiar.

I went up to bed, hoping that I would continue with the same dream. Instead it took me over an hour to get to sleep. I woke up the next morning feeling irritable with a banging headache.

Chapter 17

It was two weeks later when I eventually had a chance to pay a visit to my mum and dad's house. I had waited until William was having a weekend with Greg again. The thought of William asking all sorts of probing questions about what I was looking for and then telling my parents about what I had found was a scenario that I wanted to avoid.

My dad answered the door. "I've linked the laptop up to the telly," he informed me. "I've got all the photos of your grandma on there!" He was as excited as a child on Christmas morning. "Help yourself to a cup of tea and a biscuit and have a look!"

I took off my shoes and jacket and left them at the bottom of the stairs, before going through to the kitchen where my mum was throwing some chopped up vegetables into the slow cooker.

"You know what your dad's like with his technology," she laughed and rolled her eyes. "You'll probably get through three cups of tea before you've seen all the photos and had a running commentary from him."

"I don't suppose he's got that much to say about the photos since she was your mum and not his though," I hoped.

"Well if you think that your dad and I have been together since we were teenagers ... he knew her for a long time. I'm sure he'll make the rest up!" she laughed.

I had been hoping to look at the photos for only long enough to be polite before reminding them that I wanted to look through Grandma's old things.

"Have you got anything planned for today?" I asked, hoping that I would get a chance to do what I had come for.

"Your Auntie Rita and Uncle Bill are coming round for tea later. They asked me to do them a stew of all things!" she laughed. "It's years since they had a meal with us. I think it was when you were a baby. Rita says that they've never forgotten the stew I did for them. I just hope it comes out as well in the slow cooker!"

I looked at the clock on the kitchen wall. It was only just after ten past one. I took my cup of tea through to the living room and put it on the coffee table before making myself comfortable on the leather sofa next to my dad.

"Right. Just a minute," my dad smiled, as he picked up the remote control for the TV. I looked across at the TV screen which was filled with an old-fashioned, black-and-white photo of a woman in her late teens.

"That was your grandma when she was about eighteen," he informed me.

"Your mum says that your grandma met your grandad when she was eighteen. Didn't she look pretty?"

I looked at the 1930s clothes and hairstyle and wondered what she would have looked like in modern-day clothes.

"Do you think she looks a bit like your Auntie Rita used to look?" he asked me. "I'll ask Bill when they come round later.

"I think she looks more like our Claire!" my mum announced as she entered the room and lowered herself into the armchair.

"Claire has a lot of your mum's mannerisms," my dad added, "but I'm not sure how much she actually looks like her," my dad said to my mum.

It had taken five minutes to look at one photograph and analyse it for family traits. My heart sank and then I felt guilty. Usually, I loved looking through photographs. My dad wasn't to know that I had a hidden agenda for my visit.

"How many photos are there?" I decided to ask anyway.

"About thirty," he replied. I started to do the maths. Somewhere between two and three hours I decided, depending whether each one took five minutes or whether some needed less discussion.

"Look at this next one!"

My dad pressed a button on a remote control and the screen scrolled onto the next photograph. I assumed the bride and groom were my grandma and grandad.

"When did they get married?" I asked my mum.

"Nineteen thirty-five," my mum informed me. "Apparently it was a really hot day in August."

About ten minutes were spent scrolling through more wedding photographs, during which time I was instructed on the relationship of each person on the screen to my grandma and grandad.

"Are you alright?" my dad asked.

"Yeah. Why?" I asked.

"You look a bit anxious, that's all!"

"No, it's okay," I laughed, hoping it didn't sound too fake.

"Oh. Another one from when she was a teenager."

I smiled, hoping that my dad wouldn't pick up on my impatience. Then I noticed it. The wardrobe from my dream.

"Where was this picture taken?" I asked.

"In your grandma's bedroom," my mum informed me. "She took that wardrobe with her when she got married as well. Do you recognise it?"

"I think so," I replied, suddenly a lot more interested in the photograph.

"She can't do," my dad joined in the conversation. "They got rid of it when Claire was a baby and gave it to that couple up the road who'd just got married. Do you remember?" he asked my mum.

"Oh yes," my mum nodded. "You were about three months old. You wouldn't be interested in furniture at that age!" my mum laughed.

"Oh," I blushed.

"Where are those old books and things of Grandma's then?" I asked, changing the subject and wondering how long it would be before I could start looking for whatever it was that I needed to find.

"Why? Are you bored of looking at these?" my dad asked, sounding slightly offended.

"No, I just thought that I'd look through those as well while I was here!" I explained, hoping that I wasn't blushing too much.

A few minutes later the phone rang. My mum answered and spoke for a few minutes before passing the phone to my dad.

"It's your Uncle Bill," she explained. "They are in town already and will be here in about an hour. Bill just wanted to ask your dad for directions although why he couldn't ask me, I don't know!"

I looked at the clock. Half past two. I now only had an hour to find what I was looking for.

"Just nipping to the bathroom!" I informed my mum as I got up from my seat.

I got to the top of the stairs. I could hear my dad going into details about the new one-way system. The sound of clattering knives and forks from the kitchen told me that my mum was doing something in there. I carefully opened the door of the spare room. There was a pile of cardboard boxes against the wall on the right-hand side. I carefully lifted the flap on the top box. The first thing I saw was a wooden photo frame which surrounded a photo of my grandma and grandad. I lifted out a few more and looked down into the box. It seemed to contain only photographs.

"Oh. There you are!"

I jumped as my mum came and stood next to me.

"The books are in the bottom two boxes, if that's what you've come to look at," she informed me.

"They'll be here soon!" my dad said, appearing at the doorway. "Are you going to stay for a bit to see them?" he asked.

"Okay," I replied. "We can look at the rest of the photos when they get here!" I suggested, hopefully.

"That's a great idea!" he replied, before heading back downstairs.

I lifted the top two boxes off the pile before opening the third box. The first book I saw was an orangey-brown, hard-backed book entitled *'My Book of Bedtime Stories 1950'.*

"That was mine when I was a little girl," my mum informed me.

"Are all these yours then, or are some Grandma's?" I asked, wondering whether what I was looking for would be here at all.

"I think Grandma's might be in the other box," she replied.

I lifted the box and placed it on the floor next to the last box. If whatever it was I was looking for wasn't in here, then I didn't know what I'd do. I lifted out three hard-backed cookery books, a book on how to run a household and a book on herbs. My heart sank. I busied myself, pretending to be looking through the book of herbs in an attempt to hide my disappointment.

"Your grandma used to love this bag," my mum announced, pulling a big, brown handbag out of the box which had contained the book of bedtime stories. "It's a bit heavy though. I wonder what's in it?"

She had just started to open the bag when my dad called from downstairs announcing that someone was on the phone for my mum. I listened to one of the stairs creak as she made her way downstairs. I knew that she must be nearly at the bottom because the third stair up had always creaked.

I quickly grabbed the bag and opened it. Inside it was a thick, brown book. My heart started to race. I carefully pulled the book out and turned it so that I could see the front cover. It was blank. I opened the cover and read the handwritten title on the first page.

Book of shadows

I had no idea what it meant and quickly started to turn the pages, hoping for a clue. Each page seemed to list various ingredients and I wondered whether it was another cookery book at first, until I came to pages with headings such as *"How to attract good fortune"* or *"How to attract money"*. I felt my heart start to race and heard my mum coming back up the stairs. I quickly closed the book and grabbed the book on herbs, holding it on top of the one with the blank front cover.

"Have you found some interesting ones?" she asked.

"Yes, I've always fancied growing my own herbs," I lied.

"I'm not sure why your grandma had that book," she exclaimed. "She only ever cooked traditional meals like meat and veg!"

I was beginning to think that I knew why and couldn't wait to get the books home for a proper look.

"Claire. Your auntie and uncle are here!" my dad shouted up the stairs.

"Okay, we're coming down," I shouted back. I quickly shoved the books under my bag and coat at the bottom of the stairs before going through to the living room where my dad was just loading up the first photograph again.

"Is Claire staying for tea as well?" asked my auntie.

"Have we got enough stew for Claire?" shouted my dad through to the kitchen.

It was going to be a long evening.

****

It was half past nine by the time I finally got home. I had managed to smuggle a large carrier bag out of my mum's kitchen into which I put the books. The last thing I wanted was for anyone to ask me which books I was taking home and why. I wasn't even sure whether I was on the right lines, although the combination of the dream I had and then finding a book which seemed to contain spells made me at least feel hopeful.

As soon as I got home, I went through to the kitchen and started to turn the pages of the book entitled *Book of shadows'*. I had no idea what this book was for, or why my grandma used to have it. I re-turned the pages which I had seen earlier, hoping for something which seemed appropriate for my current predicament. *'How to attract luck'* or *'Healing Spell'* looked vaguely of interest, but it was when I eventually turned to *'How to remove a hex or curse'* that I sat up and started to read more carefully. The spell listed all sorts of stinging plants like nettles and others that I hadn't even heard of. These then had to be placed inside a red felt doll. The idea was to go a long way from home and then throw the doll where it would be destroyed. It was then important to take a different route home and not go anywhere near where the doll had been discarded for a few days.

I imagined trying to make a doll shape out of red felt and then collecting all the necessary plants. This could take a while, and how would I do all this without William wondering what I was up to? I wondered whether witches were usually single or widows, or whether they just did everything in secret without their husbands knowing. I couldn't imagine any man walking into the kitchen at home and thinking that the sight of his wife chopping things up and putting them into a doll and then throwing it out of the car window was normal! *Did my grandma try out any of these spells?* I wondered, *or was this a book that had been passed down untouched?* Alice had said that my grandma's real parents were witches, but then I remembered that she had been adopted. So how did she get this *'Book of shadows'* unless it was one she had started up herself?

I suddenly remembered Alice. With all the events of the last three weeks, I had forgotten all about the appointment I had made to see Alice again on the twentieth of September. It was the eighteenth now, meaning that I should be seeing Alice at seven o'clock on Monday night. *Who would look after William?* I wondered.

I decided that the best course of action would be to get in touch with Steve. I had loads to tell him about what I had found. Also, if he could look after William on Monday night, I would be able to tell him what Alice had said as soon as I got back.

Chapter 18

I phoned Steve late morning on Sunday and told him that I had found something at my mum and dad's house that might be what I was looking for.

"What is it?"

"It's a book," was all I said. I suddenly felt embarrassed saying that it was a book of spells. This whole situation seemed so unreal and make-believe that actually saying it out loud made me feel silly.

The research I had done over the last few months told me that quite a lot of people out there still believed in witchcraft but it was one of those subjects that was rarely talked about and was difficult to just drop into a phone conversation.

"I'll show it to you later. Would you like to come round for lunch?" I found myself saying. I hoped that if a few drinks were consumed with our Sunday roast, it might make the whole thing easier to discuss.

Steve arrived at about one o'clock as planned. Dinner was to be ready for about one thirty.

"So. What is it that you've got?" he asked almost as soon as he'd taken his shoes off and was walking through to the living room.

I realised that the idea to give him a few beers before broaching the subject was an unrealistic one. If you tell someone you've got something you want to show them, they are going to want to see it as soon as possible!

"Just a minute," I said, before dashing upstairs and grabbing the carrier bag containing the books which I had hidden in the bottom of my wardrobe.

I walked back into the room to find Steve sitting on the sofa. I pulled the large volume out of the bag and passed it to him.

"'*Book of shadows*?" he asked before starting to turn the pages.

"'*How to attract money*?' That one sounds useful," he laughed.

"Keep turning," I told him, afraid to sit next to him and get too close in case it caused him some sort of physical pain.

After reading out several headings, he eventually got to the one entitled '*How to remove a hex or curse*'.

"Are we gonna do it then?" was all he said after reading the step-by-step instructions.

"I think so. Oh, I don't know!" I suddenly felt a sense of fear at dabbling with this sort of thing.

Steve raised his voice and became more agitated as he said, "Well, we've got to either do something to stop what's happening or just not come into contact with each other again. Which would you prefer?"

"What if it makes things worse?"

"I think it'll either work or nothing will happen so we may as well try it!" Steve replied, all matter-of-fact.

"Okay. Shall we go out for a walk this afternoon and try to find the correct plants?"

"Sounds like a plan," he agreed. "Have you got any red felt?"

"We can call at the Sunday market straight after dinner."

We left the pots in a heap next to the kitchen sink and drove to the local market square almost as soon as we had finished eating.

"Can I help you?" the older lady asked, after she had finished placing some reels of cotton into a white paper bag for another customer.

"Do you sell felt?" I asked, feeling a bit self-conscious as though she might be able to read my mind and know what I was buying it for.

"Yes, here we go," she said, as she picked up a pile of assorted colours of felt from the back of the stall.

I looked through the sheets of felt which were each about a metre square. I eventually found a dark reddish-pink one.

"I'll just have one of these," I said, pulling it out from between the others and holding it up for her to see.

"That'll be three pounds please," the woman said, as she took the felt and carefully folded it into a large paper bag.

"Oh. Do you have some cotton as well?" I thought about a time when I had bought loads of material and a pattern to make some skirts when I was a student. I had got the sewing machine out, the pattern cut out and pinned to the material, when I realised that I had forgotten to buy cotton. By the time I had gone back to the shop and got home again, I had been in such a foul mood that there was no point in trying to sew that day; the end result would have been a disaster.

"Yes. Would you like it in a matching or contrasting colour?" she asked, as she held up two reels of embroidery cotton in a bright yellow and a dark red. They reminded me of the stuff I used to sew with at school.

"Oh. Just ordinary cotton will do. It doesn't really matter too much about the quality," I told her.

"A toy, is it? You want it to be strong though?"

I wasn't sure about this. If I had to discard the doll somewhere where it would be destroyed, then I assumed that it needed to come apart eventually. If I had to avoid the place where I had thrown it for a while, then I didn't want the stitching to be so strong that it would still be intact weeks or even months later. However, I didn't want it to come apart within seconds either.

"I'll take red in that one and also this one here," I replied, pointing to the cheap cotton which usually broke in the sewing machine and then the more expensive brand.

I handed her a ten pound note, not really knowing how much it was likely to cost because I hadn't bought any sewing stuff for years.

"You've not got anything smaller, have you?" she asked.

I opened the pocket at the back of my purse and pulled out a five pound note. She took it and handed me the ten pound note back and some change from the five pound note. I had forgotten how cheap these markets were and made a mental note to shop here more often.

We went straight back to the car.

"Where to now?" Steve asked.

"How about those woods near the Woodlands estate?" I suggested.

I remembered walking through those woods as a teenager when I was seeing a boy who lived on the Woodlands estate. The houses had been newly built then, and I remembered his family going on about how they had done really well to afford a house on there. The 1980s-style houses looked nothing special now, since loads of identical ones had popped up all over the city since, followed by newer developments over the last twenty years.

"Okay, we can give it a try."

Finding the nettles and a whole host of other spiky, unfriendly-looking plants wasn't a problem. Working out how to pull some of them up without getting stung was!

"We've not brought anything to cut them down with!" I stated the obvious as we both stood there staring at the overgrown walls of the things on either side of the footpath. I rummaged through my handbag, hoping for inspiration. I found a tiny pair of nail scissors and tried to cut through the stalk of one of the plants in vain.

"We'll have to go back and get some proper gardening gloves and proper gardening equipment. Some strong carrier bags as well," Steve added.

I agreed as the nail scissors missed the stalk of the nettle and my hand went straight into the nettles. Five minutes later I was sitting in the car rubbing the palm of my hand with a dock leaf as Steve drove back to my house.

After a thorough search of the garden shed, we eventually found some gardening gloves and secateurs which I had used the previous year for pruning roses. I grabbed some carrier bags from the cupboard under the stairs and after locking up, we headed back towards the car.

We had just put all the necessary nettle-collecting equipment in the boot of the car when a familiar car pulled up behind us.

"Oh no, that's all we need!" I said under my breath to Steve as Greg and William got out of the car.

I looked at my watch. It was quarter to four.

"I wasn't expecting you until six. We were just going out somewhere," I announced to Greg.

"Can I come?" William begged.

"Sorry about this," Greg started to explain. "Sarah seems to have got some sort of a sickness bug. I thought I'd better bring William back so that I can help her, and we don't want William getting it, do we?"

Pity he hadn't thought of that when William was eighteen months old and Greg had swanned off to a cricket match at Leeds all day even though I was ill with a sickness bug. This had then been followed by a day of looking after a sick toddler.

"No!" I replied, a little more curtly than I had intended.

We set off again with William in the car after telling him that we were just going for a walk in the woods.

I had just grabbed the carrier bags and gardening equipment out of the boot of the car when William informed me, in the authoritative voice which was becoming more and more common these days, that you weren't supposed to remove plants from the woods.

"We're just cutting down a few of the nettles so that people get can along the path without stinging themselves!" I hoped he'd buy my explanation.

William looked suspicious.

"Your mum stung her hand earlier and we don't want it to happen to anyone else," Steve explained.

"Oh. Can I cut the nettles down?" William asked. *This job would have been difficult enough without William*, I thought to myself.

William had stung his hand twice before he finally admitted that maybe one of the adults should do the job. We had filled two carrier bags, but hardly made an impression on the wall of nettles.

"I think that'll do!" I announced, holding up the carrier bags.

"But we still can't get along the path!" William announced. "You should have brought those big gardening shears," he added.

I looked at Steve, wondering how we were going to get out of this one.

"We'll just have to walk that way instead," he said, pointing to another, wider path leading down through some trees.

"Why didn't we do that to start with?" asked William.

"Because I wanted to go this way," I said, pointing towards the overgrown path and realising that I sounded like a petulant child. "Never mind we'll go that way instead," I said, pointing towards the other path, "but let me put these back in the car first."

The car was less than a minute's walk from where we had been gathering the plants. Steve and William followed a few paces behind me and I was grateful for Steve unlocking the car with the remote key just as I reached it. I'd walked off and forgotten for a moment that we'd come in Steve's car and therefore I wouldn't have the key. I was glad to put the bags and secateurs down. I took off the gloves and flung them into the boot next to the other stuff and turned to face William and Steve.

"Right, let's go for a walk," I said, making a conscious effort to sound more cheerful than before.

I was just double-checking that the car was actually locked; a habit which I performed without even realising I was doing it, when I saw a familiar blue car heading down the hill on the main road and coming towards us.

I stared at it, wondering whether Glenda was in the car on her own, or whether she had come out with Ted, and whether by some stroke of bad luck they were also coming out for a walk in the woods. I realised too late that if I didn't want to be seen, I would need to get out of the way before the driver of the car got any closer. As the car pulled up next to Steve's, I quickly turned my back and jogged towards Steve and William.

"What's up?" asked Steve.

Without speaking, I turned and looked towards where the blue car was parked, hoping that his eyes would follow and he would get the message without William becoming aware of anything. Glenda and Ted were both getting out of the car.

"Is that her?" he whispered.

"Yes. Don't you recognise her?"

"Not from this distance!"

Steve had only seen her that one time when we had turned up at her house, whereas her face was etched in detail into my memory.

William started to run on ahead and I was glad for an excuse to put a bit more distance between myself and the enemy. I started running after William. "Race you!" I cried, gesticulating to Steve that he should join in too.

I had caught up with William before Steve had even got started. We ran down the bank which was lined with tall, well established trees on either side of the pathway. William started to run even faster, then turned to check whether Steve was following.

"Mind the ..." I shouted, but it was too late. William had tripped over some tree roots and was screaming in pain. On closer inspection, I couldn't help but notice that his left leg seemed to be twisted at an unnatural angle.

I pointed to William's leg as Steve approached, knowing that if I shouted about what I was looking at, it would make William even more upset.

"My leg hurts Mummy!" William told me what I already knew between his cries.

I realised that the only way to get William out of the woods would be to pick him up and was glad that he was of a small and slim build. I looked at Steve, wondering whether his back would be up to carrying a child. Before I could ask him, he had picked William up and had started to head back towards the car. I was busy trying to console William and hadn't noticed Ted and Glenda coming towards us until we were face-to-face with them.

"Oh dear. That looks bad," Ted spoke in a friendly tone of voice.

I glanced at Glenda and quickly took in the unfriendly look in her eyes and the scowl on her lips.

"Come on, we'd better get him to the hospital," I urged Steve, avoiding further eye contact with Glenda.

I got into the back of the car with William. The fifteen-minute journey to the children's hospital seemed to take an age with a screaming child in the car, and I was glad it was a Sunday afternoon and not a busier time.

Several hours later, after waiting for William to have X-rays and have his dislocated knee put straight, followed by having a cast on his leg, we were back home trying to persuade him that he would feel much better after a sandwich and a drink.

It was getting close to midnight by the time William finally fell asleep that night. I had been up and down the stairs several times in response to cries from William that he couldn't sleep because the cast was uncomfortable and he couldn't lie on his side with it on. Steve had hung around wanting to make sure that William was okay before he went home. He had got into his car and driven out of view before I remembered that the felt and bags of nettles were still in the boot of his car. It was too late that day to do anything with them anyway. I would have to remind him the following day, I thought to myself. That's when I remembered the appointment with Alice which was supposed to be the next day on Monday 20th September.

I hadn't arranged for anyone to look after William on Monday evening and should I really be leaving William anyway, now that he'd dislocated his knee? I asked myself. I suddenly felt guilty that my thoughts had turned so quickly to what I was going to do with William on Monday night. *I'd just have to cancel the appointment*, I told myself. *Did I really need to see her anyway, now that I'd already seen Angelica in Whitby?* I wondered. I decided that I'd phone her the next day. I rummaged through my handbag and took out my mobile phone. I sent Steve a text message telling him that we'd left the nettles and gardening stuff in the boot of his car.

I went to bed realising that there was nothing more I could do about anything that day.

The following morning, my mum and dad arrived at eight to look after William so that I could go to work.

"So I assume it's all back on between you and Steve, then, if you were out walking together yesterday?" my mum enquired.

"We're just friends," I told her, feeling the heat rise up my cheeks.

"Passion wore off did it?"

I opened my mouth to reply but realised I had nothing to say.

"Pity. He's really good with William and would have made a good stepdad."

I'd never really thought of it like that, but realised my mum might be right. He'd waited with me at the hospital and then back at the house until he was sure that William was alright. He'd looked after William at Whitby when I was visiting Angelica. William seemed to really get on with Steve, and I knew that I could trust Steve to take care of William.

I said bye to my mum and gave William a hug before setting off for work. I realised then as I was driving that I really didn't want to lose Steve. I imagined us together as a family with William and smiled. If only. Our future depended on a spell working which would miraculously end all our problems. *How ridiculous*, I thought to myself. *How could it possibly work?* But then I told myself that if a comment made in anger by someone a long time ago could have such long lasting consequences, then maybe something as weird as putting some nettles in a felt doll and flinging it into busy traffic could get rid of the inadvertently-cast spell. *Or maybe the whole lot was a load of fiction*, I told myself. Maybe Steve was just prone to illness and injury and it was a coincidence that the symptoms seemed to flare up when he was with me. Maybe Glenda was just a paranoid old bat and the dreams I'd had were just my way of trying to make sense of things.

I pulled up in the car park at work, still wondering what to do about my appointment with Alice. I didn't really want to leave William with my mum and dad all day and then go out again at night. It seemed really selfish. *Did I really need to see Alice anyway?* I wondered.

I looked at my watch. Five to nine. I scrolled through the menu on my mobile phone and came to Alice's number, then selected call. There was no answer and I was eventually diverted to voicemail. I left a message saying that I would have to cancel the appointment and then hung up, wondering whether I had done the right thing.

The morning at work seemed to fly by. Two members of staff were on holiday and the constant ringing of their extension numbers kept the rest of us busy. I took my mobile phone out of my bag at lunchtime with the intention of phoning home to check how William was getting on. I noticed that I had a message informing me that I had received a new voicemail.

"Hello, this is Alice," the voice in the message said. "Don't worry about cancelling our arrangement. You are doing all the right things at the moment. You may need my help in a few weeks' time. I'll keep a slot free for you then."

Chapter 19

Steve called round again on the Monday night just after I had put William to bed.

I opened the door, saying "Shhhh," as I held my finger up to my lips. "William's just gone to bed," I whispered.

"I'll just pop back to the car and get your stuff out of the boot then," he whispered back.

"Aren't you going to make it now?" he asked five minutes later, as I started to put the bags of nettles in the understairs cupboard.

"Oh. I suppose I could!" I felt rather embarrassed at the idea of sitting and making some sort of felt, nettle-stuffed doll.

"I think nettles stain, though, so we'd better do it in the kitchen and put a waterproof cover over the table. I'll go and get the table ready first and then if you wouldn't mind bringing the bags through," I smiled, trying to hide how ridiculous the whole situation seemed.

Steve sat at the table, sipping his tea as I cut a doll template out of card and then drew round it twice on the felt. After cutting these out, I got my sewing kit out of the kitchen drawer. I picked up the box containing various needles, pins and part-used reels of cotton which I had collected between the ages of about seven and thirty. I hadn't sewn for quite a few years now and hadn't imagined using my skills for this!

I quickly cut a piece of the thread which I had bought from the market, wondering why on earth I had bothered buying more when I had a boxful already. I started at the head and sewed round one of the sides and both legs.

"Right. How do I get the nettles into this without stinging myself?" I asked Steve.

"I suppose you need to cut them up first, then find something to pick them up with!"

I grabbed the kitchen scissors from the drawer and tipped some of the nettles from one of the bags.

"I don't think we need this many nettles!" I laughed as I looked at the other two bags overflowing onto the table.

I cut the nettles up into manageable bits and then got a fork and spoon from the cutlery drawer.

"Can you hold it while I stuff it?" I asked Steve as I picked some of the nettles up between the spoon and fork.

"Ouch," he exclaimed several times as the nettles didn't quite go into the gap in the doll properly and brushed against his hand.

By the time I had finished sewing the doll up, I also had stung my hands several times.

"Maybe we should just take the nettles round to Glenda's and threaten to sting her to death if she doesn't reverse the curse!" Steve jokingly suggested.

"I think she has to do it willingly!" I replied, unable to think of anything humorous to say back.

"Well, how does this doll thing work then?" he asked.

"I think the nettles represent all the bad stuff in the curse, so when they are destroyed, the curse is stopped. I think I have to say something as I throw it out of the car as well."

I noticed a few dock leaves poking out of one of the bags and grabbed these, stinging myself on the nettles again in the process. I passed one to Steve and we both sat there rubbing our fingers.

"Right, let's put all this stuff in my car," I said. "I'll do it on the way home from work tomorrow."

Both my hands itched like crazy the next day as I sat at my desk, typing on the keyboard. I hoped that a few years later I would be able to look back and see the funny side of this. I imagined myself living happily ever after with Steve and William and even let my mind wander to the idea of us having a child together.

"Is that eczema?" Derek, one of my work colleagues asked, bringing me back to reality.

"No, I stung myself on some nettles the other day and I can't stop scratching!" I said, knowing that there was no way he'd guess what I'd been doing with the nettles.

Derek opened his mouth, probably about to give me some unwanted advice, when luckily he was called from across the office by Gemma, the sixteen-year-old junior, telling him that there was a phone call for him.

Derek headed across the office and I was left once more with my thoughts. I looked at my watch. Two o'clock. Time seemed to be crawling by. I worked until five on Tuesdays and my mum picked William up from school. Luckily the phone rang and I suddenly found myself a lot busier as Jennifer at Shaw's Advertising Agency informed me that there was a last minute ad from the HR Department at the local hospital and asked if I could possibly fit it in that Thursday's jobs page.

I eventually got away at half past five as extra work seemed to keep coming up from all over the place. I had turned the key in the ignition before I remembered that I needed to get the doll out of the boot. I left the engine running and quickly got out and opened the boot, looking round to check that no one was looking. I flung the doll onto the passenger seat before fastening my seat belt and setting off. I automatically started to take my usual route home from work and had gone about three miles before I decided that I'd have to change my route soon to one which I didn't usually take. I quickly took a left turn and headed down a country lane.

Remembering that I would have to go somewhere really busy, I continued about three miles to the end of the road. I took the second exit at a roundabout and found myself queuing at some temporary traffic lights. This was all I needed. I felt my stress levels rising as I looked at the clock on the dashboard which already showed 5:45. I was usually at my mum's by 5:20 and, in my rush to get to the car, I hadn't thought to phone her to say that I was going to be a bit late. I looked past the queue of about nine or ten cars in front of me, noticed that the lights were still red and realised that I wouldn't be going anywhere just yet. I rummaged around in my handbag for my mobile phone. By the time I had eventually dug it out from amongst the keys, tissues, lipsticks and hairbrush, I was startled by the driver of the car behind beeping his horn impatiently. I looked up to see a big gap in front of me and that the lights had turned to green. I quickly accelerated but managed to get to the lights just as they changed to red. I decided to quickly dash through anyway, as did the driver behind me. As we got towards the end of the row of traffic cones, a Ford Fiesta had already come through the lights in the opposite direction. Its driver must have assumed that because the cars had stopped coming through then our lights must have changed, so he just set off anyway. By the time the driver of the Fiesta and the Land Rover behind it had carefully reversed into a side road, then the driver who had beeped me earlier and I had got through the lights, they had changed from green back to red. I drove past about half a mile of very impatient-looking drivers, some who glared at me and others who beeped their horns. Those further back in the queue just looked perplexed, wondering why the queue hadn't gone down.

By the time my stress levels had reduced, I had driven about another mile. As I approached a roundabout, I noticed a queue of cars waiting to get out of a busy supermarket car park. There were also a lot of cars coming towards me. I quickly decided that this was just the sort of place to throw the doll and then drive away. I also had no reason to come here again as far as I knew. I pressed the button to open the window and dropped the doll out just as I entered the roundabout, bidding it to return all harmful intentions whence they came. I continued straight along the road after I had left the roundabout and pulled into a side road. I remembered that the *'Book of shadows'* had said to go home a different way. I didn't want to go home the same way anyway and have to queue at those traffic lights again! I felt my heart sink as I realised that to go home without going the way I had just come would mean continuing into Chesterfield and taking about a ten-mile detour. What would my mum think when I turned up over an hour late? In fact it was already after six, I realised as I looked at the digital display. It could be quarter to seven by the time I got there! I picked my phone up from the car seat where I had left it earlier and dialled my mum's number.

"Mum, it's me," I said, before she had even had a chance to speak.

"Is everything okay?" she asked, sounding worried.

"Yes, it's fine," I said, trying to sound relaxed. "I ended up working late and then realised I had to call at the shops to get something for tea. I'm on my way now," I tried to reassure her.

"I wish you'd phoned earlier, Claire. We could have given William his tea. He said he wanted to have pizza with you!"

I felt my stress levels rise even further as I realised that I'd promised William that I'd get a pizza from Morrisons on the way home. I could still get one from Tesco or Sainsbury's because I would be going past those on my way but that would make me even later. If I turned up without the pizza it would be obvious that I'd just lied about my reason for being late.

"Yeah, tell him I'll be there soon!"

I hung up and quickly phoned Directory Enquiries from my mobile and asked for the number for the pizza takeaway near home. I asked if they could get a large ham and pineapple pizza ready for quarter to seven.

I eventually picked William up, giving the vaguest possible answers to my mum's questions, and drove to get the pizza. William was so excited that we were getting it from his favourite takeaway that all questions about where I'd been quickly halted.

By the time we'd eaten it was time for William to have his bath and go straight to bed. I felt guilty that his evening at home had been rather short, but quickly told myself that it was only one evening and if things went according to plan then it would all be worth it in the end.

"Haven't we got time to play a game, Mummy, before I have my bath?" William asked.

"I'm sorry, but it's already time for your bath. I had to work a lot later today. I'll try to get out earlier tomorrow."

I read him a longer story than usual to make me feel less guilty. By the time I sat down it was nine o'clock. I sat for a couple of minutes before getting up again and looking around for my mobile phone but couldn't find it anywhere. It eventually turned up under the passenger seat of the car where it must have dropped after I had phoned my mum earlier. There was a missed call from Steve and two text messages, also from Steve.

I returned Steve's call, re-telling the story of how I had had to work late and then how I had got rid of the doll.

"So how long does it take for the doll to work then?" he asked.

"Oh. I don't know!" I hadn't really given this much thought. I had no idea whether it was supposed to work straight away, take a few hours, days or even weeks.

"Did it say in the book?"

"No. I don't think so, hang on a minute," I said, as I went to find the book and looked from cover to cover to check whether anything was written about how long these things took to work. There was no information on this at all.

"I suppose we just have to wait then!" Steve stated the obvious.

After I hung up the phone, I wondered how I would know if it had worked. I supposed the only way would be to come into close physical contact with Steve and find out whether anything happened. *Would Glenda be affected in any way?* I wondered. I hoped that nothing bad had happened to her because then that would be my fault. Or would it be her fault since she had started this whole thing? But then I realised that she was supposed to have done this by accident in a former life. It wasn't something she had consciously done in this life. Oh, I didn't know. I just wanted whatever was causing Steve to be ill and in pain so often to go away and for Glenda to stop bothering me.

After sitting and worrying about whether I had done the right thing and whether it would work or not for about an hour, I decided to browse through some Internet pages on the subject.

I was surprised how much information had been posted on the subject. Most seemed to be of the opinion that the important thing was to think positive thoughts about what you wanted to happen. You had to really believe in what you were doing. Some said that you then had to stop thinking about it all together. It had to somehow get to your subconscious before it could become a reality. While ever it was in your conscious thoughts and you kept thinking about it, you might start to imagine it not working or start to have doubts. These doubts would stop it from working.

Had I already had enough doubt to stop the spell from working, I wondered? Should I do it again on another day when I was feeling calmer and more positive and be sure to think about something else straight away? What could I do in the meantime to make sure I thought about something else?

I opened a bottle of wine, hoping that if I had a few glasses I would be able to get straight to sleep and stop thinking about things. While I drank the wine, I looked through cinema listings on the Internet and decided to treat William to a trip to the cinema the following evening. There was nothing like a good film to stop you thinking about the here and now, I thought to myself. I jotted down a few titles and times and decided that I'd ask William in the morning which one he wanted to see.

I continued to look at the Internet and, by the time I'd browsed through a few online clothing stores, I'd sipped three glasses of wine and had managed to just about block all thoughts of what had happened earlier out of my mind. I took myself up to bed and hoped that I would sleep really well.

The alcohol must have knocked me out for a while, but then I started to have a really vivid dream. I was in someone's bedroom. There was a huge oak dressing table with hairbrushes and bottles of perfume neatly arranged. Behind this there was a wide expanse of curtain. It was difficult to make out the colour because it was dark, but there was probably some sort of floral pattern on it. Next to the dressing table there was a king-sized bed with a man and woman sleeping in it. The man was sleeping soundly but the woman was tossing and turning and mumbling something in her sleep. I tried to look closer. Who was it? The woman sat up in bed and opened her eyes. It was as though I was face-to-face with Glenda. I jumped and woke up from my dream.

I wondered whether Glenda had been dreaming about me right at that moment or whether the spell was causing her to have a particularly restless night. Or maybe it was just me having an ordinary dream, I told myself. After all, I had been worrying about whether anything bad would happen to her.

I told myself to think about something else. Something that would make me happy. I imagined me and Steve being able to go out again properly as boyfriend and girlfriend like other happy couples. I must have fallen back to sleep eventually because I jumped out of my skin when the alarm went off at seven o'clock.

I was really busy at work again the following day and had to rush to get to the cinema on time with William. I managed to get really absorbed in the film and was glad I'd chosen that as a diversion from everything that was going on. It wasn't until later that night, after William had gone to bed, that I had time to think. Should I get in touch with Steve to find out how he was feeling? Was it too soon? Should I wait for him to contact me? Should I keep myself busy and try not to think about the events of the last few months? Before I had really had time to think, I found myself sending Steve a text message with the simple question *"How are you?"* After I'd sent it, it occurred to me that I really didn't know where I stood with Steve. Were we just friends? Would we go back to being boyfriend and girlfriend? I knew that if I was relying on a spell from an old book to put things right, then I was probably setting myself up for disappointment. I waited, looking at the screen on my mobile phone. Nothing. I scrolled through the Sky menu on the TV hoping that there would be something to watch. My favourite soaps had already been on and weren't repeated until well after my bedtime. Everything else was either a repeat of something I'd seen at least twice already or a film that was either part way through or went on until after 1 a.m. I put the news on and picked up a catalogue, aimlessly scanning the pages of the women's clothing section.

I looked at my phone at quarter to twelve. Still no text message from Steve. I hoped he was okay. I went to bed. There was nothing more I could do.

Chapter 20

I had occasional contact with Steve over the next week, during which time he made the briefest of replies to my enquiries about how he was and how work was going. I had decided to avoid mentioning the spell in the hope that forgetting all about it would make it more likely to work. I had no way of knowing whether it had worked yet, or if it was going to work at all. I really wanted to see Steve, not only because I wanted to know if there had been any change, but also because I was missing him. We had been through so many things together recently, that to have a whole week without seeing him had left a big gap in my life. I decided to arrange something. I picked up my mobile phone.

"Fancy meeting up for a drink or something?"

I waited, looking at the screen on my phone. After a few minutes had passed, I decided to occupy myself with something else. Maybe he was busy and hadn't looked at his phone yet. I scrolled through the TV channels. There was nothing on that I wanted to watch, but there seemed to be a lot of cricket on. I decided that this was probably why Steve hadn't replied. He'd be at home absorbed in the cricket. I eventually settled on a repeat of *Ten Years*

Younger when I heard my phone vibrate. There was a reply from Steve.

"I'm going out with the lads on Saturday night but I can make any evening next week."

I tried to convince myself that waiting until next week was probably a good thing, but deep down felt disappointed as I typed.

"How about Monday? I'll check if Mum and Dad can babysit."

Saturday would have been ideal. William was due to be at his dad's which would have meant that I wouldn't have needed a babysitter and therefore wouldn't have had to answer questions from my mum about whether Steve and I were back together again. I knew that the weekend would seem really long if I didn't find something to do to keep my mind off things, so I got in touch with Lucy and suggested a night out at the cinema with the girls. Going to the cinema with William recently had really helped to take my mind off things, and it was a good way to have a night out without having to talk too much. I really wasn't sure whether talking about the whole nettle-stuffed, felt doll thing was a good idea or not. If we were watching a film, there would be less opportunity for the others to ask me about recent events. In fact, now I that I thought about it after the event, it all seemed rather weird. I cringed at the thought of what I had done. The last time I had spoken to any of my friends was when I was about to look through my grandma's old things. They knew nothing of events beyond that.

I met the others at the cinema half an hour before the film was due to start. The original arrangement had been to meet up at seven in the nearby pub and then make our way to the cinema at eight thirty. By the time I'd got back from the shops in town and had something to eat followed by a shower, it was already quarter to seven. I texted Lucy and apologised that I was running late and would see them there. I hadn't intended to spend so long at the shops that afternoon, but after looking around six different department stores, I eventually decided that I liked the top best that I'd seen two hours earlier in the first shop and went back. When I got back to the first shop, I had to queue for ten minutes at the changing rooms before realising that the top looked dreadful on anyway!

Once I eventually arrived at the cinema, talk for the next twenty minutes or so was centred on the size of the queue for tickets followed by whether we were sharing those big buckets of popcorn or just getting our own individual bags of sweets to take in. Eventually one large bucket of popcorn and a couple of bags of sweets were bought between the four of us and we found our seats in the room marked *screen nine*. We had made quite a dent in the popcorn by the time the advertisements and trailers had finished. It was about quarter past nine by the time the film actually started.

We dashed up to the pub afterwards to find that last orders had already been called. We managed to order a quick round of drinks before the bar finally closed for the evening. Most of the talk was about the film. The bar had closed and we had gone our separate ways, agreeing that we should do this sort of thing more often without me even being asked about Steve, or whether I had found what I was looking for amongst my grandma's things.

Monday evening soon came round and I checked my appearance in the mirror as I waited for my mum and dad to arrive for babysitting. I felt guilty that I hadn't seen William all weekend and hadn't spent any time with him on Monday either. I'd rushed him through breakfast that morning so that I could get to work early and now I was rushing out again after a quick oven chips and convenience food meal. I drove to the Yellow Lion and knew that this was going to be awkward. Usually Steve would either arrange to pick me up or talk me into driving so that he could have a drink. He had seemed so business-like on the phone and it didn't feel like a casual meeting with a friend and certainly not like a date.

I spotted Steve's car in the car park and walked towards it until I could see in through the window, hoping that he'd waited for me so that we could go in together. The car was empty. The inside of the pub was dark. There were a couple of older men at the bar who turned and glanced at me as I came through the slightly creaky door. I looked around, not knowing whether to go to the seats to the right or go up the five or six steps to the left which led to a larger area with several alcoves containing tables and stools. At that moment Steve appeared from round the corner, just at the top of the steps and beckoned me to join him up there.

After asking what I wanted to drink and buying me an orange juice from the bar, plus a shandy for himself, he returned to the seats in one of the quieter alcoves and sat opposite me. He sipped his drink quietly and studied my face for a few seconds. I knew that something wasn't right. The Steve I usually knew would be making a joke to lighten the mood. This was a different Steve that I hadn't seen before and it brought back memories of that feeling you got when you knew you were about to be dumped by a boy at school.

"The Sheffield branch are closing down and I'm being re-located to London," Steve eventually announced.

"When?" was all I could think of to say.

"In the new year," he replied.

"That's three months away," I stated the obvious. "Will you be applying for jobs round here in the hope that you won't have to move?" I asked hopefully.

"If the perfect opportunity comes up, then I'll apply for it, but they're offering a really good re-location package with all rent and expenses paid on accommodation down there for the first three months."

"Oh," was all I could think of to say.

"If things had been different between us, then I would have taken a lower-paid job and stayed, but how can we have a future together when we can't even touch each other?" Steve took a breath and then continued, "I think the world of you, Claire, but realistically it's pointless us being anything other than good friends."

Tears started to well up in my eyes. I just hadn't seen this coming at all. I thought we'd have months or even years ahead of us, imagining that eventually things would be different and we would be able to have a normal relationship which wasn't cursed.

Steve continued to talk for a few minutes but I wasn't really listening. This just didn't make sense. We had seemed so close over the last few weeks and now, suddenly, everything that I thought we had been building up to was no longer there. The future was blank with nothing in it.

About ten minutes later I was back in the car, where I trembled with shock and watched Steve drive away. I sat there for a few more minutes before I made a move. I drove to the end of my road, but instead of turning left I went straight past and kept going. There was no way that I could face my parents yet and William probably wouldn't even be asleep. I pulled into the next housing estate and stopped at the end of a quiet cul-de-sac. The tears started to flow and I used up all of the tissues that I had stuffed into my handbag earlier. I decided to phone a friend and tried Lucy's number.

"Hi, Claire," she answered, sounding her usual cheerful self. "I've not heard from you for ages. Is everything alright?" she asked in a tone of voice that was far too cheerful to be spoilt by my tears.

"Not really," I felt the tears starting to well up again. "It's Steve. He's re-locating to London in January with his work."

"When did you find this out?" she asked, now sounding concerned.

"Just now." I told her the details of what had happened over the last hour.

"Where are you now?" she asked.

"In the car. My mum and dad will wonder what has happened if I go home at half past eight."

"Come round here," she suggested.

My knock at the door fifteen minutes later was met by a hug from Lucy. I followed her through to the living room where she passed me a box of tissues.

"Have I got panda eyes?" I asked her.

"Err, sort of," she smiled, rummaging through her handbag and then passing me a small mirror.

"Why is he moving to London then?" Lucy asked. "Can't he just find another job up here?"

I told her what he had said about the company paying his rent for three months and how he had said that he would have stayed if things had been different. "He obviously doesn't think it's worth risking his career for a relationship that's doomed anyway. I can sort of see his point," I told her.

"Do you really think all the problems you two had were down to some sort of curse, or do you think it just wasn't meant to be?" Lucy asked.

"I don't know. I can't believe we've been through so much to try to make things work out and now he's just leaving like that."

I wondered whether to tell her about my attempt at a spell but thought better of it. The whole thing just seemed like something that had happened to someone else.

After a cup of tea and biscuits, I had composed myself sufficiently for Lucy to offer me her make-up bag, so that I could at least attempt to hide all signs of crying before I went home. Mum and Dad were surprised when I returned at just after ten.

"I've got work tomorrow, remember!" I said, trying to sound cheerful. "It's alright for those of you who've retired; you can go to bed at whatever time you want!"

"Oh yeah. I'd forgotten it was Monday!" my dad laughed.

They filled me in on the details of what William had eaten and drunk before he'd gone to bed and told me what a good boy he'd been. I thanked them for coming round. My dad was about to say something, but my mum shot him a glance which silenced him. She must have known that something was wrong. Mums could always see through make-up and false smiles.

I curled myself up on the sofa and just lay there wondering what would happen next. January was still three months away, I told myself. There was still chance that Steve might find work around here and stay. If he stayed and things didn't work out though, would I ever be

255

able to move on and meet someone else? Maybe he was doing us both a favour by moving away, I tried to convince myself by replacing what I really felt with logical, sensible thoughts. The thought of severing all ties and making a fresh start was just too painful. *Maybe I should just take things a day at a time*, I told myself. My head was just too full of thoughts at the moment. I needed to stop thinking and go to bed.

During the next two weeks I tried to concentrate on doing a good job at work and then, when I was at home, being really attentive to William. My sudden interest in his PlayStation games was met with suspicion at first and then annoyance that I was so useless at remembering which button did what on the controller.

"Can I just play it on my own today?" he asked, when it came to the third day of me trying to join in. I went through to the kitchen and started looking through the fridge for ideas of what to cook. I was trying my best to keep busy so that I didn't have time to think about what had happened. I checked my phone, hoping for some sort of contact from Steve. Nothing. Eating was a struggle, and William kept asking why I thought it was okay to leave half of my dinner when he was expected to eat all of his.

The first time that William was at his dad's for the weekend and I was left alone with no child to fuss over and no work to go to was really hard. I started to tidy the house, wondering who I was doing it for. No one would come round to see it and William wouldn't care whether it was tidy or not. I decided to go for a walk to clear my head and get some exercise. I had walked about half a mile and was just going into the park when I felt my phone vibrating. My heartbeat started to go twice as fast as I reached into my pocket. I was disappointed to see Becky's name and number displayed on the screen when I'd hoped it would be Steve, but tried to sound cheerful as I answered.

"Hi, Becky. How are you?" I asked.

"I'm actually in Sainsbury's car park at the moment," she informed me. "I've just seen something on my way here that I thought you'd be interested in."

I waited for her to continue.

"I drove past that Glenda woman's house on the way here and it's up for sale!" she informed me. "Let's hope they're moving a really long way away so that she can't bother you any more," she added.

It would be good to know that she was far away, I thought to myself, although I hadn't seen her for the last few weeks anyway.

"Lucy told me about Steve." Becky's words made me jump slightly at the mention of his name. "I'm sorry things didn't work out between you two, I know you really like him."

"How are things between you and Dave?" I quickly asked, trying to change the subject.

"Good. We've decided to move in together."

"That's great news!" I was genuinely happy for my friend and glad that things were working out for her. She had been single for so long prior to meeting Dave.

"I'm moving in with him so that we don't have to uproot his kids. I'm renting out my house with most of the furniture. That way, if it doesn't work out, I'll have somewhere to go back to."

"Do you get on well with his kids?" I asked her.

"Yes. They're with their mother most of the time anyway and with them being a bit older, fourteen and sixteen, they have their own things that they like to do at weekends anyway. They're mostly out with friends. They seem to like my cooking and say it's much better than their dad's. I think that's what helped them to accept me," she laughed.

I shared her happiness for a moment and managed to forget my own self-pity. We said our goodbyes, promising to meet up soon, and I continued my walk through the park. I looked at the browns and oranges of the autumn leaves and pulled my jacket together against the wind. The trees would soon be bare until next spring when the whole cycle would start again. By then, my whole life would have changed, I thought to myself. I just hoped that it would be for the better.

Chapter 21

I turned the page on my calendar to December. I had only had contact with Steve twice since our meeting in the Yellow Lion. The first was instigated by me, four weeks later, when I sent him a text message asking how he was. *"Fine thanks,"* was all I received in reply. The second contact was at a shop where I had called in for some bread and milk on my way home from work. As I walked towards the check-outs, Steve appeared from another aisle carrying a four-pack of lager. I hadn't expected to see him around that part of town and hoped that I didn't look too surprised. "Hi," was all I could think of to say. He smiled awkwardly and gesticulated that I should go in front of him in the queue. After a few seconds of wondering whether to start up a conversation, I turned to face him. "How are you keeping?" I asked.

"Not too bad. I'm letting the house through an agency from January. I'm just in the middle of sorting through all the rubbish I've collected over the last few years."

"Are you letting it out fully furnished?" I asked, pleased that we'd found something to talk about.

"Yes," was all he had time to reply before it was my turn to pay at the till. I put the bread and milk into a carrier bag and paid. Should I wait for him to pay so that I could talk to him on the way out of the shop? I waited a few seconds and then said, "if you need any help sorting things out or packing, just give me a ring."

That had been two weeks ago and no such phone call had been received. I imagined him packing up his belongings and getting ready to leave. I felt the tears starting to well up in my eyes. Would I ever see him again? Was that the end? Should I forget him and move on, or should I wait? This was no good. *I had to be stronger*, I told myself. I wished there was someone who could tell me what to do. It was then that I remembered Alice. She had said that I might want to get in touch with her again later. I dropped William off at school and then phoned from the car. She answered straight away. An appointment was arranged for five o'clock on the following Friday. I would ask my mum to pick William up from school and say that I was working late.

Friday soon came round and I approached Alice's front door, knocked, and bit my nails as I waited for her to come to the door. The cold December air blew around my face and legs and I hoped that her house was warm. Snow had been forecast for that night and I hoped that it would wait until much later once I was back home. I heard the key turn on the other side of the door and within seconds I was face-to-face with Alice. Her welcoming smile helped to calm my nerves a little bit and she showed me through to a large kitchen, inviting me to sit at one of the chairs placed round an antique pine table.

She filled a large glass jug with water and placed this on the table with two glasses before taking a seat opposite me. She looked at me for a moment before placing the fingers of her right hand on her cheek, a mannerism I noticed last time I saw her which she seemed to take on just before she spoke.

"You can't stop thinking about someone called Steve," she informed me. I nodded.

"You need to get on with your life and move on," she told me. I was gutted. This wasn't what I wanted to hear.

"Your paths will cross again, eventually," she added, "but other events need to pass first."

"How long?" I asked.

"Maybe two or three years but if you don't move on you'll end up stuck where you are."

I wondered what I was going to do with myself for that amount of time.

"Glenda or Glyniss or something like that," she started to say. I nodded. "You won't see or hear from her for a long time but your paths will cross again, also in about two to three years. It will be on much happier terms than before, though," she informed me before pouring herself a glass of water. I copied and poured myself a drink.

I wondered whether to ask her about the spell. She seemed to know what I was thinking, and before I could decide what to say, she added, "things will work out eventually but you have to stop thinking about them. You just need to put things that have passed out of your mind and move forward."

The first week in January came and went with no further word from Steve. I decided to try my best to put him out of my mind. To mark the beginning of the new me who was going to enjoy herself and stop looking back, I invited the girls round to my house for a party. To begin with, talk was about how Becky was settling in with Dave, Lizzie's sleepless night with a very light-sleeping toddler, and Lucy's job. Lucy had taken on a completely different role with a company selling beauty products. We looked at some of the brochures as we drank our wine and ate the home-made pizzas which I had made earlier. Lucy worked from home arranging parties at customers' houses. Her enthusiastic air and friendly disposition meant that she was doing really well. Becky agreed to have a party at her house soon where she would invite Lucy to sell her products. She would make sure that there were plenty of women to sell to.

Later on, once more wine had been drunk, we let our hair down and danced to various 1980s pop tunes and 1970s hits by Abba. It was soon midnight and taxis were called. My friends had all had more than enough to drink and couldn't have stayed much longer, even if they had wanted to. They had all done such a good job of not mentioning Steve that I went to bed that night for the first time in months without even thinking about him. Despite waking up at ten the next morning with the worst hangover I had had in years, I decided that it had been just what I needed. I had real friends who I could count on and a son who meant everything to me. I didn't need a man and would be fine without one.

I threw myself into my work, and when I was at home I made sure that I spent some quality time with William every day. I also vowed to see my parents more often, rather than just calling them when I wanted a babysitter. *This was what had happened over recent years*, I thought to myself guiltily.

"We never found out why your grandma had been adopted or who her biological parents were," my mum announced one Sunday afternoon when my dad brought out a copy of the family tree that he and my mum had been working on.

I had forgotten that the information I had been given about my grandma was from Alice on that night at Lucy's house all that time ago. "Oh. I thought that her parents were ..." I stopped, suddenly realising what I was saying.

"Have you found something out, Claire?" my dad asked.

I blushed. "Err, not really. I don't know,"

"People always thought that your grandma had special powers," my mum added.

"Really?" I asked.

"Yes. She told me that when she was at school, if anyone lost anything, they always asked her to help them find it. She always seemed to know exactly where to look, even if it was in the most unlikely of places."

"Your mum lost a watch once and spent ages retracing her steps through all the shops she had been in that day. She left a description of the missing watch in every shop in case someone had handed it in."

"Anyway, your grandma came round that night," my dad added, "and asked your mum to get out all her handbags. There were about fifteen handbags all lined up on the bed and your grandma pointed to a brown one that your mum hadn't used for a couple of weeks."

"It's in there, she said," my mum continued to recount events. "I told her that it couldn't be because I hadn't used that bag for a while, but she insisted that I looked anyway. I looked inside and, sure enough, there was the missing watch!"

"How come it was in that bag, then, if you lost it at the shops? Had you taken that bag after all?" I asked.

"No. I remembered a few minutes after finding the watch that it had come off when I was out at the cinema with your Auntie Susan and I had put it in my bag for safe keeping. I can't have been wearing it when I went shopping after all!" my mum laughed.

By the time they had recounted all the lost items my grandma had retrieved and told me stories about her just seeming to know things that she hadn't been told, they had forgotten that I had started to admit to knowing something and they didn't quiz me any further on the subject.

That night I started to think about what Alice had told me about my grandma's parents being threatened for being witches and how they had had their daughter taken from them. Despite my earlier attempts to research the subject, I still wasn't really sure whether people just chose to become witches and spent their lives hoping that the spells they cast would come true, or whether some people really were born with special abilities, beyond what so-called normal people were capable of. *Were some people just naturally wise because they understood people and the ways of the world better than others, or did they really possess magical powers?* I wondered.

I thought about the *'Book of shadows'* that I had found amongst my grandma's things. Because she had been adopted and hadn't seen her parents since she was a baby, the book couldn't have been passed down to her. She must have had a strong interest in witchcraft and had either started the book up herself or been given it by someone else. I found the book out and turned the pages one at a time, looking at the handwriting. It all looked as though it had been written by the same person, so the best way to find out whether it was my grandma's writing was to get something else that had been written by her and compare the two, I decided.

I pulled a box out of the bottom of my wardrobe that contained special birthday cards that I had kept over the years. My mum had given me all the cards that people had sent when I had been born. I opened each one, one at a time. "Congratulations on the birth of your daughter," read the first one, "Love from Susan and Ian," in what I recognised as Auntie Susan's neat, schoolteacher writing.

"Best wishes on the birth of Claire, she's beautiful," read another card from Lisa and Pete, whose names I didn't recognise. I looked through quite a pile, smiling at what people had written, but getting disappointed that none of these were from my grandma. Eventually, when I had almost given up hope, I opened a white cardboard box, tied with pink ribbon. Inside the box was a card wrapped in pink tissue paper. I carefully folded back the tissue paper to reveal a beautiful card showing an angel looking over a baby. Inside the card the most careful and perfectly formed handwriting said, "Wishing your beautiful baby daughter luck and happiness throughout her life, Mum and Dad." I compared the writing to that in the *Book of shadows'*. It was a perfect match. It was even written in the same dark blue ink from a fountain pen. The spells must have all been written by my grandma.

I was about to replace the card in the box, when I noticed another small piece of tissue paper which had been carefully folded up in the bottom of the box. I opened it, making sure that I didn't tear the delicate paper, which took a lot of doing when I was trembling with excitement and impatience. Eventually, I took out a silver chain which had a pendant threaded onto it. The pendant was a silver pentagram with a purple stone in the middle. There was also a small envelope containing a handwritten note which read,

"Wear this as protection from harmful forces and bad luck."

If only I had found this sooner, I sighed to myself and put the chain around my neck.

I turned the pages again in the *'Book of shadows'* until I got to the spell which I had tried. All that had happened for me was that Steve had gone further away. *Maybe the book shouldn't have found its way into my hands and I should have left it where it was*, I thought to myself. I reminded myself how badly things could go wrong if magical spells got into the wrong hands and thought about the spell inadvertently cast by Glenda all those years ago. I closed the book and put it away in the bottom of my wardrobe along with the cards. Alice had told me to forget all about Steve and everything that had happened before. I vowed not to get the book out again and not to think about Steve, the spell, or Glenda. I continued to wear the pendant since my grandma had given it as a gift with the intention that I should wear it, judging by the note that was with it. I went to bed, deciding once more to put the past behind me and hoping that the future would bring better luck.

Chapter 22

It was six months later that Becky announced her engagement and a year after that when I turned to catch a glimpse of her in her wedding dress, which had been kept a secret to all except her older sister. I had only met Becky's father a couple of times when he had been wearing attire suitable for helping Becky with the decorating. I certainly wouldn't have recognised him dressed in what was most likely a very expensive suit. It clearly showed in his face that he was proud of his daughter and was happy with her choice of husband.

Adoration for his bride showed all over Dave's face as the couple turned to face each other to say their vows. Both mothers searched through their handbags for tissues on several occasions throughout the ceremony.

The wedding and the reception were at Thorncliffe Hall. The grounds were beautifully maintained with gardens, water features and large lawned areas. Luckily the weather was good and it was a pleasure to stand outside and sip wine during the photographs. I remembered my wedding to Greg all those years ago. It was a very windy April. Posing for photographs in the churchyard, especially once the rain started, was not a happy start to married life.

Hopefully this lovely day would bode better luck for Becky and Dave's future together.

I chatted to Lucy and Lizzie and meanwhile their husbands started up their own conversation about cricket. I turned to look towards Becky and Dave during the conversation and noticed a man looking in our direction. I wondered whether he was someone that Lucy, Lizzie or one of the men knew. I didn't recognise him, but whenever I turned to admire Becky's dress or comment on the proceedings, he seemed to be looking our way.

It was near the end of the photograph session, when all the guests had been photographed together, that he started to walk towards me.

"Hi, I'm Keith," he said by way of introduction. "I don't think we've met before."

The man was probably aged around forty. He had wavy mid-brown hair and brown eyes. Slight dimples formed in his cheeks when he smiled. He was around five feet, ten inches tall and of medium build. There was a confident air about him but not arrogant.

"Claire," I said, shaking the hand that was offered.

"Are you a friend or relative?" he asked.

"I'm one of Becky's friends," I explained. "How about you?"

"I'm Dave's cousin," he answered. "Would you like a refill?" he asked, pointing towards my empty wine glass.

"Yes, please." I wasn't sure whether to follow him back indoors as he went for more drinks or just stand there.

"That took a long time!" Lucy exclaimed.

"What did?" I asked, wondering whether she was talking about the man who had just spoken to me.

"The photos!" she sighed. "What else do you think we've been standing out here for all this time?"

I glanced in the direction of the conservatory where I could make out Keith as he headed towards the bar. Lucy didn't seem to have noticed me talking to him only a minute earlier. She had had her back to me and was talking to Lizzie during my conversation with John.

"Who was that then?" asked Lizzie, who had clearly witnessed everything.

"Dave's cousin, Keith," I explained.

"Have you met him before? I noticed him looking at you earlier," she winked.

"No. He's just introduced himself," I said, trying not to blush.

"You look like a fourteen-year-old again," laughed Lucy. "Do you fancy him?"

I really didn't know what to say. The last thing on my mind had been meeting someone. It had been eighteen months since Steve had left and I had almost managed to convince myself that I was ready to move on with my life.

If I said yes to dating someone else, it would mean that Steve and I as an item were definitely in the past and there would be no turning back. All that we had been through would become history.

"He's probably just being friendly," I said.

"Is that why he's coming back across the lawn with two drinks?" laughed Lucy.

"And heading towards you?" added Lizzie.

"Are these more of Becky's friends?" he asked as he passed the glass of red wine to me.

"Don't let her have too much red wine before the meal," laughed Lucy. "She'll fall asleep."

"No, she'll tell you all our secrets and then fall asleep," laughed Lizzie.

"Secrets?" Keith raised his eyebrows.

"Oh, don't listen to them," I smiled. "They'll all have nodded off in a corner long before me!"

"Are you here on your own?" I found myself saying.

"No. There are about two hundred people here, aren't there?" he joked.

I laughed but wondered who he would be sitting with for the meal. I was about to probe further when an older gentleman called from across the lawn.

"Sorry. Best man duties call," he explained.

"Oh. I didn't know that you were the best man," I smiled as I watched him dash across the grass.

During the ceremony, my view of the best man had been limited due to someone wearing a rather large hat. There were three men in addition to the groom, all of around the same age, dressed in matching suits. They looked related. I later discovered that one was Keith's older brother and the other was two years younger. I wondered why Dave had chosen Keith to be the best man rather than the oldest of the three male cousins.

Most of my questions were answered during the speeches. I discovered that Keith and Dave had been through school together and were the same age. They were best friends as well as cousins. The other brothers were married to the two bridesmaids. Keith didn't have a partner or wife sitting with him at the top table, but I wondered whether he had a girlfriend sitting at one of the other tables who hadn't been given an important role at the wedding. I looked around the room for possible matches. There was a round table seating ten. I looked at the occupants for a moment. There seemed to be an equal number of men and women, their ages ranging from about thirty to mid-fifties. I guessed that these could possibly be either Becky's or Dave's work colleagues but then wondered again since work colleagues were only usually invited to the evening celebrations. Everyone seemed to have a partner on that table and whoever they were, there didn't seem to be a spare woman who might be Keith's girlfriend or wife. I looked over at Keith. He didn't have a wedding ring on. He smiled and laughed easily with the other guests. I must have looked at him for a moment too long, as he seemed to become aware that someone was watching him. He looked up, smiled and lifted his glass in my direction. I smiled back and then looked away, unsure how to react. I wasn't sure whether I wanted to encourage him or not.

"You do fancy him, don't you?" laughed Lizzie. "I saw you looking at him!"

"I'm having a look at everyone," I replied. "There are a lot of guests here, aren't there?"

"Yes, and you're having a look at some of them more than others," joked Lucy.

Once the cake had been cut and all the formal stuff was over, guests started to leave their tables and either head towards the toilets, the bar, or outside for some fresh air or a smoke. I walked over to Becky and Dave as they started to make their way outside for some fresh air and congratulated them on how well the day was going so far. There was quite a gathering of people wanting to have a quick word with the happy couple and I stepped back to let someone else talk. At that moment, I felt a gentle tap on my shoulder. I turned and found myself face-to-face with Keith.

"Oh, hello again!" I said, trying to sound as natural as possible but feeling like a schoolgirl who had just spotted the boy she had a crush on in the school corridor.

"Hi. It's a bit warm in here. Do you fancy a walk outside?" he asked.

"Yes. I was just on my way outside anyway," I replied.

"You don't smoke do you?" he asked.

"No, I want fresh air, not polluted air," I laughed.

"Good. I don't like cigarette smoke either!" he smiled and led the way out into the gardens.

I found out that he worked at one of the large banks in the centre of town and lived at the north of the city, about twelve miles from where I lived at the south-east. I told him about my job for the local newspaper and that I had a nine-year-old son.

"We never had any children," he replied, his smile fading.

"Oh," I wanted to ask who the other part of *we* was, but wasn't sure how it would sound. He answered the question without me having to ask it.

"I was married for eight years but she was killed in a car accident," he informed me.

"Oh, I'm sorry to hear that. That must have been horrible for you." I didn't know what else to say.

"That was five years ago. I've been single ever since," he continued.

"I was married and divorced. I've been single for the last eighteen months," I informed him.

"So you haven't been seeing anyone since the divorce then?"

"Oh, the divorce was a few years ago. I was seeing someone after that but it didn't work out. It was that which ended eighteen months ago," I said. Hearing myself say the words sounded really final.

"Have you got over him yet?" Keith asked.

"I think so. You can't just wipe out the past though, can you?"

"No, but you can't go back there either," he smiled.

I looked down at the ground, wondering what to say next.

"So we're both here on our own," he stated.

"No, there are about two hundred people here, aren't there?" I laughed. Keith laughed back at my reference to what he had said earlier.

There was definitely a spark between us, and about fifteen minutes later when he asked for my phone number, I didn't hesitate in giving it out.

"I thought I'd better get your number before I have any more to drink," he laughed. "The evening guests will be arriving soon, and once the disco starts it'll be much too noisy to talk, so all there is to do is drink!"

"I know what you mean!" I smiled.

As predicted, the evening was very noisy and very busy. The bar area and dance floor were all full and it was difficult to make out who was who once the lights were dimmed. At one o'clock, Lucy informed me that she had phoned a taxi and asked whether I wanted to share it with her, Lizzie and the two men. I said yes, feeling glad that I wouldn't be travelling alone.

"Are you seeing him again, then?" Lizzie asked, once we were in the taxi.

"He's got my phone number, so we'll see," I replied.

"He must really like you," said Lucy. "Apparently, he's been on his own for years since his wife died. He's not looked at anyone else since," she added.

"You know how nosey Lucy is," laughed Lizzie. "She's been doing a bit of detective work!"

"I didn't hear anything bad about him. I think he's a good catch," said Lucy.

"It'll do you good to start seeing someone," chipped in Lizzie.

Luckily, the drink knocked me out that night so I didn't have chance to think. The hangover the next morning also prevented me from wondering whether letting Steve go was the right thing. I hadn't heard anything from him or about him since shortly after he had left for London.

Later on Sunday evening, once William had returned from Greg's and had been tucked up in bed, I began to think about things a bit more. I thought that Steve would probably have met someone else by now anyway and wondered whether he was still prone to injuries and illnesses or whether he was better now that he had moved away from me. *If this was the case, was it just coincidence or was it really the case that he was in good health as long as he and I were apart?* I wondered. What would happen if I saw him again? Could my spell have worked? There were so many unanswered questions but, since Steve was at the other end of the country and didn't seem to be interested in getting in touch, I could only assume that he had moved on. *Maybe we would have better luck in another life*, I thought to myself, thinking about the dreams I used to have. I hadn't had any of those strange dreams since Steve had left and thought how unreal the whole thing seemed now.

It was Tuesday when I heard my mobile phone ringing. I searched through my bag and found it just as it stopped. I didn't recognise the number and wondered whether it might be Keith. I quickly returned the call, not wanting him to think that I had deliberately ignored him.

"Hello!" Keith answered.

"Hi, it's Claire. I think you just rang me but I couldn't get my phone out of my bag in time!" I explained.

"Would you like to meet up this Friday?" he asked.

"Yes. Where are we going?" I inquired.

"Do you like Chinese food?"

"Yes," I replied.

"Good. I'll pick you up at seven, if that's okay?"

"Yes, it should be," I said.

He wrote down my address and said he looked forward to seeing me. He would make all the arrangements for the restaurant in the city centre.

Chapter 23

Friday evening arrived. William had been taken round to my mum and dad's to stay overnight and I was back at home nervously checking my appearance in the full-length mirror in my bedroom. I had decided not to dress too formally and opted for some flattering, black jeans with a pretty, pale-blue top which fell in the category of somewhere between a blouse and a shirt. I carefully applied dark grey eyeliner and a subtle pale blue eyeshadow to highlight my eyes which I thought of as being one of my more attractive features. I decided that any sort of foundation was unnecessary since my skin was quite good over the summer months. I finished my make-up off with a dark pink lipstick and gave my hair a good brush. It was now in a just-below-the-shoulder, low-maintenance style which just needed a bit of hairspray around the front to keep it under control. I finished off with some high-heeled, slingback sandals and matching handbag into which I crammed my purse, mobile phone, hairbrush, lipstick and a few tissues. I still had fifteen minutes to spare before Keith was due to pick me up and I headed downstairs where I paced the living room floor nervously. I wondered whether he would arrive in more formal attire and make me look underdressed, or whether he was one of those men who always wore a shirt and jeans for all but the most formal occasions. I had only seen him dressed as Best Man, which definitely counted as the latter.

Every time I heard a car drive past the house, I looked out of the window, wondering whether it was him. The fifth car which went past caught my eye, especially since it wasn't one I recognised as belonging to any of my neighbours, and it stood out due to being exceptionally clean and shiny. The black paintwork put the unwashed, dusty car on my driveway to shame. I wasn't sure what make of car it was since my knowledge was limited to only the most common makes. William would have told me immediately if he had been there. I was more interested in the driver who pulled up outside my house and looked across to check the number on the front door before getting out of the car. I quickly jumped back from the window, hoping that he hadn't spotted me. I wanted to look calm and in control, not like an excited child who had been waiting impatiently.

I opened the door and my nerves were instantly calmed when I was met by his friendly smile and warm brown eyes.

"Hi," he said.

"Come in, I'll just get my bag," I said, realising that I had left it upstairs and ran back up to get it.

I came back down to find him standing at the bottom of the stairs looking at a photograph of William and my mum and dad. This had been taken on a day out to York the previous summer.

"Is that your son?" he asked.

"Yes, and my mum and dad," I answered, remembering that I had told him that I had a child when I met him at Becky's Wedding.

He smiled at me. "You look very pretty tonight."

I looked at his dark blue chinos and casual shirt and then down at his very shiny black shoes.

"Your shoes are as shiny as your car!" I laughed, trying to hide my embarrassment at his compliment.

"I took the car to be washed and valeted this lunchtime!" he joked. "It didn't look like that yesterday!"

After making one last check that the windows were closed and the door was locked, I followed him up the driveway and out to the pavement where he held open the door on the passenger side of the car for me.

"Do you always check things that many times?" he asked, as the cheeky dimples started to form in his cheeks.

"Yes. I can't rest unless I do," I giggled and blushed.

"Have you been to Chinatown before?" I asked him.

"Yes but it was a long time ago. I think it was for a friend's thirtieth. There was a group of about twelve of us there. One of the couples got a bit loud and embarrassing," he informed me.

I wondered whether he had been there as a couple with his wife.

"How about you?" he asked.

"Oh. Yes," I replied. "I've been a few times. I think the last time was a couple of years ago." It had been with Steve but I thought it better not to mention that.

Keith pressed various buttons on the radio, tuning into the preset channels. He stopped at one playing "Gold" by Spandau Ballet and started to sing along. I was surprised that he had such a good singing voice. The previous men in my life wouldn't have listed singing as one of their strong points and would have probably just sung along to the chorus unaware that it wasn't quite in time or in tune. 'Gold' was one of my favourite songs from the eighties, but I felt too self-conscious to sing to it in the car on a first date. I regularly sang in the car on the way to and from work when there was no one else there to listen, but on this occasion I just sang along in my head.

We arrived at the restaurant and were seated at a small, candlelit table for two. I looked around at the other diners. The restaurant had seating for about two hundred people and was already almost full with a mixture of couples, families and larger parties.

"Could I take your drinks order please?" we were asked by a young waitress who looked no older than twenty three. I wondered what drink Keith would order. Everything was new and I suddenly felt nervous again.

"Do you drink wine?" Keith asked me.

"Yes. I prefer white with food," I answered.

He ordered a bottle. At first I wondered whether he was expecting me to down a bottle all to myself and was relieved when he asked for no other drinks.

By the time the food arrived, I was already on my second glass of wine and started to feel more at ease. Conversation was based around topics such as some of the teachers we'd had at secondary school, 1980s music and work. Not really all that exciting, but safe. If we were to go on further dates, conversations of a more personal nature would eventually take place, I assumed, but I didn't want to make any assumptions at this stage about whether there would be further dates.

The evening continued at a bar further along the same road. The music was loud and we had to lean towards each other to be heard. I liked the way he smelled and felt a reaction to his touch as he gently put his hand on my shoulder when he leaned in to ask whether I wanted another drink in there or whether I wanted to go somewhere quieter. I opted to go somewhere quieter and he kept his hand on my shoulder as he gently led me out through the very busy pub.

The wine bar he took me to next was in complete contrast to the lively bar we had left. I looked around the large room across the stained wooden floorboards and saw couples sharing quiet conversation in dimly lit corners on leather sofas. Gentle background music played, the sort that was advertised on TV to relax after a stressful day at work.

"There are some seats up there," said Keith. "I'll get the wine."

I wandered over to the steps which took me up to a carpeted area. The area was about twenty feet square and contained more sofas and low coffee tables. Apart from one couple, who were probably in their mid-forties, this area was empty and I chose a sofa in the far corner, away from the other couple.

Keith came with a bottle of white wine and two glasses. I hadn't been out much over the last couple of years and was only used to having a couple of drinks. I tried to drink slowly, hoping that I wouldn't get really drunk and make an idiot of myself. Conversation flowed from Becky and Dave's wedding through to more talk of secondary school in the 1980s. Before I knew what had happened, Keith was sharing out the last dregs of the wine.

"Come on, let's find a taxi," he said as he stood up and got hold of my hand. I followed him outside, feeling slightly dizzy as the fresh air hit me. He managed to flag down a taxi almost straight away and before I knew it, we were seated side by side in the back.

"Where to?" the driver asked.

Keith had reeled off my address before I could even get the words out. I felt unsure of what to do next. It was years since I had been on a first date. Would he get the taxi to drop me off first and then instruct the driver to carry on to his house, or would he expect to come in for a coffee or something? My head was spinning and I couldn't think straight. Before I had decided what to do, the taxi had pulled up outside my house.

"Are you coming in?" I found myself asking, although I'd said this because I didn't know what else to say rather than intending it as an invitation.

"If you're sure," Keith smiled. I wasn't sure at all but let Keith hand over some money to the driver and follow me into the house.

Almost as soon as I had turned the key in the lock, Keith put his arms around me and ran his fingers through my hair. He gently pulled my head towards his and started to gently kiss my mouth in a way which I had never been kissed before. I felt my body responding. He ran his hand down my back and gradually seemed to be working back up towards my breast. I pulled away, unsure whether this was what I should be doing on a first date.

"Shall we have some coffee?" I asked, my breathy voice seeming to come from someone else.

"Okay," Keith replied.

I looked at his face. There was a look of arousal in his eyes and his breathing was coming fast and shallow. I showed him through to the sitting room before heading into the kitchen. I filled the kettle and then steadied myself against the worktop. My pulse was racing and I couldn't decide what to do. I felt so aroused, but should I let things go any further with someone I had only met once before? Had I really come to terms with Steve no longer being part of my life? Would Keith expect me to say no or had my invitation into the house led him to believe that he would be staying the night?

I took the coffees through to the sitting room, hoping that the correct answer would come soon. Keith was looking comfortable and relaxed on the sofa in contrast to the bag of nerves that I now felt. I sat opposite him and sipped my coffee.

"It's been five years since my wife died," he said, his face and voice now much more serious.

"And you've been on your own all that time?" I asked, remembering what Lucy had told me after Becky's wedding.

"There have been a few that haven't got beyond the first date. I haven't met anyone special," he said, looking me in the eyes, "until now," he added.

I wondered whether he meant that he'd had a string of one night stands or had been celibate for the last five years. I certainly didn't want to become a one night stand. I'd never done that sort of thing before and didn't intend to start now. I told him about my marriage to Greg and how that had ended when Greg played away from home, then how my relationship with Steve had ended when he moved away to London with work.

"If he really loved you, he wouldn't have gone," Keith stated in a matter-of-fact tone of voice.

The hurt must have shown in my face, because he said, "You loved him, didn't you?"

I didn't know what to say. I didn't want to go there.

"There were just too many things against us," I stated, hoping to sound as vague as possible.

"I'll call a taxi," Keith said, getting up from his seat. I looked at the clock. It was half past one. All the passion from an hour ago had been replaced by sadness. He left without saying whether there would be a next time and I didn't want to ask.

Chapter 24

Two weeks passed and I still hadn't heard anything from Keith.

"Maybe he's afraid to have a proper relationship," suggested Lizzie, as we sat in her sitting room, sipping lager and nibbling crisps.

"It sounds as though he's never seen anyone more than once since his wife died. Five years is a long time though. Maybe he'll never get over her," Lucy added.

"I'm glad I didn't let him stay over. I don't want to be another of his one night stands." I rolled my eyes and reached for a handful of roasted peanuts.

"His wife looked a lot like you apparently," Becky announced.

I had forgotten that Keith was Dave's cousin and therefore Becky probably knew more about Keith than me. "I'm definitely glad I didn't take things further!" I exclaimed. "Have you seen Keith recently?" I asked, realising that Becky and Dave would probably be seeing Keith on a regular basis, even if I wasn't.

"No. Not since the wedding," Becky replied. "We only came back from our honeymoon a week ago, remember!"

"Oh, yes. Have you got the wedding photos back yet?"

"Yes, I've brought them with me. I was waiting until everyone was here!" Becky announced.

The next hour was filled with cooing over the photographs.

"I could invite Keith round for tea one night next week and try to find out how the land lies?" Becky suggested as she saw me looking at a photograph of Dave and Keith together.

"I don't know. If he was interested, he'd have got back in touch by now," I sighed.

"Maybe he's waiting for you!" Lucy said.

Later that week, Becky phoned. "Hi, Claire," she said sounding excited.

"Hi, Becky, how are you?" I asked, not sure whether I was even bothered about what she had to say about Keith or not.

"Apparently he hasn't been in touch because he thinks you're still in love with Steve."

"Oh," was all I could think of to say.

"What did you say to him?" she asked.

I relayed the conversation that had taken place about our marriages and relationships.

"Do you want to see him again?"

"I don't know," was my reply.

"Why don't you make the first move and give him a ring?" Becky suggested. "Give it another chance and if it doesn't work out at least you'll know."

"I'll think about it," was my answer.

I thought about it for two days and then got in touch. We met up at one of the local pubs the following weekend. I decided not to mention Steve or either of our pasts and give Keith a chance. I was too young to be left sad and lonely for the rest of my days.

Drinks were coming my way even faster than on our previous date and the pair of us soon forgot our worries about what the other one was thinking and we started to have a really good time. The pub was only a short walk away from my house and we walked back once last orders had been called. This time it was me who made the first move and put my arms around him as soon as the door was closed. I looked up into his eyes and smiled before standing up on my toes and kissing him. He responded immediately with much more passion than before, pressing me up against the wall. I didn't protest when he put his hand inside my top and undid my bra. Instead I put my hand on the front of his trousers and felt his hardness against me. We removed each other's clothes and ran upstairs leaving them in a heap at the bottom of the stairs. Neither of us needed much foreplay. It had been a long time for both of us and within minutes he was inside me. I shook as my body spasmed with the intensity of my climax. He followed soon after and we lay there breathing deeply. We must have both dozed off because it was half an hour later when I woke to find the pair of us sprawled naked across the bed. He must have sensed my movement and woke to look at me.

"That was a bit quick, wasn't it?" was the first thing that came into my head to say.

"Let's see if we can make it last a bit longer this time," he grinned, pulling me towards him again. This time he carefully caressed every part of my body until I couldn't take any more. When he eventually moved inside me, I climaxed almost straight away, but this time with even more intensity than before and I screamed out loudly in pleasure.

The third time was at eight in the morning. After a small amount of sleep we got up just after nine and both showered before breakfast. At that moment the past didn't matter. I had just had the most amazing night of sex. The past was forgotten. Lust had taken over.

"When can I see you again?" Keith asked, after I had given him a lift to his house later that morning.

"Well, William only goes to his dad's on alternate weekends," I explained. "I'd need to arrange a babysitter if you wanted to see me before then."

"Could you get someone to babysit next Saturday?" he asked.

"I'll ask my mum and dad if William can stay over at their house next Saturday night, shall I?"

"Yes, that would be great," Keith smiled.

As soon as I got back home, I phoned to make the necessary arrangements. It was all set up. I was seeing Keith again the following Saturday.

Saturday came round and I dropped William off at my parents' house.

"Who is this new bloke then?" my dad asked. "When are we going to meet him?"

"It's early days yet, Dad!" I answered.

"Has he met William yet?" my mum asked.

"No. I've only seen Keith a couple of times; it's too early to introduce him to William."

"Yes. You're probably right there," my mum agreed. "Decide whether you like him first before you go getting William involved. He still misses Steve, you know!" Mum informed me.

Back at home, I waited like an excited teenager for Keith to arrive and almost skipped to the door as soon as I heard him knock.

"Where are we going?" I asked.

"Let's start with this," he said, pressing me up against the door and kissing me urgently.

"Hey, patience now!" I grinned.

"I've brought some wine. Let's drink it here," he said.

I felt slightly disappointed since I had expected a night out somewhere.

"No taxi to pay for, no noisy music to shout over, and cheap booze!" he announced.

"Well, when you put it like that!" I laughed.

The wine was consumed within an hour and before I knew what was happening he was unbuttoning my top. Part of me wanted to protest, wondering whether he had only come round for sex but my body responded and lust took over again. He stayed the night and there was a repeat performance on Sunday morning.

It was the following weekend when Keith came round again, bottle of wine in hand, that I stopped him just as the feeling of déjà vu was coming on.

"Keith, can we sit down and talk for a few minutes please?" I asked.

"Why the serious tone of voice?"

"Sit down a minute please?"

"Okay. What is it?"

I waited for him to sit down and look as though he was going to take me seriously.

"Are we going to have a proper relationship, or is this just about sex?"

There, I'd said it. I stood at the end of the sofa, wondering what his response would be.

"Why don't we just see where it leads?" he replied. "That relationship word is a bit heavy, don't you think? We've only seen each other a few times!"

"Exactly. We talked the first time and ever since all we've done is had sex. We're not finding out anything else about each other and not doing stuff together."

"You weren't complaining!"

He was right. The sex was good but I didn't want to build a whole relationship on sex and then discover we had nothing in common. I voiced these concerns to Keith.

"Okay. Where do you want to go out to?" he asked.

I wasn't really in the mood to go anywhere now. "Can we just sit down and talk?"

"Oh. About what?"

"Well, I'd imagined us going out on dates and having days out. You know, doing things together. As well as the sex!"

He seemed to be struggling with something. He went very quiet and an awkward silence filled the room.

"I really like you, it's just ..."

"Just what?" I asked, sitting down opposite him.

"You remind me so much of Trina."

I realised that Becky had told me before that I looked like Trina. I'd conveniently put this to the back of my mind until now though, hoping that it was just a coincidence.

"Well, why did you ask me out in the first place then?" I started to raise my voice. "You've got to like me for who I am. It's got to be me you are making love to. In fact ..." I started to feel sick at the thought of what might have been going on here. "Have you been pretending that I'm Trina when we're in bed together?"

The way he lowered his eyes to the floor confirmed my suspicions.

"I think you'd better go!" I grabbed his jacket off the rail at the bottom of the stairs.

"Seriously, I think you'd better get help. You need to meet someone who doesn't remind you of her!" I was as angry with myself as I was with him. Why had I given him another chance after that first date instead of following my gut reaction?

Keith left and I sat fuming on the sofa, tears welling up in my eyes. I felt like an idiot. If he'd just said that he wanted a no-strings-attached arrangement based on sex I would have been disappointed, but to think that every time we were together he was thinking of his dead wife was just wrong. It was sick. He wasn't just having a bit of a fling. He needed his head seeing to.

The months passed by. Christmas came and went. Lucy, Lizzie and Becky were disappointed that things with Keith hadn't worked out. I didn't go into all the details with them but said that it was mainly because I reminded him of Trina. I tried to be philosophical about it. At least it had taught me that a relationship needed to be much more than sex. I thought of all those times I'd felt let down because the physical side of my relationship with Steve had been problematic. At least we got on really well, did lots of things together, he got on well with William and even stood by me when I was busy trying to deal with a curse. It had been two years since Steve left and I hadn't seen him since. I had no idea how he was finding his new life down in London. Did he like his job? Was he seeing someone else? Was he happy?

I decided to do something to cheer myself up and I booked a holiday cottage near the Norfolk Broads for Easter time. In the meantime, the occasional nights out to the cinema with my friends continued. Steve and Keith were both banned topics of conversation and my friends were under strict instructions not to try and set me up with anyone! I needed time to get myself together before jumping into anything else. I began to enjoy being single. I could please myself on what I cooked for meals, where I went out to, and I kept myself busy at weekends by taking William out for days out in the countryside or to the coast if the weather was up to it. When William was at Greg's, I treated myself to a day out shopping at Meadowhall or went running. I had recently discovered that there was nothing quite like running through the fields on a spring day to make myself feel alive and remind me of all the good things in life.

Easter time soon came round and it was time for my holiday to Norfolk with William. The car was packed with clothes for both warm and colder weather since April could be so changeable. Basic food supplies were packed in case I didn't find a supermarket straight away and we were ready to go. I had bought a satnav. especially for the trip since I hadn't driven that distance myself before. I programmed in the postcode and we were ready to go.

Four and a half hours later, we eventually arrived at the cottage and settled ourselves in before finding a fish and chip shop within walking distance from the cottage. I took William for a long walk around the area to get rid of that restless feeling after being stuck in the car for so long. This was followed up by watching a DVD back in the cottage whilst we shared a big bar of chocolate. William was allowed shandy as a special treat and I had a can of cider. We both slept well and woke up on the Sunday morning ready to have a really good week's holiday.

We had walks through country lanes which ran alongside the Broads, taking picnics to eat for lunch as we sat and enjoyed the fresh air and scenery. We had a day exploring Norwich, and I drove to the coast at Yarmouth on Thursday so that William could have a day on the beach with his bucket and spade making sandcastles and digging moats. I bought an extra bucket and spade and joined in the fun. It was like being a child again. I really enjoyed myself and was so glad I'd made the decision to have a holiday with William.

It was on Friday, when William and I stepped off the boat at Wroxham after a trip along the Broads, that something unexpected happened. I held my hand out to steady William as he stepped off the boat, making sure that I didn't lose him amongst the crowd leaving the boat or the queue of tourists waiting for the next trip. The guided tours lasted forty five minutes each and were an hour apart to allow time for one lot of passengers to disembark and the next group to take their places. I was walking along the roped off area with William when I saw a familiar face looking straight at me from within the queue of tourists waiting to board the boat. I tried to avert my eyes and pretend that I hadn't seen her, but the way in which the lines of people were directed by ropes meant that I had no other option but to walk straight past her. The queue of people leaving the boat came to a halt just as I found myself standing side by side with Glenda.

"Why have we stopped, Mum?" William asked.

"They're selling half-price tickets for a trip on another boat this afternoon," Glenda piped up in response to William's question, which in turn caused William and me to turn towards her."

"Can we go on that Mum?" William asked.

"I don't know. I was hoping to have a look round the shops," I said, really for something to say more than any other reason. There didn't actually seem to be that many shops in Wroxham and we'd probably seen most of them already that morning.

"I'm glad I've seen you. I need to talk to you about something," Glenda said.

"Oh," was all I could say. Something in the softness of her voice told me that any anger she had been feeling towards me in the past had gone and she had changed her mind about things.

She smiled kindly as she said, "will you meet us in the café over there in an hour please?"

I glanced down at William, wondering whether what she wanted to talk about would be suitable for him to hear.

"It's okay. Ted can take him to play on the slot machines for a while whilst we have a chat, if that's alright with you."

I looked at Ted's kind face. There was nothing about Ted that would make me distrust him in any way and so I agreed to meet them back at the café at one o'clock.

Chapter 25

I looked around a nearby department store with William to try to fill the time until one o'clock. I ended up buying two new T-shirts for William and some sunglasses for me. *Maybe it would have been cheaper to take the half-price trip on the second boat, rather than going shopping,* I thought to myself as I put my debit card into the card reader.

I headed for the café at five to one and saw Glenda and Ted walking towards me amongst a large group of people. Some were elderly, others tried to negotiate pushchairs through the crowd and a young couple held up the proceedings as they stopped to give each other a kiss. Ted and Glenda eventually made their way over to where I was standing.

"How about a quick go on those machines over there before your mum gets your lunch?" Ted asked William.

I handed some loose change to William and told him that it was okay to go with Ted.

"Ted used to live near us, William. You'll be alright with him for a while," I said, as William's questioning glance said that he didn't know this man.

I went inside and took a seat where I could see William and Ted but talk to Glenda as well.

"I had one of those past life regressions done," Glenda said smiling at me.

"Oh. Really?" I said, wondering what she was going to say next.

"It turns out you were right. We used to be sisters in a former life."

My heart started to beat faster and I didn't notice the waitress standing next to me waiting to take our order.

"Can we order in five minutes please? We haven't quite decided yet," Glenda smiled at the young woman.

The waitress went to another table and Glenda continued.

"It seems that I was jealous of you and Steve, or Edward as he was called then, and in my anger, I inadvertently put a curse on your relationship with him."

I nodded and moved forwards onto the edge of my seat.

"I'm really sorry. The therapist said that I needed to apologise to you and you needed to accept my apology in order to get rid of the curse and any bad feelings that are still out there."

I thought of how things could have been between Steve and me and wondered whether I could ever forgive her for causing things to go so badly wrong. But then it was Steve who had decided to take the promotion in London.

I had no way of knowing whether things would have worked out between us because he wasn't with me any more and there was nothing more I could do about it.

"I'm not just apologising because I've been told to," she continued. "I'm really genuinely sorry for accusing you of having an affair with Ted and following you around for all that time. I'm sorry for anything that was said that's had an impact on your life. I'm sorry for what was said when we were sisters all those years ago. Can you forgive me?"

I looked into her grey eyes. She really meant what she had said and had no hard feelings towards me any more.

"Yes. I forgive you," I replied.

She held out her hand and placed it on top of mine. "Thank you," she said, before signalling to Ted and William that they should come over and join us.

"What are we having for lunch?" asked Ted, picking up a menu.

I hadn't planned on staying to eat with Ted and Glenda, but William followed Ted's lead and started looking at the menu. I looked around and noticed that all the other tables were now taken. Glenda must have noticed me looking around.

"We might as well all eat here now that we've got a table, dear," Glenda smiled.

I couldn't believe the transformation in this woman, who at one time was hunting me down with a scowl on her face and bitter words. She had become a sweet old lady who smiled and called me 'dear'.

Once the food was ordered there was an awkward silence for a minute before I asked, "I noticed that you sold your house and moved away. Where did you move to?"

"We've got two cottages in Sheringham. We used to rent both of them out except for when we came down for holidays. Now that we've both retired, we live in one of them and just rent the other out," Glenda explained.

"It's such a lovely day today that we just fancied a ride on one of the boats, so we drove down to Wroxham for a day out. Here's one of our cards," said Ted after he had produced a black leather wallet from his trouser pocket and took out a small business card. "If you fancy a holiday down in Sheringham get in touch. It's much cheaper than booking through agents."

"Thanks," I said, getting my purse out and placing the card in with my bank cards. "I'll remember that."

Once lunch was over, we said our goodbyes and I promised to get in touch if we wanted to take a holiday in Norfolk in the future.

I felt as though a weight had been lifted from my shoulders. As I packed our bags that night it was as though I was packing to start a new life back at home. I was no longer being accused of something I hadn't done. I had been apologised to and I had accepted the apology. That brief conversation had made so much difference to how I felt and all the stress which had built up over the last three years seemed to be leaving my body. I felt a new energy that hadn't been there for a long time.

The next day was bright and sunny, so although I had to vacate the cottage by ten o'clock in the morning, I decided to spend a few hours on the beach with William before setting off home. We had a great time paddling in the sea, playing cricket on the beach, and paying a final trip to the amusements, before I finally decided that we should start our journey at three o'clock. Once we were home, I bought a pizza from the local takeaway and we crashed out in front of the TV until it was time for William to go to bed.

As I unpacked the cases, I wondered what Steve was doing. It had been over two years since I had last seen him. I thought back to the conversation Steve and I had had with Glenda that day when she had collapsed. I wondered what he would have made of the recent turn of events. Glenda had apologised and, not only that, she had heard from another source that those dreams I had been having were actually true. I wished that Steve was around so that I could tell him what had happened. During that time between the trip to Whitby and him leaving for London, I felt as though we had grown really close, but Steve had realised that to be so close but be unable to take the relationship any further than best friends was just too painful. Accepting the move to London and trying to move on was all he could have done. I wondered whether phoning him as a friend and updating him on recent events would be a good idea, but then it had been so long since we had spoken. I wondered whether he had met someone else by now. The last thing he would want would be me phoning for a chat if he was on a date with someone or even living with someone. The thought brought a bad feeling to the pit of my stomach. I had no way of knowing unless I got in touch and found out for myself, but the thought of the trouble that this might cause or the upset if he didn't want to talk to me prevented me from taking any action.

"Please, oh please let me see him again!" I whispered as I looked out of my bedroom window into the starry sky, hoping that some greater force was listening.

It was two months later that my wish was answered, but not in the satisfying way I had hoped. I was driving on one of the outer roads to the city centre on my way to a park at the opposite side of the city from where I lived. It was the school holiday at the beginning of June and I had decided to take William to a different park for a change.

We were passing some large office blocks to our left when William suddenly called out.

"Mum, it's Steve!"

"Where?"

"Look, there, going into that building!"

I glanced to my left and saw the back of someone who could have been Steve going into the office block. He was wearing a suit and carrying a briefcase. I didn't have chance to look for more than a second because I was driving towards a roundabout and needed to change lanes.

"Did you get a proper look, William? Was it Steve?" I asked.

"Yes, I'm sure Mum. He came down the hill and I saw his face before he went into the building."

I took the second exit at the roundabout and carried on driving. I felt like parking up and waiting in the hope that he would come back out later, but he could have been going in for the rest of the day and I could hardly go into the office block after him! If he was back in Sheffield maybe I stood a chance of seeing him on another day soon. *But why was he back in Sheffield?* I wondered. The office block he had gone into belonged to the bank where he worked. *Had he managed to get a promotion and move back to Sheffield?* The smart attire and briefcase would certainly suggest something more important that the position he'd held before.

"Do you think Steve's come back, Mum?" William asked, as we ate our ice creams in the park.

"I don't know, William. He might have just come up for a meeting."

"Do you still miss him, Mum?"

The question took me by surprise. I didn't know whether to tell him the truth and say yes or to come out with some cliché about people moving on and relationships not always working out. William was now a bright ten-year-old and capable of understanding something of how relationships worked. I was still wondering what to say when William spoke again.

"Do you think you'll start seeing him again if he's living in Sheffield?"

"I don't know," was all I said.

The thought that he may have moved back up north and still not want anything to do with me made me feel worse rather than better. *How long had he been back in Sheffield? Where was he living?*

Chapter 26

I woke early the next morning to the sound of birds all singing their different songs. Why did they all do that the minute the sun came up? I tossed and turned thinking about Steve. He had been so near and I missed him so much. I supposed that my wish had come true. I had wanted to see him again and that was exactly what had happened. I had seen him. If I wanted to speak to him I would have to give fate a helping hand rather than just wait around hoping that our paths would cross again. I would have to take a risk and phone him. If he wasn't interested it would hurt but at least I would know. I couldn't carry on like some lovesick teenager. It was only four in the morning though. I would have to wait at least another four hours before it was a decent time to ring and then he would probably be getting ready for work. Not the best time to take someone by surprise and update them on two-and-a-half years' worth of news.

I decided to wait until midday in the hope that he would be having a lunch break and have time to talk. I tried to keep myself busy during the morning with long overdue chores. The front door and window frames shone white for the first time in months, in fact, probably that year. I looked over at my neighbours' clean and well-presented houses. *When did they find time to keep their houses looking so tidy?* I wondered.

William was quite content to sit in his bedroom and play on his PlayStation. I felt guilty that I'd just left him up there all morning, but then told myself that we couldn't go out doing things every minute of every day and we'd had a day out yesterday. Sometimes cleaning just had to be done! I peeped into his room to check that he was still occupied before heading back downstairs and selecting Steve's name from my contacts list on my mobile phone.

After only a couple of rings someone answered. It wasn't Steve.

"Oh. Is this Steve's number?" I asked, wondering who this person was.

"No, love. You must have the wrong number," replied a friendly older man.

"Oh sorry. This used to be Steve's number!"

"Probably love. I've just got a new phone and it came with this number. Steve must have a new phone or something. Sorry, love."

I hung up. I had taken comfort all this time knowing that I still had Steve's phone number and that he would be there on the other end of the phone if I rang him. Now I had no way of getting in touch with him. Or did I? I quickly grabbed the phone directory from the window ledge and started looking for banks. The number for the

Sheffield head office where I'd seen Steve going the day before was listed before the various local branches.

I rang the number, my hands shaking with nerves. Eventually a voice came on the line.

"If you know the extension number you want, please dial it now or stay on the line and wait for main reception to answer."

I stayed on the line and waited. Eventually a woman answered.

"I'm trying to get in touch with Steve Clarke," I told her.

"Steve Clarke," I heard her repeating. "Do you know which department he works in? I don't know anyone of that name. Could he be new?"

"Yes he might be new," I said. "He probably works in something to do with IT," I informed her, hoping that I was right.

"I'll put you through to IT and you can ask up there," she said, and before I had time to say anything else, I heard another dialling tone and was waiting nervously.

The phone was answered by a young woman. I asked her whether Steve Clarke worked there.

"I'll just check if he's in," she said. I heard her calling across the office. She obviously hadn't become acquainted with the privacy button. My pulse raced as I heard her conversation. She was on the line a few seconds later, confirming what I had already heard.

"He's in a meeting until one and then he'll probably be going straight for lunch. Can I take a message?"

I wondered whether to leave a message or just phone back later. I decided to leave a message.

"Could you tell him that Claire phoned please?"

"What's it in connection with?" the girl asked.

"Oh, I'm just a friend with some news," I informed her.

I hung up wondering whether I had done the right thing in leaving a message. I had no idea what Steve's circumstances were these days. What if he was married and news that a woman was phoning him at work was now going round the office? I felt upset at the thought that he could have got married since I last saw him. I hadn't thought of that before. *As for a female friend phoning him at work, surely these days that would be nothing out of the ordinary would it?* People had friends of either sex. It didn't necessarily mean anything worth gossiping about.

I called William downstairs for his lunch, although I had trouble eating mine due to wondering whether Steve would call back and what he would say if he did. I was relieved when an hour later, one of William's friends knocked on the door, asking if William wanted to play out. At least William wouldn't be around listening to my side of the conversation if Steve phoned back. I tried to keep myself busy by tackling the ironing, all the while glancing at the clock each time I took an item of clothing from the pile. Two o'clock came and went. He must have come back from lunch and got the message by now I thought! Half past two. Still nothing. It was six o'clock when I was in the middle of cooking that the phone finally rang. I looked at the caller display but didn't recognise the number, although it had a Sheffield dialling code at the beginning.

"Hello. Is that Claire?" I was asked by a familiar voice.

"Yes," was all I could say in reply, my heart in my mouth.

"You phoned me at work. Is everything okay?" he sounded worried.

I explained how I had seen him the day before and how I had tried his mobile phone.

"Something interesting happened and I just wanted to tell you about it. We're still friends aren't we?" I found myself saying, feeling suddenly ridiculous and wanting the ground to swallow me up.

What had I been thinking? I didn't give him a chance to answer before I carried on speaking. I told him how I had seen Glenda and Ted during my visit to Norfolk and about Glenda's apology.

"When I saw you yesterday it just made me think that you might be interested to know, after everything we went through together," I said, by way of explanation for suddenly getting in touch. "I hope I didn't worry you by phoning you at work. I hope you don't mind?" I found myself going on.

"Well, at least she's finally admitted that she'd got it wrong," Steve replied in a very matter-of-fact tone of voice. Not the Steve I once felt close to. "Yes, that's good news, Claire. I did wonder what had happened to her. It was strange you bumping into her like that, wasn't it?"

"Yes, but I'm glad I did. How are you anyway?" I asked.

"Good thanks. I moved back up to Sheffield last week. One of the IT managers moved abroad and I managed to get the job. How about you?"

"Okay. Still at the same house and same job. William's ten now," I told him.

"Time flies doesn't it?"

It was a polite conversation between two adults and nothing more. If he had been desperate to let me know of his return to Sheffield he would have got in touch last week, I thought to myself. He sounded business-like on the phone. I had hoped for some reunion to have been arranged, but it clearly wasn't to be. I ended the conversation feeling flat. He had my phone number and knew where I lived. If he wanted to make contact he could do. I doubted that he would though.

"I really thought that I was going to get that happy ending," I told Lucy on the phone later that evening. "Glenda has apologised for any upset she has caused me and Steve has moved back to Sheffield."

"What happened to your plan to forget about him and move on?"

"I've tried really hard but it just seems as though things could have been different. I just wish there was some way that I could get Steve to give it another go."

"But what if nothing has changed?" asked Lucy. "What if he does agree to give it another go and then things are just the same as before? Won't that cause even more hurt?"

"But at least we'd know!"

"I think he ended it because he has really strong feelings for you and the pain of knowing that things couldn't progress any further was just too much for him to bear".

"So, you're saying that he probably wouldn't want to take the risk?"

"Yes, and it's been two-and-a-half years. He might have moved on."

"How do I find out without looking like a stalker?"

"Not sure. You could check whether he's listed on one of those Internet sites like Facebook, but if he works in IT he'll probably be sensible enough to have his account on the highest security settings."

She was right. I joined the popular social networking site just for the purpose of checking whether Steve was a member. I scrolled through pages of Steve Clarkes and finally saw a photograph of the correct Steve. I clicked on it hoping that details of his current status would be displayed but was greeted with a message saying that *only friends of Steve Clarke are allowed access*. I would need to add him as a friend if I wanted to view more. My finger had already clicked on the *send friend request* option before the part of my brain expressing doubt started to work. *What if he looked at my profile and saw that I had no other friends listed? I would definitely look like a stalker then!* I spent a further hour typing in names from the past in the hope that I would acquire a friends list soon and not look like a desperate woman who had joined solely for the purpose of keeping tabs on her ex.

I turned the laptop off and went to bed. I turned it back on it at half past six the following morning and paced the floor as I waited for it to start up, hoping that my online friendship status had changed. Three women and a man who were once in my year at school had added me, but there was still no word from Steve.

I decided to check later that day at work. I bought a sandwich from the local shop at lunchtime and took it back to my desk. I bit into it as I waited nervously for the social networking site to load up. There was a friend request from Lucy with a message attached saying '*I knew I'd find you on here! Any luck?*'

I answered that "No. *The friend request had been ignored by Steve.*"

By the time I left for home that evening, I was thinking a bit more rationally and decided that what I really wanted to know was whether the spell had worked or not. After all, some of my ancestors had been witches and I had found the '*Book of shadows*' amongst my grandma's things. Steve had left before we'd had a chance to find out if the curse had been removed. Also, Angelica from Whitby had said that there were several solutions to the problem. The other had been for Glenda to take back the curse which she had inadvertently caused in a previous life. *Did her apology that day in Norfolk count? How could I find out for sure unless I had some sort of physical contact with Steve?* I couldn't even get him to communicate online, let alone be in the same room as me at the moment. I didn't blame him. The whole thing must have seemed pretty weird. I could see that avoiding me altogether would be an easier option. After all, he was an attractive man and could probably have the pick of any woman he wanted. Except me.

I decided that one way to find out whether I had any special powers would be to try casting another spell. Nothing too life changing. Just an experiment. This would at least give me some indication of the chance of my earlier efforts working. Maybe I could pay Alice or Angelica another visit, I thought to myself. After all, it had been quite a long time now since I had taken any advice from either of them and things had certainly changed since then.

Chapter 27

I carefully pulled out the carrier bag from the back of my wardrobe. I put it down on the bed before gently sliding out the heavy, brown book. I turned the pages of the thick parchment slowly. *Dare I attempt to cast another of these spells? Was there one which looked easy and wouldn't have any bad consequences if it worked?*

I looked at some of the neatly written headings *'How to attract new friends'*. I didn't really feel as though I needed any new friends. The ones I had already were really good, knew me really well, and would stand by me whatever happened. *'How to attract love'*. This one sounded tempting, but what if some man turned up who wasn't Steve and was madly in love with me but I didn't feel the same way? I would be stuck with someone I didn't want and there was no way I would get Steve back if this happened. *'How to attract money'*. *Now this one might be worth a shot*, I decided. I read the spell carefully.

<u>What you will need</u>:

One thin slice of horseradish;

One paper bill of money;

One coin;

Your purse or wallet.

When you have gathered all these items, sit at your altar, close your eyes and visualise what you want. Don't be too greedy; only ask for what you need. Think about what you would do with the money and what you need it for.

I thought about this. *Was I being greedy if I asked for money?* Working part-time as a single parent meant that there usually wasn't any money left over at the end of the month for luxuries, even with the maintenance payments coming in from Greg. If I asked for enough money to keep me and William fed, clothed, and with a roof over our heads, then it wouldn't be greedy would it? I could do with just a little bit more to prevent that overdraft from getting any further into the red. Yes. I would try this one and I supposed that if the powers that be thought that I had enough money, then I just wouldn't get any more. No harm done. I read on.

Place your hand over the horseradish and say:

"I charge you with the power of prosperity, to attract my next thought into being."

Wrap the horseradish and the coin in your paper bill.

Place it in your wallet or purse and carry it in there for the entire year.

If you change your wallet or purse for any reason during the year, be sure to transfer the bill (and the contents) to your new wallet/purse.

On the next January 1st, do the ritual again with a new piece of horseradish, new bill and new coin.

Place the new items wrapped in the new bill into your wallet/purse,

and THEN *remove the old one.*

It's very important to put it in

BEFORE *taking out the old one.*

Would this spell still work if I did it part way through the year? I wondered. Well, there was only one way to find out. I carefully put the book away and went to the supermarket in search of horseradish. This wasn't as easy as I had thought it would be. I looked carefully at all the vegetables on display. Turnips, carrots, potatoes, and all the more common vegetables were there in plenty. I went over to where the salad items were displayed; lettuce, cucumber, tomatoes, but no horseradish. I suddenly remembered that some of the smaller items were on a separate display such as root ginger and mange-tout. I found these items alongside those mini sweetcorns and asparagus. Still no horseradish. I looked around for someone who worked there. I spotted two young men in green overalls chatting as they unloaded some oranges onto the fruit display.

"Excuse me, do you sell horseradish?" I asked hopefully, as the two of them stopped their conversation about the date one of them had had last night and turned to face me. They looked at each other again before the spotty one answered.

"It's on the isle with the jars of sauces and pickles love."

"No. I mean fresh horseradish, not horseradish sauce!" I explained.

The spotty youth looked at me blankly. The other one spoke up.

"I don't think we sell that."

"Thanks anyway!"

I grabbed the bread and milk, which I decided to get whilst I was there, before leaving the shop, disappointed. Where would horseradish be sold?

As I was eating my toasted cheese sandwich that lunchtime, I remembered that there was an outdoor market in town every Tuesday afternoon. It always boasted of having a lot of vegetable stalls, including one which sold the less common ones. It was worth a try. This week my days off were Monday and Tuesday which meant that I could give the market a try the next day.

I dropped William off at school on Tuesday morning and headed for town. I had forgotten that the roads would still be busy and wished I had waited another half an hour or so. I sat on the dual carriageway in the queue, hoping that my efforts were worth it. These spells always seemed to demand shopping trips!

It was forty minutes later when I finally managed to park the car in town. I checked the prices. I hoped that I wouldn't be more than an hour, but realised that the minimum which could be paid in this car park was two pounds for two hours. I rummaged through my purse. I only had a five pound note and wondered whether I should try a different car park. I was relieved to see that the machine accepted notes and I inserted the five pound note. I waited for my change. Nothing happened. I pressed the button again to select the *'up to two hours'* option. Nothing. I scanned the instructions again. *'Change not given. Overpayment accepted.'* I took my ticket and stormed back to the car. Great. This was already turning out to be a very expensive spell!

Once I had secured my ticket to the inside of the windscreen, I headed for the outdoor markets. The first two stalls were selling bags and footwear. I rushed past those wondering where the food stalls were. The next looked more hopeful. I scanned the items on the stall to see black and green olives alongside peppers and chillies which were arranged enticingly on the display. No horseradish here. I passed a jewellery stall and one selling second-hand CDs. There had to be more stalls selling food! I started to dash in and out of the isles between the stalls looking for what I wanted. Two elderly women turned and looked at me suspiciously before it occurred to me that I must look like either a crazy woman or one who was up to no good. I made an effort to slow down and go with the pace that the other shoppers were setting. After all, I'd paid enough for parking to shop all day!

I eventually saw a stall selling turnips and other various root vegetables. I went over to have a closer look. I hadn't bought horseradish before and suddenly realised to my embarrassment that I didn't know what it looked like. I decided to ask and was glad that I did. The old man behind the stall untied a bunch of dirty horseradishes with leaves still attached from the frame supporting the top of the stall.

"Is that everything?" he asked, as he pushed them into a white paper bag.

"Yes, thanks," I replied handing over a ten pound note. I now had a purse loaded with pound coins.

I spent another hour wandering around the shops feeling that this would somehow make the long journey to get there and the amount spent on parking a bit more worthwhile. The amount that I ended up paying on a new pair of jeans, however, meant that the shopping trip for horseradish turned out to be the most expensive ever at forty pounds.

Almost as soon as I got back to the house, I was in the kitchen getting everything ready for the spell. I carefully washed one of the horseradish plants and sliced a thin piece off one of them. I took a pound coin and a five pound note out of my purse and put them together on the table. I ran back upstairs to get the *'Book of shadows'* to check the exact wording of the spell. It mentioned an altar! I didn't know whether the kitchen table would do, but it would have to, I decided. I followed the spell carefully, holding the horseradish in my hand and telling it what needed to be done before visualising myself better off financially with money left over at the end of each month. I then wrapped the coin and horseradish in the five pound note and placed them at the bottom of my purse. I had no idea how long this might take to work (if it ever did), but I was now stuck with a load of horseradish! I looked through my recipe books as I ate my lunch, wondering what to do with it!

Two weeks passed and life hadn't changed at all. Steve hadn't been in touch, I had no idea if the curse from my former life had been lifted, and I didn't seem to have any spare cash in my bank account or in my purse. I had no idea how long these things were supposed to take, but since the spell had said that the horseradish and money had to be left in my purse for the whole year, maybe that would be how long it took! I probably should have chosen a different spell, I thought to myself, although the horseradish sauce I had made had gone down well with roast beef, according to my mum and sister. The mystery still hadn't been solved though. I either had to choose another spell that looked as though it might be fast at acting or try to get in touch with Steve again and ask if we could meet up to find out what happened if we came into contact. I looked through the spell book again but they all seemed to be either for things which I didn't need or just looked too risky to try. I either had to walk away from the whole thing and forget the past or be patient and wait. Unfortunately, I wasn't a very patient person. I needed answers now. Then it suddenly occurred to me. I knew just the person who would have the answers. I rummaged through my handbag and found the card with the contact details for Angelica on. It would mean another trip to Whitby, but it had to be done. I picked up the phone and dialled the number.

Two weeks later I drove up to Whitby with my only companion during the trip being the voice on the satnav. Luckily, Greg had phoned and asked to swap the weekend which he saw William which fitted perfectly with my new plans for this weekend.

I arrived far too early for my two o'clock appointment and found a bench overlooking Tate beach. I sat and ate my pre-packed tuna and cucumber sandwiches, salt and vinegar crisps, and drank my carton of fresh orange juice. It was still only half past one when I finished my lunch so I sat and watched the boats go past on the sea below and thought about the last time I had been in Whitby with William and Steve. Since that time I had tried different paths to put my life onto the right track. The required apology from Glenda had eventually been given and Steve had even moved back to Sheffield, so something must have worked. *Why wasn't I back with Steve? What else did I need to do?*

I looked over at the bay for a few minutes, trying to calm myself, before getting up and slowly walking back to the cottage which I had passed earlier. I arrived just before two and knocked on the door. Angelica answered the door. Something about her warm smile and the way she held herself immediately had a calming effect on me and she showed me through to the kitchen at the back of the house as before.

She passed me a large glass of lemonade and poured another for herself. Even though this had been only the second time I had met Angelica and nearly three years had passed since we last met, it felt as though this was a meeting with an old friend.

"A lot has happened since we last met," she smiled, "but you're very impatient, aren't you, Claire?"

"Well, yes. It's the waiting and not knowing what to do which I can't cope with!" I laughed.

"You won't rest until you're back with Steve, will you?" she asked.

Before I had time to answer she continued. "You need to clear your head of all that has gone before and start afresh. While ever you are obsessing with the past it can't be put to rest. You have done some good work but you now need to stop. There will be a time of waiting in which positive energy must be allowed to build. Have faith that there will eventually be a happy ending. Negative thoughts will only attract negative energy and you do not want that to happen."

"What should I do in the meantime?" I asked.

"Take up a new interest. One which will take your thoughts completely away from Steve. When the time is right he will return of his own free will," she advised me. "The ball is in Steve's court now. Remember, he must return because he has chosen to. Do not use magick to try to speed up the process."

After saying my goodbyes to Angelica, I went out through the entranceway as before and left a donation in the hanging basket at the end of the corridor. Rather than rush back home, I took my time to look round the shops on my way back down Church Street. The shops selling Whitby Jet and Amber were so inviting and after I had browsed the stock in each of these, I passed a further twenty minutes in the old-fashioned little bookshop with rickety stairs. I bought a couple of books about the history of Whitby before heading to a pretty little café with polished wooden floorboards and clean white tablecloths. I ordered a large scone with clotted cream and jam with a pot of tea for one. I sat and looked through the books as I waited for my order to arrive. I was instantly drawn to a chapter about witchcraft in Whitby and was so absorbed in my reading that it took the waitress a few attempts to attract my attention so that she could put my order down on the table. I was quite pleased to read that witches had not usually been killed in Whitby but often respected for their special skills. The worst punishments usually given included being put in the stocks and pelted with vegetables, being ducked in the village pond (but not drowned), or made to walk through the village wearing only a petticoat. Basically they were humiliated in public and made to repent of their ways. This was far better news than my earlier reading which had told me that witches had been killed. The book also said that any educated person able to prescribe medicines or write might have been thought of as a witch, because they could write out a prescription that someone else could read and then the drugs or herbs prescribed would make the person feel better. To the uneducated, this may have looked like magick. I finished my afternoon cream tea, paid, and walked back to the car wondering whether I had been really gullible and silly believing in all this witch business. What I had just read seemed much more plausible. I thought about what Angelica had told me. Was she purely giving me sensible advice that any agony aunt looking in at someone else's situation would do, or was her advice based on her ability to see into the future? Was everything in life down to a series of random decisions that we might make, of which some were just better than others, or was there really a predestined path? If so, could this path, or fate, be altered by outside forces such as magical spells? What if we were born, lived, and then died and that was all there was to it?

I felt quite depressed at these thoughts as I approached my car and flung my handbag into the passenger seat. This only lasted a couple of minutes though, and by the time I was driving out of Whitby I had turned my thoughts to what sort of interest I could take up which would stop me obsessing about Steve.

Chapter 28

My first piano lesson had been arranged for two weeks later on the Monday morning. I had phoned several teachers whose details I had found via the Internet. I had chosen a friendly-sounding woman of around my own age. I asked if it was alright to book a trial lesson to check whether it was the right thing for me before I splashed out on a piano.

I had some basic music reading skills from when I used to play the recorder as a child. However, the first piano lesson only really dealt with getting the correct posture, hand shape, and only a few notes with each hand, so it didn't really matter what my background had been. I really enjoyed the feeling of the keys under my fingers and imagined myself as an accomplished musician playing music which others would want to hear. I booked a second lesson for the following week and started looking into buying a piano. New instruments were much too expensive, and the second-hand or really old ones that I saw were often in need of care and attention and sometimes so out of tune that I wondered whether even the most gifted piano tuner would be able to bring them up to pitch.

It was the Friday of the same week that William announced, as I met him in the school playground, that there was a piano going spare at school which they wanted to sell. I went round to the school office and asked the secretary if I could speak to someone about the piano they had for sale. At first Mrs. Bridges, a very serious-looking woman in her mid-fifties, looked at me as though I was speaking nonsense and I began to wonder whether William had misheard.

"Piano?" she asked frowning.

"Yes, Mr. Jones mentioned it in assembly today," William informed her.

I was pleased that William was confident enough to be able to speak to this rather serious looking woman who immediately left her seat and went to get Mr. Jones.

"Hello. Ian Jones," a friendly man in his mid-thirties held out his hand to shake mine by way of introduction. "I don't think we've met before. I'm the new music coordinator in the school," he informed me.

"I hear there's a piano going spare and I wondered whether I could have a look at it?"

"Yes, yes, come this way," he instructed.

He led me across the schoolyard and into one of those mobile classrooms where a piano stood in the corner. Piles of books were heaped on top of it.

"It seems to be used more as a bookshelf at the moment," he told me as he started to rearrange piles of history text books. "This classroom used to be used purely as a music room but, due to rising pupil numbers, it now houses one of the Year Four classes."

He lifted the lid to reveal a full set of black and white keys which were in much better condition than I had expected.

"This room used to be locked when it wasn't in use for music lessons which is why the piano is in such good condition, but now we just haven't got the space for it any more and want to sell it before it gets neglected."

I ran my fingers over the keys. There were none of the twangy sounds that I had expected from an old piano.

"It will need tuning once it has been moved," Mr. Jones continued, "but pianos always do if you move them. It sounds as though it was regularly tuned before though, because it's only a little way below pitch, so it should be easy to put right."

"How much do you want for it?" I asked, expecting to hear an amount which I couldn't afford.

"Only a couple of hundred pounds. We'll put the money towards more cupboards for this classroom. We'd much rather know that the piano was going to a good home than ask for a larger amount of money for it," he explained.

The deal was done and, the following Wednesday, specialist piano movers had been arranged to deliver it to my house at the end of the school day. I arranged with work to finish at lunchtime and do an extra half day the following week so that I could get my house ready for the new arrival. I met William outside his classroom and was pleased to see the piano was already out of the mobile classroom and was being wheeled across the playground by two men towards a white van parked in the car park. Groups of parents speculated with interest about where the piano might be going. William proudly interrupted one group of mums to tell them that it was going to our house. I introduced myself to the men as they pushed the piano and checked that they knew how to get to my address from there.

Ten minutes later I was standing at my front room window with my very excited son waiting for the white van to arrive. I had to wait a further fifteen minutes before it finally pulled up outside and we had both been getting worried that something had gone wrong. The man who knocked on the door, a fifty-something, stocky man of about five foot nine, explained that they couldn't reverse off the school drive until all the parents and children had moved out of the way and then, just when they had thought it was okay to move, a car had pulled up behind them and blocked them in. I offered them a cup of tea, which was gratefully received, while I explained where I wanted the piano putting.

"Can I have a go? Can I have a go?" screamed William, as he danced around the piano as soon as the men had been paid and left the premises.

"As long as you are gentle with it. I don't want it spoiling before I've even had it tuned!" I warned.

I let William have a turn for a few minutes before getting out the music which I had been playing in my lessons. I played through the simple exercises several times, feeling really pleased that I could practise at home. The piano had travelled well in spite of being wheeled across the bumpy tarmac at school and sounded okay to play even before the piano tuner turned up a couple of weeks later. From that day I was practising every day and really enjoying my new interest. After a few weeks, William started to have lessons as well, giving him something to do which didn't involve a games console or TV screen, for which I was grateful.

Two months passed by and I had put the *'Book of shadows'* and the spells to the back of my mind. If thoughts of Steve popped into my head, I quickly busied myself with some piano practice, or if it was too late in the evening, I would go upstairs and read one of the many cheap paperbacks which I had purchased via eBay until I fell asleep. I was feeling much happier with myself and really began to feel as though my life was moving forwards at last.

One evening, about four months later, I turned on my laptop to check whether I was the winning bidder of some second-hand novels and a piano tutor book. I decided to check my emails whilst I had the laptop on, just on the off-chance that something worth reading had actually been sent amongst all the spam. I scrolled down the pages of unread messages, deleting most of them without even reading them.

I came to two messages from Facebook which had been sent about ten days earlier. The first one informed me that Rachel Brown, who had been in my year at school, had added me as a friend. The second one told me that I had received a message from Steve Clarke. My pulse rate immediately quickened and I quickly logged into Facebook with mixed feelings about this unexpected contact. I had done so well over the last few months in not thinking about him and now there was a message which forced all thoughts of Steve to the front of my mind again.

I waited impatiently for my received messages folder to open, wondering what he had decided to say to me after all this time. The message was short and to the point:

Hi Claire,

Sorry for not getting in touch or adding you as a friend on Facebook. I have a girlfriend in London. She wouldn't be very pleased if I was keeping in touch with an ex-girlfriend and therefore I won't be adding you to my friends list.

Steve

I stared at the computer screen, feeling more annoyed than anything that he had got in touch with this message. I had assumed long ago by his lack of contact that he was no longer interested and I had been following Angelica's advice to take up a new interest and stop thinking about him. If the message had said that he wanted to meet up, I would have thought that my patience in waiting for Steve to contact me of his own free will, as Angelica had put it, had eventually been rewarded. To receive a message saying that he had a girlfriend and therefore wouldn't be keeping in touch was just unnecessary and opened up old wounds. I really didn't need to know about his girlfriend in London or anything about him if he wasn't interested in me. I closed the laptop down angrily and flung myself down into the armchair. Tears welled up in my eyes, and the more I thought about his message, the angrier I became.

The following day, I had difficulty concentrating at work and had to correct so many mistakes in an advertisement which I was getting ready for close of business that day that I almost missed the deadline. I almost went through a red light on the way home and snapped at William later that evening when he asked if it was time to do our piano practice. I realised that I would have to be stronger than this if I was going to get past this setback and decided to phone Lucy. I apologised to William for my bad mood and suggested that he did his piano practice first while I phoned my friend who would hopefully be able to cheer me up. After reassuring William that my bad mood wasn't his fault, he set to work on playing some scales whilst I phoned Lucy.

"Hello, Claire," she answered as cheerfully as ever. "It's a long time since I've heard from you!"

I told her about the piano lessons and how I had done really well in forgetting about Steve until now. I told her how this one message from him had set me back months and how my head had been all over the place since the previous night.

"It's a bit strange that he's got in touch just to tell you that!" she continued before I had a chance to comment. "Why would anyone get in touch to say that they wouldn't be keeping in touch, if you know what I mean?"

"I know. Why couldn't he just continue to ignore me?"

"Maybe he's saying that he would keep in touch if he didn't have a girlfriend in London. Maybe he does still think about you?"

"I've only just got rid of a jealous woman from a previous life. I don't need a jealous girlfriend in this life to screw things up for me."

"Are *you* jealous, Claire?" Lucy asked. "You know, that he's got a girlfriend?"

"I don't know. I would have felt a whole lot better not knowing anything about him though!"

"Maybe it'll help you to stop thinking about him if you know that he's got a girlfriend. Maybe it's a good thing!"

"I *had* stopped thinking about him!" I explained. "The piano practice was doing the trick and now he's messed everything up!"

"Ignore him. Forget about him and just get on with learning the piano!" Lucy advised. But it was easier said than done.

Later that night, even though I knew it was a bad idea, I couldn't help opening the message from Steve again and reading it through. I felt myself getting angry all over again and then even more angry with myself for sending him the 'friend request' in the first place. Before I had given myself time to think more rationally, I had replied to his message:

Steve,

I had already worked out by your lack of contact that you didn't want to keep in touch. The message you sent me to say that you have a girlfriend in London was unnecessary.

Claire

I poured myself a glass of red wine and put on one of those compilation CDs of 1980s hits. I thought about what I had just done. When Steve read my message he would most likely think that I was being very childish. I wondered what his girlfriend was like. I imagined one of those well-dressed and well-spoken businesswomen. I wondered how long he had been seeing her and whether she would be moving up north to come and live with him? If not, how was he going to keep a relationship going with someone who lived so far away? He wasn't prepared to keep in touch with me when he moved to London, was he? But then things had been different, hadn't they? There had been a problem, a curse. Maybe Rachel, all those years ago in a former life, had felt just how I felt now. Someone else was with the man she wanted and she couldn't do anything about it. I mustn't let history repeat itself. I had to be better.

I opened up my Facebook page again with the intention of wishing Steve well and found that there was a message in my inbox from him already. It said:

Claire,

The message you sent me to say that my earlier message was unnecessary was also unnecessary. LOL

Steve

LOL? What did that mean? I was unfamiliar with these new abbreviations. Was it a term of ridicule? I texted Lucy. She would know.

I decided to send Steve a more grown up message anyway to let him know that there were no hard feelings and no jealousy and then that would be the end of it.

Steve,

I hope that you and your girlfriend are very happy together. I just wanted to let you know that there are no hard feelings from me. We had some good times together didn't we? Even if some of them involved cutting up nettles. LOL

Claire

Lucy's text message to explain what LOL meant had arrived when I was part way through sending Steve this last message. Reassured that it indicated that you were smiling or laughing in a friendly way seemed an appropriate way to end my contact with Steve. No hard feelings. No jealousy. No chance of repercussions in the future.

I poured myself another glass of wine and, by the time I had finished it, I had managed to convince myself that all was well with the world, things between Steve and I had ended amicably, and if I was meant to ever be with him again, then maybe it would be in a future life (if such things really existed). Maybe there was someone else out there for me who I hadn't even met yet. I closed my laptop down and flicked through the TV channels. I stopped for a few seconds on one of the sports channels. I looked over to the chair where Steve used to sit when we were going out, or rather staying in together. I could picture him sitting down and checking the latest football scores whilst passing me some chocolate to try to appease my annoyance that he was taking charge of my TV. The cheek of it! I remembered the bar of chocolate that I had put in the fridge earlier and went to get it before continuing to scroll though the Sky menu. There wasn't anything on that I wanted to watch and I had no one to share the chocolate with. A tear rolled down my cheek and dripped into my empty wine glass.

Chapter 29

William had started secondary school. It had been an expensive summer once new school uniform had been paid for, including two sets of trousers, three shirts, tie, blazer, shoes and full sports kit. Several nights out with the girls had been arranged and I had also been on quite a few dates, although the longest any of these potential romances had lasted was three weeks.

First there had been Ian. He seemed like a nice enough man but that word just about summed him up. Nice but boring. He was a divorcee with two teenage sons. He seemed reliable and wasn't bad looking either but I just didn't feel any spark. I ended things after four dates. Next there had been Danny. He was a bit younger than me. His cheeky grin and sparkly eyes caused me to be instantly attracted to him. Unfortunately, he was also attractive to other women and he knew it. When we were out together, on more than one occasion, I returned from the ladies' to find him chatting up another woman at the bar. The first time it happened I thought that maybe it was just a friend that he had bumped into and was being friendly, but as I got nearer he didn't even offer to introduce us. In fact, by the time I had reached the bar, he had his arm around her waist and was close enough to her face-to-have kissed her. He explained it away and apologised, saying that he had had too many to drink and she had come on to him. This sort of thing happened two more times with different women, although the third time he practically had his tongue down the woman's throat. He was very quickly dumped after this.

By mid-August, I had met Jack whilst on a night out with the girls. He was attractive, had a good sense of humour, and didn't look at other women when we were out on dates. After three weeks and several dates he decided to go back to his wife. When I had first met him and he had told me he was separated from his wife, he had led me to believe that this had been a long-term separation that would shortly be leading to a divorce and therefore he was a free agent. However, it turned out that he had been staying at his brother's house for two months while he 'sorted his head out' as he had put it. He was sorry that I had got hurt in the process, but he now knew that he couldn't love anyone like he loved his wife and had decided to continue with the marriage. I wondered whether he would tell her that he had stayed over at mine on more than one occasion whilst he was deciding what to do. I decided to just forget about him.

Even though William was at secondary school, I was still only working three days a week. On my days off I found myself doing hours of piano practice. On the days I worked, piano practice was done in the evenings. My teacher seemed to be having trouble keeping up with me. At one time, most of each lesson would have been spent correcting the mistakes in what I had practised and the same work would be set again until I had got it right. Now, however, I was really getting the hang of it and new pieces of a more difficult nature had to be found for me to play on a weekly basis.

I felt as though I had become a different person. I still had the same job. I was still a single mother, but a new talent had been uncovered which I hadn't realised was there before.

The message I received from Steve that October took me completely by surprise. He had sent this one directly to my email address rather than going via Facebook.

"Hi, Claire," it read. "Sorry about before. How are you?"

I really didn't know what to think. I had had enough of men stringing me along that summer and had become more cautious than I would have been even a few months before. I decided to reply but to be as business-like as possible until I knew why he had changed his mind about being in contact with me.

"I'm good thanks. How about you?" was all I said.

The next day, I checked my inbox as soon as I got in from work. There was another email from Steve:

"I've been offered a promotion at work; in fact I've been offered two positions. One is in Sheffield and the other in London. I'm trying to decide which one to accept. How is your work going?"

"I am still working three days a week for the newspaper but, now that William is at secondary school, I wouldn't mind more hours. There isn't anything available at the moment though. I suppose your decision about which position at work to accept depends on your girlfriend, doesn't it? What does she think?"

I had no idea whether she had moved up to Sheffield to be with him, or whether she was still in London and he was going down there every weekend to be with her. It really hadn't been any of my business. I wondered why he had chosen now to get in touch.

The reply came later that evening.

"Since I have been back in Sheffield I have got used to seeing all my old friends again. Well, most of them anyway. I like it round here. It still feels like home, even though I was away in London for all that time."

There was no mention of what his girlfriend thought.

Another message appeared two days later.

"Can we meet up?" it said. "I need to talk to you in person."

I really didn't know what to make of this. Part of me was over the moon that after all this time Steve finally wanted to see me face-to-face. Part of me heard alarm bells. What if I built my hopes up all over again for him to shatter them by deciding to take the job in London, and this was assuming that he hadn't still got a girlfriend? I would have to be on my guard and assume that he still had a girlfriend in London unless I found out otherwise. I would have to meet up expecting nothing more than a chat between two friends. I mustn't read too much into it. I had spent all this time trying to put him to the back of my mind, and now Steve had taken the first move and got back in touch. I needed to proceed with caution. I reminded myself of this several times until the time came that weekend to meet up.

We had arranged to meet at a quiet pub on the outskirts of Sheffield where we were unlikely to meet anyone either of us knew. We both agreed that there would be no chance to have a proper talk if we met up at a local where many of the regulars would know at least one of us. I pulled up in the car park of the Fox and Hounds just as Steve emerged from a very sporty-looking silver car. My pulse started to race as I got out of my tatty old Ford Fiesta and started to walk towards him. He walked towards me and we came face-to-face a few feet from the door of the pub. He smiled at me and all the years since we were together before seemed to disappear. He had gone a little bit grey in places and a few more lines had appeared around his eyes, but he looked even more attractive than ever. This was going to be difficult. How could I be on my guard and behave like someone who was just meeting up with an old friend when I only had to look at him and all those old feelings were stirred up. I wondered what he was thinking as he held the door open for me and asked what I wanted to drink.

We sat at a table which was tucked away in a quiet corner. I sipped at my soda and lime and wondered what to say. Steve broke the silence.

"So, how are you?"

I told him how William and I had started to learn the piano and that I was finding that I had hidden talents.

"I think I've told you that William has started secondary school now. He's a lot more grown-up than when you last saw him," I added. "How about you?"

"Well, I told you that I had been offered two promotions and it was up to me to decide which one I wanted."

"How long have you got to make your mind up?" I asked, wondering how long there might be until he potentially went back to London.

"I've got until the end of the month to decide, although I wouldn't be taking up the new position until the end of the year."

I wanted to ask him about his girlfriend but couldn't bring myself to ask. He didn't volunteer any information either.

"Do you like London?" I asked, hoping that the answer would throw some light on his situation.

"It was exciting for a bit. I enjoyed the idea that I was one of those professionals working in the capital for a while, but really I feel much more at home here."

"Why don't you accept the job here then?"

"My girlfriend ..." he stopped.

"Will she move up to Sheffield?" I asked.

He suddenly looked awkward and the colour started to rise up in his cheeks.

"I don't know," was all he said.

"You mean that you can't make a decision until she has decided as well?"

"Something like that."

I wondered whether he thought enough of her to sacrifice his own happiness to make her happy.

"How easy would it be for her to find another job if she moved up here?" I asked.

"She would have to work in London until something suitable was available close to Sheffield and then move up. She's worked in London since she was twenty two though, so it would be a bigger upheaval for her than me."

"It sounds as though you both have a lot to think about then!"

Steve escaped from the awkward silence by getting up and getting two more drinks from the bar. So, he felt that home was Sheffield, but she was used to London. If she moved to Sheffield now, she wouldn't have a job. This sounded too much of a risk to me. I felt deflated at the thought that Steve would most likely take the position in London and I probably wouldn't see him again.

He returned and put the drinks down on the table.

"She earns a lot more than me. She has worked really hard to get where she is."

So, that's it then. It sounds as though the decision has been made, I thought to myself.

"Has she got any children?" I asked.

"No. Work has always come first with Pippa, but now she's in her late thirties I think she might want to settle down and start a family."

Start a family? I imagined some businesswoman in her late thirties playing at happy families with my Steve. She'd probably be the sort to employ a nanny or pay for expensive day care and continue with her career just as before. The children would have posh names like Virginia or Rupert. My heart sank. I realised that even now I still thought of Steve as my man. This meeting had been a mistake.

"I think I'd better be going soon," I said, tracing the shape of a beer stain on the table with my finger and avoiding eye contact.

"Why? It's Saturday night. Have you got to go somewhere in the morning?"

I looked at him for a moment. Why was he here with me on a Saturday night anyway?

"How come you're not in London anyway this weekend?"

He looked at me as though he was unsure what I was getting at.

"I thought that you would travel down to see Pippa at weekends?" I added by way of explanation.

"Oh. She's away on a hen weekend."

"I suppose she wouldn't be very happy that you'd met up with me, would she?"

He didn't answer. Why had he wanted to meet up with me? He had said that he needed to talk to me in person. Why? He'd told me a bit more about his job offers and I had found out a bit more about his girlfriend. Why did he need to see me face-to-face?

"I really should be going, Steve," I said, getting up out of my seat.

He stood up and put his jacket on as he followed me to the door. We stood face-to-face in the car park.

"Bye, Claire," he said with a sad look in his eyes. "I'll let you know which job I take."

"Bye, Steve."

I felt pretty sure that his mind had already been made up for him.

Chapter 30

As the weeks passed I found myself feeling angry with Steve. He had implied that he had something important to say but all he had done was tell me what I already knew and had managed to upset me all over again. Why had he done this? Why had he wanted to see me again? Nothing had changed. Steve was out there. My soulmate. But he wasn't with me.

December came and I still hadn't heard anything from him. I still didn't know which life-changing decision he had made. But then what did it matter? I had to start the process all over again of putting him to the back of my mind and hoping that time would make the pain go away. I decided to concentrate on preparing for Christmas. Maybe some retail therapy would give me something to focus on? Pushing through the crowded shopping mall and queuing for twenty minutes per purchase would at least give me something to feel annoyed about other than Steve!

It was as I was doing my third lot of Christmas shopping in town that I heard a familiar voice say my name. The hairs on the back of my neck stood on end as I turned round and found myself face-to-face with those gorgeous blue eyes set in that handsome face and framed by wavy brown hair.

"Steve!" I gasped. "You made me jump there!" I said by way of explanation for the abrupt tone in which I said his name.

"I'm glad I've seen you, Claire," he said, looking straight into my eyes and making me go weak at the knees, despite my annoyance at seeing him. I remained silent waiting for him to speak again.

"I felt as though you were angry with me for some reason. You left suddenly without me getting chance to find something out."

I wanted to shout at him that I'd found enough out to know that we could never be friends. It was impossible to be friends with someone who you were in love with. It had to be all or nothing for me.

"I don't think it's fair on your girlfriend for us to keep in touch," was what I actually said. "I don't think she'd like the idea of you keeping in touch with an ex-girlfriend. I know that I wouldn't."

Before he had time to say anything, I continued, "I hope that whichever job you have chosen to take that you'll be happy with it. Bye, Steve," I said, trying to sound business-like and keep all emotion from my voice. I turned and walked away.

"Wait!" I heard Steve shout after me. Within seconds I felt myself being grabbed by the shoulders and turned round. I was face-to-face with Steve again. Before I had time to argue, I felt his arms around my back holding me close and he was pressing his lips to mine. I responded automatically, all thoughts of anything other than how good this felt erased from my mind. I had just about got my breath back and was about to speak when I felt his lips pressing against mine again. Eventually the kissing stopped and we stared into each other's eyes, neither of us bothered by the shoppers who were passing on either side of us and probably tutting their disapproval at two people in their early forties kissing with such passion in public. It was the most amazing kiss I had ever felt. Steve had never kissed me like that before. He couldn't have done even if he had wanted to. I stood staring at him, waiting for some crippling pain to take hold of him ... Nothing.

"I've wanted to do that for so long," he said, and I could have sworn there was a tear in his eye. "I needed to know."

I nodded. The feeling was mutual.

"What about Pippa?" I asked, the moment of joy suddenly disappearing as I realised that he was meant to be with someone else.

"I've never loved her like I love you, Claire!" he said.

"What about your job?" I asked.

"Can we go back to my flat and have a proper talk?"

He gave me the address and we met there twenty minutes later. It was in an exclusive block at the more expensive part of the city. *He must be earning a lot these days to be able to afford this*, I thought to myself.

"David at work is renting it out to me," he said by way of explanation as he unlocked the outer door. David's loaded but he let me have it at a very reasonable rate until the end of the year. After then I'll have to pay full whack."

"So, what's happening at the end of the year?"

"I've decided to stay in Sheffield."

"What about Pippa?" I asked.

"She's got some interviews up here."

"Oh."

"But I needed to know, Claire. I needed to know if there could ever be anything between us."

"And?"

"Everything has changed, Claire. I want to be with you."

Before I could ask any further questions, his arms were around me again and he was pulling me down onto the sofa. We kissed again and again. The passion started to build up to such an extent that I felt as though I might explode. He pulled me up from the sofa and led me into the bedroom. We made love for the rest of the afternoon.

"I don't want to lose you again, Claire," he whispered. "Now that I know that we can be together properly I never want to let you go."

I stared at him, unable to speak. The Steve I knew would never declare his feelings so openly. He must really feel strongly about this to have spoken up. As for the sex, that had never before been like it had been today. I couldn't believe that I finally had my Steve after all these years.

"Marry me!"

I thought that I was imagining things. "What?" I whispered, finding that my voice wouldn't work.

"I mean it, Claire. I want to marry you. Please say yes."

I nodded. Still unable to get any words out.

Steve spent most of Sunday at my house. William was at his dad's and so we had the house to ourselves. We made love in my bed before going out for Sunday lunch. It was just as we finished eating that Steve's mobile phone rang.

"It's Pippa!" he whispered before answering it and going outside to continue the call. I sat looking at him through the window, trying to work out from his body language what he had said to her.

Five minutes later he came and sat down opposite me. He finished the rest of his lager before speaking.

"She rang to say that she'd just got back from her friend's wedding ... you know, the one whose hen night she was at a few months ago. She found a letter on the doormat inviting her for an interview at the bank where I work!"

"What did you say?"

"I told her that I'd phone later for a proper chat and that I was out having a drink with a friend at the moment."

"Oh."

"Well, it's sort of true. I could hardly say that I've proposed to someone else!"

"What are you going to tell her?"

"I don't know. She'll be very shocked and she gets jealous very easily. I'd better break it to her gently."

Steve went back to his flat that evening. We decided that it probably wasn't a good idea for him to still be at my house when William got back from his dad's. William would have so many questions to ask and it didn't seem right to answer them until Steve had spoken to Pippa.

At ten o'clock, I sat on the sofa feeling restless as I wondered whether Steve had spoken to Pippa yet and if so, what he had told her. I couldn't imagine her being very happy at Steve breaking the news to her in a telephone conversation and wondered whether he would go through with it. I flicked through various TV channels, hoping to find something to take my mind off things and fill the time until Steve called with some news. It got to quarter to eleven and I still hadn't heard anything. I tried to phone Steve on the landline to his flat but got the busy tone. I wondered what was happening. Why had it taken until this time for him to speak to her? What if she got really jealous and history repeated itself all over again? The last thing I needed was another wronged woman inadvertently, or even deliberately, putting a curse on me!

Steve phoned at half past eleven.

"It was awful, Claire!" he began. "Before I could even start talking she started telling me all about her friend's wedding and how the chief bridesmaid had got really drunk. She seemed so happy and I felt really bad spoiling her weekend for her."

"So you didn't tell her then?" I asked, my heart sinking.

"Well, I decided to test the water by asking her about the interview in Sheffield. She told me that with her having to travel a long way, they've given her an interview time of four o'clock so that she has time to travel up from London in the morning. I tried to put her off coming, saying that it didn't seem fair for her to give up a career she loved for a lower-paid position in a different company and suggested she waited until a better opportunity came along. I thought that if she changed her mind and it was her idea, then there would be no jealousy and anger directed towards you."

"What did she say?"

"She said that she'd come up for the interview anyway and think about what to do afterwards if they offered her the job."

"So what did you say?"

"I told her that moving up here would be a big change for her and I had been wondering whether it was the right thing for her to do. She started to get upset and asked whether I had changed my mind about being with her. I told her that I didn't want to be responsible for spoiling her career. She started to get angry and asked me if there was someone else."

"Did you tell her?"

"I wanted to, but then I thought of all that business with Glenda. I told her that if she moved all the way up to Sheffield away from all her family and friends and then discovered she hated her job, or if things didn't work out between me and her, then she'd be really unhappy. She said that she was coming for the interview anyway and had booked Monday and Tuesday off work so that she had time to come and see me. She said she'd talk about it then. I left it at that, thinking that it might be better to sort things out face-to-face tomorrow rather than continue over the telephone late at night."

"Okay, so you'll let me know what happens tomorrow, then?"

"Yes. I'll get in touch as soon as I've spoken to her."

I got up early on the Monday morning after a bad night. William set off for the school bus at eight o'clock and I went into work early, hoping that clearing some of my to-do list would take my mind off things. My weekend with Steve had been something I had been hoping for for years now. I should have been ecstatic that the curse had gone and that we were finally going to be together properly.

Pippa gave me a bad feeling though. I had never met her, but until yesterday she had been planning to change her whole life to be with Steve, and if she was anything like me or most women, she would have been hoping that after a couple of years of living together that a wedding would follow. She would be very unlikely to accept this sudden change of mind from Steve without either fighting to keep him or getting nasty if she was as jealous as Steve had made out.

I managed to keep myself busy all morning by trying desperately to meet deadlines at work whilst constantly being interrupted by phone calls. I struggled to eat my lunch as worries of how Pippa would react started to take over my thoughts. *Was Steve strong enough to find a way of ending things with her, and could he do it without there being any backlash? Would she turn into a 'bunny boiler' and make our lives hell for years to come, or would he be afraid to tell her and string her along whilst secretly planning to marry me?* I hoped that, after everything we had been through, he wouldn't be so weak that he would choose the latter.

I managed to get through work that afternoon and drove home knowing that before the end of the day, I would know what had happened. Events would have moved on in one way or another.

When I got home, William was sitting at the dining table doing his homework. I wondered what he would think of Steve coming back into our lives after all this time. It had always felt right when the three of us were together before and I hoped it still would.

It was half past six, just as I was clearing away the pots in the kitchen, that the phone rang. Before I could wipe my hands and get to the phone, William had answered.

"It's Steve, Mum," he announced, handing me the phone and giving me a questioning glance.

I took the phone upstairs and went into the bedroom. I closed the door before starting to speak.

"Have you seen her?" I asked, feeling my pulse quicken.

"Yes," he replied, the tone of his voice telling me that what had happened hadn't been very easy.

"I told her that I had been having second thoughts about her moving up to Sheffield and that she should stay in London."

"Did you tell her why?"

"I told her that I didn't think that she was the one I wanted to settle down with and therefore she would be making a mistake if she moved up here. I said that we should go our separate ways because it wasn't right to continue when I wasn't sure about her."

"Did she accept that things were over though, Steve?"

"I think so. When I was with her she got a phone call in which she was offered the job in Sheffield. She turned it down saying that she had decided to stay in London. I felt awful but at least I know that she's taken what I said seriously."

"At least if she doesn't know about me there won't be any jealous revenge or anything."

"No, there shouldn't be."

Chapter 31

It was close to midnight when my mobile phone started to ring. I looked at the display but didn't recognise the number. I decided to ignore it since no sane person would phone at that time of night, and if it was someone I knew, their number would be in my contacts list. I turned over in bed and was just making myself comfortable when it rang again. I stared at the screen for a few seconds before deciding to answer it.

"Hello?"

"Hello, Claire." It was the voice of an unknown woman with a very business-like tone.

"Who is this?" I asked.

"This is Steve's girlfriend, that's who."

I sat up but couldn't think of anything to say.

She continued, "I've seen all your little text messages. Thought you could get away with it, did you? Hoping to get your hands on my boyfriend? Well, think again, bitch. He's mine and you're not having him!"

She hung up leaving me trembling with shock. My first instinct was to phone Steve. I rang his mobile. It rang a few times before the same woman's voice answered.

"Hello, Claire. Don't bother trying Steve's phone. I've got it right here in my hand and Steve's in bed next to me. He can't speak to you at the moment. He's got better things to do." My eardrums were assaulted with a loud, cackling, evil laugh before she hung up.

I imagined Steve curled up in bed with some other woman. Some woman who he said he had finished with a few hours earlier and who was meant to be in London by now. What should I do? I wanted to drive round there and confront them but I couldn't just get in the car and drive off in the night leaving my son in the house on his own, and also, what could I say or do anyway without looking silly and losing any self-respect that I had left. Why would he do this? The way he had been when we were together over the weekend seemed genuine and when he had proposed marriage he had sounded sincere. Why was she still there with him? Had she managed to talk him round? Was Steve hoping to keep the two of us on the go? But no, if he was really there in bed next to her he would have heard the phone conversation. He would know what she had said. Was she lying? What was she doing with Steve's phone?

I went downstairs and made myself a cup of tea. I didn't know what to do. Then it came to me. If I phoned his landline and she answered again, then I would know that she was really there. I picked up the cordless handset from the window ledge in the front room and dialled, my heart in my mouth. No answer. What if he had gone back to London with her? I sat down on the sofa, suddenly feeling cold and alone. I finished my tea before deciding to phone one more time. Still no answer.

I was just putting my empty mug in the kitchen, when the sound of the phone ringing made me jump out of my skin. I dashed through to the front room and picked it up.

"Hello!"

"Claire? Is that you? Are you alright?" It was Steve.

"No. Not really." I couldn't continue, as tears started to well up in my eyes.

"What's happened, Claire?"

I continued to cry and it was a few seconds before any words came out.

"Is she there with you?"

"Who?"

"Who do you think? Pippa!" I cried, giving up all hope of keeping the emotion I felt from my voice, as the tears started to flow.

"What do you mean, Claire? You know that I ended it and she's gone back to London. She went as soon as I had spoken to her and I won't be seeing her again. What's brought this on?"

"She phoned and said that you were together!" I cried, reaching for the box of tissues.

"What! She's got your number? How? I swear I haven't given it to her, or told her your name or anything!"

I told him the story from beginning to end of what had occurred.

"Just a second!" Steve said, and I heard him put the phone down on a hard surface.

About twenty seconds later he picked up the phone again.

"I can't find my phone, Claire. She must have taken it."

"Why would she choose me to phone out of all your contacts?"

"Because you're the only woman I've sent and received text messages from over the weekend. I haven't deleted any of them."

"What are you going to do?"

"Well, she doesn't know your address, and if I just cancel the contract on that phone, then she won't be able to phone you from it and she won't be able to get in touch with you again."

"She must have put my number on her phone as well though, because she phoned me from a different number to start with!"

"Cancel your number as well in the morning and then she won't be able to call you again!"

"Okay."

"Do you want me to come round now?"

"I don't know. It must be about one in the morning!" I said, even though I wanted nothing more than to have him there next to me.

"I'm coming round. I'll be there in about twenty minutes."

While I was waiting for Steve to come round, I thought about what had happened. I felt a bit sorry for Pippa. Up until the day before, she had thought that she was moving up to Sheffield to start a new life with her boyfriend. I assumed that she wouldn't know about Steve's previous relationship with me. Or, even if he had mentioned an ex-girlfriend called Claire, I couldn't imagine him going into details of events just before he had taken the job in London.

I thought about when my ex-husband, Greg, had left to be with Sarah. I had been gutted, but I would never have phoned her and made threatening phone calls, or lied, saying that he was still with me. I had phoned Greg a few times to tell him what a bad father he must be to take up with another woman, leaving his wife and son behind, but once I accepted that he wasn't coming back, I had gradually put my life back together. I hoped that Pippa would be able to accept that Steve had ended things with her and that she would be able to move on. I hoped that if we changed our phone numbers she would get the message and leave us alone.

I was feeling much calmer and philosophical by the time Steve arrived. We held each other for a while before going up to bed to try to get some sleep.

"She'll get over it," Steve tried to reassure me as he stroked my hair.

"I hope so," I whispered, as I rested my head on his shoulder.

We woke early the next morning and decided that we would both phone work saying that we were ill. Neither of us had got much sleep and wouldn't be able to rest until our phones had been cancelled. I got up at seven, telling Steve that it was probably better if he waited in the bedroom until William had left for school. I would tell William later that we were back together. I went downstairs in my dressing gown and prepared some toast and a cup of tea for William, who I could hear running the water in the bathroom above. He appeared downstairs a few minutes later asking why I hadn't got dressed yet. I told him that I had been awake all night feeling ill.

"You made me go to school when I'd been awake half the night with that cough, Mum!"

I felt guilty. I wasn't setting a very good example.

"I've got a really upset stomach though. I'll probably start being sick soon!" I lied.

He put his toast back on his plate. "Thanks, Mum. I'll probably get ill now!" He threw the toast into the bin and poured himself some cereal instead.

"I washed my hands and I haven't been sick yet, so you should be alright!" I sighed.

Steve appeared as soon as William had left for the bus.

"I felt terrible hiding up here. I kept feeling the need to sneeze and I had a right job holding it in!" He smiled, as he wrapped his arms around me and gave me a hug.

"Coffee?"

"Yes, please. I'll get straight onto my phone company while you're getting it ready."

"You'll probably have drunk it before they get round to answering!" I rolled my eyes and started to spoon instant coffee into two mugs.

Steve was halfway down his cup of coffee before his call was answered. He explained that he had lost his phone and wanted to stop the number as soon as possible. Luckily, he had taken out insurance with his monthly contract and they told him that they would send out a replacement handset with a new number which should arrive in a few days.

I phoned to get my number changed as soon as we had finished breakfast. It took even longer for my call to be answered. I explained that my number had got into the hands of someone who I didn't want to speak to.

"Are you saying that you're receiving nuisance calls?" the customer services assistant asked.

I paused. Pippa had only phoned once and the other time I accidentally phoned her. I didn't really want to file a complaint against her.

"Not really. It's just my partner's ex-girlfriend," I blushed, glancing at Steve.

The woman explained how I could block incoming calls from Pippa's number rather than going through all the hassle of replacing my SIM card.

"What if she's written it down and phones me from other phones?"

"So you're saying that you do want a new SIM card then?"

"Yes, please!"

This was arranged and I decided to keep my existing number until the new one arrived and would just ignore calls from any number which I didn't recognise.

"Feel better?" Steve asked, giving me another hug. In all the time I had known Steve, I didn't think I'd been given as many hugs as I had been given by him over the last two days.

"Are you sure you feel okay, Steve?" I asked smiling. "It's not like you to give out so many hugs!"

"Well, we have a few years' worth to catch up on," he laughed. "I'm sure it'll wear off when we've been married for a few years!"

I held him close and buried my face into his chest. It still hadn't sunk in that he had asked me to marry him and, with all the stress of Pippa phoning me, I hadn't really had time to let myself get excited about it.

"When would you like to get married?" I asked.

"I suppose it'll take a while to make all the arrangements. Sometime next year?"

"Sounds perfect."

"When do you want to start telling people?" Steve looked into my eyes.

"Well, no one even knows that we're back together yet!" I laughed. "We'll tell friends and family that we're back together and then when we've had a think about where and when the wedding is going to be we'll tell them about that."

"Sounds okay to me!"

Steve stayed at my house all day, and almost as soon as William came home from school he discovered Steve standing in the front room. William put his bag down and looked from me to Steve.

"I'm back with Steve again!" I told him before he had a chance to ask.

"Are you staying in Sheffield now?" William asked.

"Yes. I'm staying around. For good," Steve added, seeming to be aware of the suspicious tone of voice with which William had asked the last question.

"Mum was really upset when you left before!" William informed Steve.

"Well, don't worry. I know what I want to do now and I'm staying."

William looked at me.

"It's okay, William. Lots of things have happened over the last few years and they have made me and Steve realise that we only want to be with each other."

I looked at Steve and felt a blush starting to rise up my neck and into my cheeks.

"Okay, Mum. I'm gonna get a drink and then start my homework."

William went through to the kitchen with his school bag.

"He's grown up a lot. I can't believe he's at secondary school!"

"I know!"

"He's almost as tall as you!"

"Most kids his age are and some are taller!" I laughed.

"Hey, you've got a piano!" Steve said, pointing across the room.

"Well I told you I'd been having lessons, didn't I?"

"Yes, but I'm not used to seeing a piano in your house. It still took me by surprise seeing it there."

"I'll play it for you later if you like, if you're staying around that is!"

"Can't wait!"

Steve stayed around for most of the week. He called round to his flat to collect some of his clothes later that evening and then again the following evening.

"Did you say that your mate from work wanted to charge you full whack for your flat after the end of the year?" I asked a couple of days later.

"Yes. But I won't be needing it, will I?"

"No, I suppose not! Do you want to move in here?" I asked, hoping he'd say yes.

"Definitely!" he smiled. "Well I'd sort of assumed that would be happening!" he started to laugh. "I'll collect some of my things from the flat this weekend and we can gradually get all my stuff moved in."

I had been invited to a get-together with the girls that Saturday night at Becky's house. Steve decided to have a night at his flat so that he could have a really good sort through all his things and then bring some more of them round on Sunday morning. My mum and dad had agreed to come round to keep an eye on William.

There was a lot to tell my friends and they were soon getting excited that Steve and I were back together.

"So, he's moving in then?" asked Lizzie.

"There'll be wedding bells soon!" laughed Lucy

I laughed but didn't comment.

"What does William think to it all?" asked Becky.

"Well, he was a bit protective of me at first," I explained. "I think he was worried that Steve would go back to London."

"But he's definitely staying, isn't he?"

"Yes, and I think William knows that now, so he seems quite happy to have Steve back in our lives."

"Aw, that's great. You three make a lovely family!" smiled Lucy.

"We've had a bit of trouble with Steve's ex-girlfriend though!"

I continued to tell the story of what had happened with Pippa. Meanwhile Lizzie topped up everyone's wine glasses.

"I suppose you can't blame her for being upset," said Becky, "but she does sound like a bit of a nutter."

"Yeah, I'd give her a wide berth if I were you!" added Lucy.

"It wasn't as though he'd promised her marriage or anything. Sometimes people just realise that they're with the wrong person. It's one of those things. I'm sure she'll come to accept it in time," said Lizzie.

"She was on the verge of changing her whole life for him, though. I can't blame her for taking it badly, really."

"At least he broke things off before she moved up here. Many men don't have the guts to end things when they should and end up stuck in a situation that they don't want and then end up having an affair," Becky commented.

"So is Steve at your house then?" asked Lucy.

"No, he's been there all week, but because I've come here tonight he's decided to go back to his flat and sort through his things. He's going back to mine in the morning."

By the time it reached quarter past twelve, all the wine had been consumed and we were more than a little bit merry. I was almost home in the taxi when my mobile phone began to ring. I looked at the display and realised that it was her number. Pippa's. I turned my phone off, determined not to answer it. In a few days I would have a new SIM card and she wouldn't know my number. I had just had a really good evening catching up with all the latest news of what my friends had been up to and telling them all my news. I started to feel stressed again, wondering what she would have said if I'd answered. Well, I didn't want to know. She would just have to get over what had happened.

I got out of the taxi at twelve thirty-five and let myself into my house. Mum and Dad told me how they had hardly seen William that evening, since he had been in his bedroom most of the time playing on 'some computer game or other'. I apologised for William's rudeness and said I'd tell him to come and speak to them next time they came round.

"It doesn't matter," said my mum. "Lads that age never know what to say to people our age. He went to bed when we told him to after he'd had a drink and a couple of biscuits."

I wished my parents goodnight before checking that the front door was locked and sat down on the sofa with a glass of water. I took my phone out of my bag and remembered that I had turned it off. I turned it back on again in case Steve had left me any messages, then I remembered that he had cancelled his phone and wouldn't get a new one for a few days. I wondered whether it was too late to phone his landline. I decided that it was and went to bed. I was soon knocked out by the amount of wine I had drunk earlier, and the next thing I knew it was just after eight in the morning. I decided to have another hour in bed and then I would phone Steve to check what time he was coming round.

Chapter 32

I felt sure that I had dialled the correct number for Steve's flat, but in response I got a constant tone which indicated that I had either dialled a number which didn't exist or Steve's phone was out of order. I had been hoping that he would phone first thing in the morning. His new mobile phone still hadn't arrived and I was missing the text messages that I had got used to receiving on a regular basis over the last week. I told myself that, if there was something wrong with his phone line, I would just have to wait for him to arrive at my house and speak to him properly!

At one time, not that long ago really, phones didn't exist and people just had to wait! I imagined the two of us in a former life writing letters to each other and me waiting for Steve to call round on foot or horseback. I smiled to myself at the thought.

Ten o'clock came and went. Still no sign of Steve. Eleven o'clock. I hated not knowing when people were meant to be turning up. Maybe Steve had decided to have a really good sort out and had lost track of time. By midday William was starting to get upset.

"What if he's changed his mind, Mum, and he's not coming after all?"

"Don't be silly, William!" I tried to reassure him. "He'll have got up late and decided to pack a few more things before he set off, that's all!" I said, although deep down I was beginning to wonder what the problem was.

"Shall we go there to help him with his things?" William asked.

"It's a good idea but what if he's already on his way here and arrives to an empty house?"

"I'll look out for his car, Mum, and we'll just turn back if we spot him!"

Five minutes later we were in the car heading for Steve's house. We were both feeling anxious in case we arrived to find that Steve had already set off, or even worse, had decided not to come at all! Nothing could have prepared us for what we saw as we approached the flats. Two of the windows were completely smashed and what was left of the UPVC window frames was melted and brown. The brick-work surrounding what would have been the kitchen window was black. The other windows were brown and cracked. As I pulled up and got out of the car, I looked up to the small veranda where Steve and I had stood and admired the view over the park last time I had been there. The sliding glass doors which opened onto it had been left partly open. From below I couldn't see into the room. An elderly couple walking a slow, overweight King Charles spaniel approached us.

"Terrible business last night!" said the man, looking up towards the flat where Steve and I had spent much of the previous weekend.

"What happened?" I asked.

"Where's Steve?" asked William.

"Steve?" asked the elderly lady.

"The man who lives in the flat," I explained. "We were coming here to see him!"

"I don't know love," replied the man. "Apparently it happened some time around two in the morning. Wait a minute, there's that young man coming out of the next block. Maybe he'll know."

I ran towards the man who must have been in his mid-twenties. He was dressed in jeans and a brown T-shirt with one of those longish, layered hairstyles which were the fashion.

"Excuse me!" I called, as he threw a bag of rubbish into one of the large black bins.

He turned to face me as I approached.

"The man who lives in that flat," I pointed to the burnt-out shell. "Do you know where he is or what happened to him?" I started to feel sick, dreading what I was going to hear.

"I heard sirens last night and when I looked out of the window I saw a man up there on the veranda shouting for help. They got him down and took him in the ambulance."

"So he's alive then. Thank goodness!"

"I don't suppose anyone has said which hospital they've taken him to?" I asked.

"No. Sorry," he replied.

"Have you got a phone book I can borrow to look the numbers up?" (My mobile phone was quite an old model and therefore not very good for using the Internet on).

"Yeah. Just a minute," the young man replied.

We waited at the entrance to his block and he returned a few minutes later with the phone book.

"Just press the buzzer for Flat Three when you've done with it," he said and headed back indoors.

William and I sat on the brick wall outside the flats as I thumbed through the pages for the hospitals. I tried the Royal Hallamshire Hospital first. I explained to the woman on switchboard that I was trying to find a man called Steve Clarke who had been in a fire last night, and could I find out whether he was there.

"Just a minute, love," the voice answered, before I heard another dialling tone.

I explained the situation all over again to another middle-aged woman.

"Steve Clarke. Are you family?"

"I'm his girlfriend," I explained.

"Just a minute."

The phone went dead for a couple of minutes before the same woman spoke again.

"Yes, he's here, love, on Ward 3F."

"Thanks!" I hung up.

Fifteen minutes later I had managed to find a parking space at the hospital and was running towards the main entrance. Once inside I looked up at the signs hung above the glass double doors. One listed various departments and the other listed wards with arrows pointing in different directions. The arrow for wards 1A to 4C pointed straight ahead and I continued with William along the corridor and through some double doors before stopping and looking for further signs. Two sets of silver-coloured metal doors to my right had lists of various wards hung next to them, and I pressed the button for the first one after checking that Ward 3F was on the list.

We stepped out onto the corridor. The ward sister was looking through some paperwork at the desk. William and

I stood there for a couple of seconds before she looked up.

"We're trying to find Steve Clarke," I began. "I understand he was brought here last night."

"Yes, but it's not visiting time until two o'clock."

I looked up at the clock on the wall behind her which showed half past one.

"Is he okay?" I asked. "I'm his girlfriend, in fact we're getting married," I added, hoping that my status would prompt her to give out more information.

William took a sharp intake of breath and stared at me on hearing this new piece of information.

"Just a minute. What's your name?" she asked.

"Claire Turner," I replied.

"Take a seat," she said, indicating a row of blue plastic chairs further along the corridor.

Several minutes later she returned.

"He's inhaled a lot of smoke and is still rather poorly. He was asking us to contact you but he didn't know your number from memory and it wasn't listed in the phone book."

"No, it's ex-directory," I explained.

"Since he's not had any visitors yet I'll let you go in. But I think your son should wait outside. There's a waiting area just next to your boyfriend's ward with a vending machine. He'll be alright there."

"Thanks," I replied, and followed her through some double doors before taking a left turn. I made sure William was okay in the waiting area before I entered a small ward containing four beds. Only one of them was occupied. It was Steve. He turned to face me as I approached the bed.

I flung my arms around his neck before he had a chance to speak. Tears started to well up in my eyes.

"How did it happen?" I asked, as Steve tried to sit up and started to cough.

"I don't know. The smoke alarm went off and I tried to get to the fire escape, but there were flames and thick black smoke all the way along the corridor. I couldn't even see the door so I went back into the flat and got out through the doors onto the veranda and shouted for help. I tried to go back in and phone the fire service but smoke was starting to build up and I couldn't breathe properly. It wasn't long before the fire engine arrived. Someone must have phoned them. I don't know who. The firemen put a ladder up to the veranda."

"Have they said how it started?"

"No. The police came to the hospital last night and spoke to me saying that it appears to have started near the door to the fire escape but they need to investigate further."

"The door to the fire escape? But how? Did you leave anything plugged in that might have overheated?"

"No. There aren't even any sockets round there!"

When I had gone to Steve's flat the weekend before, we had entered the block by a communal entrance. He had unlocked the door with a key before taking me up to the first floor and unlocking the door to his flat with a further key. On entering the flat there was a door to the right which opened into another short corridor which led to the bathroom. At the end I had noticed another door which Steve had explained led out to the fire escape. I tried to imagine how a fire could have started there but nothing sprang to mind. I thought about how modern and expensive the flat had looked and wondered how much damage the fire had caused. I imagined Steve being woken by the smoke alarm and finding the route to the fire escape blocked by thick smoke.

"I'm glad you're okay!" I said, as I reached across and held his hand.

"I'm wondering if they've managed to get in touch with David yet!" Steve said.

"David?"

"Yeah, you know. The bloke who's renting me the flat."

"He'll have it insured won't he?"

"Yes, and I had all the contents insured, but getting it all repaired and replacing everything will take months. I'd paid rent in advance until the end of the year but it'll take longer than that to get it all fixed and ready for a new tenant."

"Don't worry about that now. Just get yourself better and everything will get sorted out in time."

"Everything will be ruined, Claire. I've not even got any clothes to go home in!"

"You'd already taken some to my house. Remember? I'll get something brought round later."

I thought about Steve's only possessions being the ones which he had already taken to my house. What a nightmare! At least he was moving in with me anyway and would have somewhere to live.

Later that week, Steve was back at my house, or rather our house, as I would have to get used to calling it. Investigations were still continuing to find out how the fire started. All evidence seemed to suggest that it had started near the fire escape and the possibility of arson had not been ruled out. Steve had been asked several times whether he was certain that the fire escape door had been closed on the night of the fire before he had gone to bed. Apparently the fire service had found the door to be slightly ajar when they had arrived at the scene and there was no evidence to suggest that the door had been opened by force.

"I never used that door during the whole time I was living at the flat," Steve told me after the investigators had left.

"And you say they were asking you where your keys to the flat were kept and how many sets you had?"

"Yes. I told them that I had two sets of keys. One set was with my car keys which I usually had on the bedside cabinet overnight. The other set would have been in one of the kitchen drawers."

"So, what do they think happened then?"

"They just said that they'd be in touch when they had more news and not to go back to the flat."

It was two days later when investigators called to say that a thorough search of the flat had taken place. They had found a complete set of keys in the bedroom with Steve's car keys, but no other keys could be found anywhere. They were now working on a theory that someone else might have got hold of the keys and let themselves into the flat. The offender had started the fire in the corridor near the fire escape before leaving via the fire exit. They hadn't closed the door properly on their way out because it was one of those which had a push bar on the inside and had to be slammed quite hard from the outside. They either didn't want to wake Steve or just wanted to get away quickly and hadn't bothered closing the door.

"Who would do such a thing?" Steve asked, horrified that he may have been deliberately targeted.

"Did anyone hold a grudge against you, Mr. Clarke?" the investigator had asked.

"No. I don't think so!"

"Not upset anyone recently then?"

The investigator must have become aware of the look on my face as I put my hand over my mouth. Both he and Steve were looking in my direction.

"Have you got something to say, Miss Turner?"

"There is someone but ... no ... she wouldn't!"

"You mean Pippa?" Steve was clearly shocked at my train of thoughts.

"Pippa?" the investigator asked.

Chapter 33

After Steve and I had told the investigating officer about recent events with Pippa, he had asked Steve for her address and said that she would be paid a visit. We would be informed of the outcome in due course. Steve was allowed to go home with me later that day. However, we were afraid to go to bed that night in case Pippa was still in Sheffield and had managed to find out my address.

"What if she tries to set fire to my house as well?" I asked.

"We don't even know that it was her and, even if it was, there was nothing in the flat with your address on and I haven't told her!"

"What if she followed you?"

"When? She went back to London after I told her that I'd changed my mind about her moving up to Sheffield."

"Are you sure about that? She managed to steal your phone so she probably got your keys as well while she was at it. Who knows what else she's been doing?"

We took turns to try to sleep whilst the other kept watch. William joined us part way through the night, saying that he couldn't sleep either. We had tried to keep him in the dark about the fire being caused by suspected arson, but he had come home from school one day when we were talking to the police and had overheard something before we had realised that he was there.

It was early evening the following day before we heard that Pippa had been arrested for arson. She had broken down saying that she had never intended to cause either of us any harm, but she couldn't deal with the idea of Steve being in the arms of another woman. She had confessed to taking the keys when she took Steve's mobile phone. The phone and keys had been on the kitchen worktop and she had swept them into her handbag when Steve had turned his back. She had got the train back to London that evening and had spent the journey looking through text messages on his phone and looking at the log of calls that he had made and received. At first she had wanted to find out whether Steve had been two-timing her with me and for how long. She had allowed her anger to build up over the course of the following week after she had spoken to me on the phone. She had got the train back to Sheffield the following weekend and had quietly let herself into the flat, originally intending to confront the two of us. She had gone to the sitting room and had seen various bags and boxes packed and had guessed that Steve was moving out. In a fit of rage, without even knowing whether Steve and I were in the flat or not, she had taken a bottle of vodka from the kitchen cupboard and had poured the contents over the carpet in the corridor, before moving out onto the fire escape. She had checked that no one was watching before pulling the door almost closed and pushing several lit matches through onto the carpet. Afterwards she had run to the phone box down the road and had phoned the fire service. She had never intended to kill anyone but had wanted to scare us and spoil things for us.

At the trial, she was found guilty of arson and put behind bars. After a few more weeks, a letter of apology from Pippa was sent to Steve's work address asking for us to forgive her for her actions. She had scared herself when she realised what her jealous reaction had caused her to do and said that she wished us well for the future.

As the months passed, Steve settled into his promotion at work and William was really happy to have him around in the evenings and weekends.

It was the end of May when my manager at the newspaper asked me into his office for a chat. I sat down nervously, wondering whether I had missed a deadline.

"There's no need to look so nervous, Claire," he reassured me. "I am really happy with your work and wondered whether you wanted to go full-time?"

"Oh!" I didn't know what to say. It wasn't what I had expected to hear.

"Tracey has decided to not return to us at the end of her maternity leave, which means that her hours need to be filled from the beginning of July," he explained. "Have a think about it and let me know by next Monday."

I discussed it with Steve that evening.

"You said that you wanted more hours now that William was getting older and could make his own way to and from school."

This was true. I thought about all those years after I had split up with Greg and had really struggled for money but had preferred to work part-time rather than hardly have any time with my son. I hadn't struggled for money since Steve had moved in and had been able to share the bills with me. The idea of wanting more hours at work hadn't seemed such a priority any more. However, I decided to accept the extra hours at work anyway. There was a wedding to pay for after all and anything spare after that could be put into a savings account.

That autumn Steve and I were married and put a deposit down on a brand new, four-bedroomed house. All the negative events of previous years seemed to have been wiped away and for the first time in years I felt truly happy. All my wishes had been granted. The curse from a former life had been lifted and I had the life I wanted with Steve.

Epilogue

I didn't feel the need to visit any more clairvoyants or text the so-called 'mystics' once I had the man of my dreams (literally). However, after hearing my story, my friends were hooked.

It was over a year later that someone hammered on my door at eight o'clock one Sunday morning. I opened the bedroom window and looked down, wondering what kind of lunatic would be up and about at that time on a Sunday. I laughed to myself as a feeling of déjà vu overcame me.

"Just a minute!" I shouted down to Lucy, as she hopped from foot to foot impatiently on the doorstep.

"Sorry. Not interrupting anything am I?" Lucy winked.

"No. We were still asleep! What's so urgent? In fact, why can't you phone like a normal person?" I laughed. I could never get angry with Lucy. She was so girly and impulsive.

"We saw Alice again last night. Even Julie was there!"

"Come in, then!" I said, rolling my eyes. "Let's get a cup of coffee and you can tell me about it."

"Do you feel alright?" Lucy asked.

"Yes! Why?"

"Just something Alice said."

"Well, you don't look worried, so it can't be anything bad. You're not going to tell me I'm ..."

Lucy smiled and started to laugh before finishing the sentence for me.

"Pregnant?"

Eight months later I gave birth to a beautiful baby girl.